Entwined Publishing books by Rachael Heinan & Kimberly Metcalf

Amber Falls
Yours, Always
Forever Yours

Amber Falls

FOREVER YOURS

RACHAEL HEINAN &
KIMBERLY METCALF

ENTWINED PUBLISHING

Forever Yours
ISBN # 978-1-80250-722-5
©Copyright Rachael Heinan & Kimberly Metcalf 2025
Cover Art by Kelly Martin ©Copyright January 2025
Interior text design by Entwined Publishing
Published by Entice, an Entwined Publishing imprint

Published in 2025 by Entwined Publishing, United Kingdom.

Entwined Publishing is a division of Totally Entwined Group Limited.

FOREVER YOURS

Dedication

Rachael
To my parents. I got my creativity from you, and you've always fostered my talent, in whatever form it took. I love you!

Kimberly
To my mom, your unwavering support meant more than you will ever know.

Prologue

Gabriel Atwood was in love. He thought love at first sight was only found in romance novels, but gave a mental shrug as he backed the hot blonde up against his hotel room door. He didn't even know her name, that would come later, but he was in love. At the risk of sounding completely shallow — and completely male — she was all legs with a killer personality. That was all he needed to know right now.

He'd met her earlier in the evening at a bar in downtown Boston. After ending a semi-serious relationship a few months ago, Gabe hadn't set out looking for any action that night. He was in town for a craft brewers convention, hoping to find some new IPAs for his bar, Finnegan's, located in western Massachusetts, a small township called Amber Falls. He'd decided to go out to see where his last night in town would take him.

The fact that he'd fallen in love was unexpected. It blindsided him. Not in a bad way, if he let himself dwell on that feeling. He pushed the philosophizing away, focusing instead on getting her skirt off, but this damn leather skirt had to have buttons down the side. *Who put buttons on leather?* The mystery blonde swatted his hands away. Her shirt was already open. She was braless and breathtaking. She gave him a gentle shove and a slow smile.

"Pants off, please," she requested with more politeness than he'd be able to muster now.

Gabe backed up toward the bed, his fingers fumbling on his fly as he watched her lean over and unbutton her skirt. She freed herself, then pushed the remainder of her clothes to the floor. She walked toward him, and he realized his fumbling hadn't gotten him anywhere, his pants were still on, he was just standing there, speechless at the sight of her. Her long hair was falling over her breasts, obscuring them enough that he ached to see them uncovered, to see if they tasted of vanilla, the scent that had floated off her all evening. He gave up on his pants for the moment — he had to know. The only thought driving him forward was to know if she tasted like perfection. She tried to nudge him onto the bed, but he held still, running his hands over her backside and up to the nape of her neck, her skin prickling along the path his hands had taken. He moved her hair aside and brushed his thumbs over her nipples before taking one into his mouth. He knew now. He knew she was perfection and he'd remember this moment for the rest of his life.

Gabe hardened to an impossible degree when she moaned, his mind drifting to what she would taste like between her thighs. If this was perfection, that would be heaven. His mystery woman had somehow unbuttoned and pushed down his pants and he only noticed when she grabbed his cock and ran her sure hand up and down its length. She traced her thumb over the tip, swiping away the moisture, before raising it to her mouth to suck it off before resuming her strokes, almost bringing him to his knees.

"Now," she whispered in his ear, and she pushed him to the bed, her long legs straddling him.

"Condom?" Gabe scratched out the word.

"I brought my own, hope that's okay." She flicked two of her fingers up, a wrapped condom between them.

Gabe wasn't sure what turned him on more, the confidence that she exuded while tearing open and rolling the latex down his shaft, or that she'd taken complete control.

Her hands were planted on his chest, and he reached down and held his cock steady as she took her time lowering herself onto him.

She moaned. "Fuck, you feel so good."

The sounds she was making were so heady and, like a siren's song, he wanted to hear more.

She rolled her hips, he felt his momentum build. He reached up and wound her hair in his fist, pulling her down with his other hand so they were chest to chest, moving his knees up to move himself deeper inside her wet heat.

"Harder," she gasped.

Gabe didn't hesitate at her command. Hooking her leg, he flipped them over as he thrust hard into her in the same motion.

"Like that?" he managed.

"Yes, fuck, yes."

He brought up her legs to his shoulders, groaning as she tightened around him.

"Don't stop!" she demanded.

He set a fast pace, bringing his thumb to her clit, rubbing small circles.

"Come for me," he ground out.

He felt her orgasm – oh yes – God did he feel it, then released her legs, bracing his hands on either side of her. He thrust in again and again and on the third, he felt himself empty. Their breathing was heavy, their bodies glistening with sweat.

"Holy," she breathed.

"Yeah."

Gabe disposed of the condom then lay on the bed facing her and raised his palm to her cheek. Her eyes were already closed in sleep. He chuckled, pulling her close, following her into slumber.

* * * *

Gabe awoke before dawn the next morning to his phone alarm going off. He reached to the other side of the bed and met an empty space. He looked over – the sheets were still crumpled; a pillow was on the floor. She hadn't needed the pillow as he recalled, the warmth of her pressed up against him in sleep now a distant memory.

"Damn," he muttered as he sat and rubbed his eyes. Looking around, he was hoping to see a note, something that would give him a clue as to who his mystery woman was. Nothing. He got out of bed, his morning erection pointing toward the bathroom door as if indicating she might be in there and could be back in his bed at any moment, to satiate his need for her once again. Their joining only a few hours ago had been fast and powerful. He'd let her take charge, feeling a sense of vulnerability in her, one that faded when she had power over him.

"Sorry, big guy." He ran his hand over his cock. "She's gone." He didn't even know her name.

Chapter One

Devlin Watkins woke with a start, her heart pounding and her breathing shallow. She had the dream. Again. She often dreamed of Boston, a time and place where she was a different person, before she'd left what seemed like a lifetime of bad decisions. She couldn't bring herself to call that night a bad decision, but her subconscious wasn't so sure. She would be going about her day and a wave of heat would wash over her and her body would tense in anticipation. That nonsense was usually squashed before it overwhelmed her, and she'd take a moment to gather herself and get on with her day. Still, her subconscious wouldn't be ignored, and she found her thoughts drifting to the man.

Her heart had stopped the first time she'd seen him in Amber Falls. On a fall day over a year ago, she'd been at the front window of Books and Beans, her downtown coffee shop, watching the leaves waltz in the street, her mind wandering as she wiped off a table. Then he'd walked by, and the leaves' rhythm changed to a tango.

He looked the same. Tall, with wheat colored hair styled in an undercut. With a face chiseled out of granite, he possessed the look of strength that only someone who did physical work for a living had. His lips were pursed, as though whistling, and his hands were shoved into pockets. *The picture of a man without a care in the world.*

She'd felt like she was in a fog and had flipped the sign of Books and Beans to closed. She'd hurried outside but hadn't had to go far. He'd pulled open the door to a business two doors down from hers and entered it. She'd walked over and stood, looking through the frosted-edged glass window and had seen the man from Boston, moving behind a gleaming wood bar top.

She'd focused her eyes on the sight in front of her. *Finnegan's.* Her heart had started beating again, fast and uncomfortable this time, and she'd reached out to steady herself, bracing one of her hands on the rough brick wall. The movement must've caught the man's eye and he'd glanced over. He'd squinted at her, the moment suspended in time, then had shaken his head and gone back to pouring a beer, a smile lighting his face as he'd handed a glass to the patron across the bar top. *He doesn't recognize me.* Feeling a little a whoosh of lightheadedness at the realization an incredulous laugh had bubbled up from deep inside and she'd backed away from the window and walked back to her shop.

Devlin shook off the memory of that day, stretched upward and yawned. She knew she looked different now. Her long bleach blonde locks had been shorn off and she'd gained a handful of pounds, still thin, but no longer painfully so. It wasn't really a surprise that someone she'd met in a dark bar, then proceeded to have sex with in a dark hotel room, over a year ago, wouldn't recognize her. She'd smoothed one hand over her natural brown pixie style, an unconscious habit she'd developed after cutting her hair, affirming to herself she was still there, that chopping off her hair hadn't also taken away her identity.

Since her move to Amber Falls, she'd become friends with two wonderful women, the curvaceous redhead Prudence Hardwick and the petite auburn spitfire Annabelle Winters. She didn't want to dwell on the past, but it was hard not to when Prudence falling in love with Greyson Atwood had brought her past crashing into her present. Devlin would've been happy to leave the blurry image of Gabe through the etched glass as the last time she'd seen him, however, Prudence's said soulmate was Gabe's brother.

Greyson was a movie star who'd left the glitz and glamor of Hollywood to pursue teaching the craft to others. He'd returned to his hometown a few months ago and won the heart of Prudence. Dark where his brother was light, Greyson was taller than Gabe by only a fraction, with the perfect smoldering looks to play his signature role of Ben Stone in a series of hit spy movies. Their happiness had made things very difficult for Devlin over the last few months, as she'd had to come up with creative ways to avoid being in the same room with Gabe.

Since then, she'd perfected the Irish Goodbye — or the French Exit or the Dutch Leave — whatever people called it. Should Gabe show up anywhere she was, she could ghost the place like a pro. But now? It had become almost impossible considering her friendship with Prudence and Prudence's relationship with…well…it all was getting very complicated. Tonight was New Year's Eve. The night was going to be rough, and she wasn't sure how to navigate it since everyone would be at Finnegan's to ring it in. She'd heard Gabe would be working, but she had a feeling she couldn't avoid him all night.

One thing at a time, you haven't even gotten out of bed. She shifted her focus back to her daily tasks, glad she'd made the decision to close early today. She'd been able to hire someone to help part time with the shop so she knew she wouldn't have to open tomorrow, giving her a rare day to sleep in. Today was not one of those days. She shivered at the predawn chill in the air as she threw back her duvet. Amber Falls had had very little snow so far this winter, but when she looked out of her loft window to the dark downtown streets, she noticed flurries.

Devlin's short hair made mornings a breeze as she hurried with her early ablutions. She locked her door and made her way down the flight of stairs that led into the Books and Beans office. Quick access from living to working was one of the reasons she had chosen this location in Amber Falls.

Her loft was above the coffee shop, which made for an easy commute. Floor to ceiling windows looked down over the town square, double-paned and soundproof. The original floors had been polished to perfection and she swore you could glide over them with socks on, and she'd just maybe tried this a time or two. It was a large open space with two updated bathrooms, a main and a master, and a cook's kitchen. One door led down to the office below and one down to the street. *This. This is home.* The deal was signed.

While the loft was a gleaming example of downtown living, the shop had been left to deteriorate. On the short walk to the shop, Devlin thought about the past year and how she had spent those first hot summer months preparing the shop to open. She had found out very soon after arriving that Amber Falls was a special town. They celebrated the changing of the seasons with a joviality that bordered on crazy, but she loved it, becoming immersed in the seasonal cheer. She'd just participated in the latest Fall Festival, getting into the spirit by having a hot apple cider stand at the hay bale maze and a coffee and dessert stand at the Funny Friday Frights Street dance. She'd even kept her shop open late on Wine Wednesday to get some foot traffic in the door by handing out samples of her new fall flavors.

The extra work had been worth it. Between the Fall Festival and running pop-up carts at farmer's markets and craft fairs, the extra attention her shop had gotten took her from steady to thriving. Over the last few months, Devlin had drafted a business plan that included an expansion of her shop. She was trying not to get ahead of herself, but she wanted both a larger book section, and something else that would keep customers in her store for longer than it took to drink a cup of coffee. She was also not quite ready to leave what she had created at this location, it had become her own little slice of paradise. Devlin entered her office and turned on the sound system to play throughout the shop. She took a deep breath as she reached the counter, the strong aroma of coffee beans calming any negative thoughts in her head. She started her morning meditation, to focus on the quiet music and just breathe. In and out, her mind drifted to which bean would be the prominent smell for the day. *Ah, hazelnut is winning out.* She grabbed the grounds and started them as her daily house blend.

Motion outside the front door caught her eye and she glanced at the clock on the wall. Six a.m. — too early for customers, she didn't open for another half an hour.

She saw the person wave and recognized Annabelle. Devlin hurried to open the door and let in Annabelle — and a frigid gust of wind.

"You're out early today, AB," Devlin observed, using the group's nickname for Annabelle as she re-locked the door and walked behind the counter.

"You know us journalists never sleep." Annabelle gave a melodramatic shiver, stomping her feet on the mat at the door to release the fine snow that had collected on the toes of heeled winter boots that were better suited for anything but winter. "His Supreme Earldom said we could all have tomorrow off, but only if we met our deadline today. I'm sure I'll get done with just enough time to get dressed before heading over to Finnegan's tonight." Annabelle spoke of her boss at *The Amber Falls Bee*, Sebastian Locke. Their hate-hate relationship was legendary.

"That makes for one long day. Are you still planning to stay here tonight after the party?"

"You know it. Slumber party!" Annabelle's mouth widened in a jaw-breaking yawn, as she peered behind the counter. "It smells so good, what do you have started?"

"I have today's house blend brewing — hazelnut." Devlin took a cup from the tall stack and filled it. "Tell you what, why don't I bring you a pick-me-up after I close and grab your dress from your place so you can get ready here? I'll have a fresh pot on."

"You know I love you, and not just because I could inject your coffee into my veins, right?"

"I was hoping you loved me for more than just the coffee, but you know I need to hear it spoken out loud." Devlin grabbed a bagged muffin from behind the counter. "Blueberry?"

"I haven't eaten a single cookie all Christmas season so I could fit into my dress tonight, but, at this point I'll eat all the sugar and carbs if it'll keep me awake."

"I sized up my flapper dress so I could enjoy Mrs. Crenshaw's apple pie, and I savored every bite," Devlin said, referencing the town's elderly busybody.

"You look the same to me, Dev. Where are these extra pounds you're talking about?"

"They all landed about here." Devlin gestured to her midsection in a vague, absentminded way.

"Well, I don't care where anything lands so, yes, I'll take the muffin. Hey, how's that new girl working out?"

"Emma's great. She'll be opening the shop in the morning."

"That's good news, we can let loose tonight."

Devlin's stomach turned as she thought again about seeing Gabe tonight. "Yeah, we all need to party a little." She swallowed down a wave of nausea. *Get it together, Watkins!*

Annabelle narrowed her eyes and peered at Devlin. "You seem to be turning an odd shade of green. Are you sure you want to go?" she asked.

Devlin felt a hint of contrition about how she'd informed Annabelle and Prudence about Gabe. *I am glad they know.* The rest of it, though? At the time it had seemed like such a teensy tiny white lie. She preferred to call it a non-truth, the word lie seemed so…dramatic. The smallest of non-truths, really. She'd told Prudence and Annabelle, at an extra boozy ladies' night, the story about her and Gabe. The part about Boston was truthful. At one point, however, she'd told the girls that she and Gabe had met in Amber Falls after her move, had talked over what happened in Boston and decided to move past it. In truth, this had never happened. She *had* seen him, but he had no clue she was there. *I'll deal with this later.*

Devlin nodded and turned away, pretending to wipe down a spot on the counter. She wouldn't be able to ghost them tonight, but she was sure she'd find a way to disappear whenever Gabe came around. "I'm a grown woman and we have a deal." She sighed then set down the rag and looked at her friend. "Sorry, AB. I'm just distracted. The night will be perfect."

Annabelle reached out and squeezed Devlin's hand. "I know it will. So, dinner at the bar is still a go? We don't have to get there until late, I'm sure I'll be working, and I want you to get a nap in."

"Tell you what, when I drop off coffee after I close, let's see where you are in your day, and we can plan more then."

"I like it. Whatever happens, we can be back here as soon as we've decided the rest of New Year's Day is better spent sleeping."

"You have no idea how excited I am to sleep past five a.m." Devlin took a long drink from her own coffee.

"I don't like to get up that early, but I know what you mean about sleeping in."

"Hey, what do you think the over-under is on Prudence and Greyson making it to the bar tonight?"

Annabelle pondered the question for a moment. "Well, they're in the honeymoon phase of their relationship, and they already ditched out on our Boxing Day get together, so I expect them to be all over each other as long as they can and not show up to the bar until, say, eleven fifty-three p.m."

"That's specific, even for you."

"I'm hoping they show up, but we'll be okay if they don't. New love is a crazy drug."

Devlin cast her eyes toward the counter, trying not to feel the slightest hint of envy for the couple. *I am human after all.*

"Hey, I'm sorry," Annabelle said. "I was so serious when I said we don't need to go."

"I'm going to be damned if I let someone, a man no less, ruin a sensible plan. Besides, both you and Prudence know my history with Gabe, so I have nothing to hide from you." She crossed her fingers behind her back.

"I was hoping you'd say that, but if you change your mind, I'll do whatever you want." Annabelle took a sip and leaned her back on the counter, pointing to the opposite wall. "You know, I just read the art gallery between you and Finnegan's is going up for sale soon. The story is going to be in the next edition of The Bee."

Devlin ignored the flush that crept over her at the mention of Finnegan's, the new information ricocheting around in her head. At that moment, she had a clear vision of expanding her shop into the soon-to-be-vacant space. She'd been in the gallery only once — it had been cluttered with art, the owner getting ready for a new exhibit. The space was small for a downtown location but perfect for her plans, and she wouldn't have to move her shop. She rested her elbows on the counter and stared at the separating wall.

"Woah, earth to Dev." Annabelle waved her hand in front of Devlin's vacant eyes. "You're cleared for re-entry, Captain."

Devlin blinked, confused, then broke out into a large grin. "I'm gonna buy the place!"

"What?"

"I haven't said anything to you and Pru yet," Devlin confessed, "but I've been working on a plan to expand

Books and Beans and I haven't found any place that fits what I wanted as well as this location."

"That's great news."

"I'd love to expand my book and merchandise area. I've researched market trends, and the college students are more apt to buy extra things when they're already there and it's convenient for them."

"How convenient," agreed Annabelle.

"This opportunity is perfect."

"I'll see what other info I can get when I'm at work and I'll shoot it off to you." Annabelle finished her coffee and looked at her now empty cup, a hint of sadness in her eyes.

"You don't know how much I'll appreciate that. How about a refill for the road, friend?"

"You read my mind. Can I get two shots of espresso in that house blend, please?"

"Are you sure about that?"

"It's going to be a two-shot kind of morning." She paused and took a deep breath as if sensing something. "I can feel something in the air."

* * * *

After Annabelle left, Devlin let her mind wander to the festivities planned for the night. The theme was the 1920's and, despite Annabelle's previous protestations regarding Devlin's weight, the dress she'd selected had turned from a loose costume into a body hugging, cleavage bearing, try not to sit for too long because something might pop off, outfit. *And I look damn good in it.* The underlying white fabric was set aglow by silver bits and bobs sewn all over and sequined accents with long strings of beads falling from the hemline at her knees to her ankles.

She could go the whole night without seeing Gabe, she knew she could. Sure, at some point he'd come over and say hi to Annabelle, but when she saw him heading over, she could make an excuse to leave. Plus, the night was going to be so busy, and since Gabe was working, he wouldn't be hanging out with them, he'd be focused on running his business.

The overhead doorbell chimed, and a regular customer walked in. Devlin put on her best business smile and told herself she'd deal with whatever happened tonight when—*if*—it happened.

The morning flew by. It had been busier than she'd expected but the stream of customers was down to a trickle by the time she closed the shop in the early afternoon. Her mind had been occupied all morning by her work and her patrons, but now that she had a moment to think, her mind wandered, as it did most days, to Gabe. She scrubbed at some dried-on caramel syrup harder than she had to then threw her rag on the counter.

"Enough of this," she muttered to herself. "You have a full and rewarding life. You came to Amber Falls to start a business, not a relationship. Get your mind off that man."

The gods were not listening. She cursed Hades as the one person she didn't want to think about strode past her shop. Gabe stopped and, without warning, turned and reached for the door, trying to yank it open then peering through the glass when it held firmly shut.

Devlin was surprised to find herself ducking down behind the counter, her heart pounding. The door rattled once more then went silent. She wished she knew who the god of good luck was and offered vague thanks that she'd remembered to lock the door, sure the right deity would intercept it. She inched up to peer over the counter, relieved to see her doorway empty once again. If that wasn't a sign to get the hell out of there, she didn't know what was. She finished her work and grabbed Annabelle's coffee. She crept to the door, feeling so much trepidation that she ended up tiptoeing. She wasn't sure what she expected, but when Gabe failed to appear outside the door, or in the immediate vicinity, Devlin hurried the few blocks to The Amber Falls Bee.

She went straight to Annabelle's office but had to go searching for her when she wasn't behind her desk. She cocked her head to the side, listening for the familiar strains of — ah, there it was — the now familiar raised voices of enemies in the wild. The thought crossed her mind to leave the coffee on Annabelle's desk, but she remembered they needed to finalize the details of tonight's plans. Plus, no one wanted cold coffee, and who knew how long they'd be if someone didn't interrupt them. She followed the raised voices to Sebastian's office.

"Winters, it isn't going to snow. They've forecast two storms this year that ended up being some wind blowing around tiny amounts of flurries. Each of those storms had front page headlines for a week predicting a 'snowpocalypse' that never happened."

"This storm is a Nor'easter, sir," Annabelle explained to Sebastian in a voice meant for school children.

Devlin leaned into Sebastian's office in time to see the most baffled expression cross his face. It looked like he'd been pacing the room while Annabelle had one of her hips propped against his desk, her arms crossed.

"I don't—" He stopped pacing and raised one of his hands to his temple like he was massaging away a headache. "What the hell is the difference?"

Annabelle mimicked his gesture. "Do you even read your own newspaper? The articles we've printed have gone into minute detail about the differences," she snapped, adding at his glare, "Sir."

"Hey, guys!" Devlin chimed in.

"Devlin!" Sebastian broke into a smile. "It's good to see you."

"I didn't know you'd be with Annabelle, otherwise I would've brought you something, too." She held up the coffee.

"That's nice of you to say, but Winters and I are done here." He turned to face Annabelle. "You're dismissed."

Devlin could see the pressure building in Annabelle's lithe frame and grabbed her hand, pulling her out of the office and throwing a quick bye over her shoulder. She whispered to Annabelle, "You have to print something about the Nor'easter."

Annabelle looked like she was ready to go back in and battle it out with Sebastian but took a deep breath and stated loud enough to hear throughout the office, "It's already done, it'll be on the front page tomorrow." A loud crash came from Sebastian's office. He'd heard. Annabelle propelled them down the hall to her office. "I was just letting him know as a courtesy that the front page was changing with the new forecast."

"You think it'll turn out to be a bad one?"

"I've heard reports of three feet, Dev, but it could be a lot more." Annabelle took the coffee and settled into her chair. She slid off her boots and took a sip. "Wanna sit? I have a few minutes."

"Not today. I do want to try to get a nap in if I still can."

"I hope you take one long enough for the both of us."

"How's the workload coming?" Devlin leaned her shoulder against the doorway. "Will you still be done early?"

"We've had to change the entire front page around now that the new forecast has come out." Annabelle glanced at the clock. "I can't see us being out of here any earlier than eight."

"That's fine by me, no need to rush on my behalf."

"How about this, I'll finish up here and grab dinner on the way over to your place. That way we're not spending the whole night at the bar?"

Devlin nodded. "Great idea. I'll run over and get your bag."

"Thanks, Dev. I'm sorry this storm is throwing a wrench into our plans."

"Hey, the new year will ring in no matter what we do and I for one find comfort in that fact. See you tonight." Devlin turned to go but stopped. "You know, this is Sebastian's first real winter. Atlanta only has two seasons—hot and rainy. You should cut him some slack."

Annabelle snorted into her coffee. "I will do no such thing."

Chapter Two

"Hey, toss me that screwdriver," Gabe called to his brother, reaching out from under the hood of the car.

"Which one? You have at least ten in here." Greyson rattled around in the drawer of the tool chest.

"Phillips, please."

"Here you go. You know, Dan down at the service station can put the new spark plug in." Greyson leaned against the side of his '86 Jeep and peered in.

"Hollywood made you soft. '86 was the prime year for this SUV, you should be able to do almost anything but replace the engine on it." Gabe swore as the screwdriver pinged off the screw and hit his other hand. "Damn, this one's almost stripped. Why'd you park down here anyway?"

"I wouldn't call it parked—this is where the Jeep died. I'm lucky I got it into this lot."

"I suppose. Hand me that spark plug. You need help with the new house any time soon? I'm almost done with the renos on my place, and I need a new project."

Greyson had just purchased a large fixer upper a few blocks from Gabe's house. The house was in rough condition, but Greyson said it would be home for him and Prudence once he could repair it. Gabe had looked at the house with him before Greyson had purchased it, giving advice about the repairs and what they'd be able to do together.

"All right, that should do it." Gabe straightened, a smile passing over his face. His smile fell right off when he saw the green tinge on Greyson's face. "You breathe in too many fumes?"

"I'm going to propose to Prudence tonight," Greyson blurted.

"Oh shit, man! That's fucking awesome news!" Gabe pulled Greyson into a hug, clapping him on the back.

"I'm glad you think so, because my pulse has not stopped beating double time since I got the ring from Mom."

"Grandma's ring?"

"No. Mom's always held that ring close to her heart. I figured when she lets it go, it'll be for her baby boy."

Gabe landed a punch to Greyson's arm. "You're an idiot, she would've been happy for you to have it."

"When I called her last week and told her I was proposing to Pru, she dropped the phone and Dad had to come on the line. They're both excited about it, but she did tell me she had a ring that would suit Prudence much better, Great Aunt Shell's ring."

Greyson pulled a small box out of his pocket, opening it to show Gabe an antique ring set in platinum with a ruby stone surrounded by diamonds. "She said with Pru's red hair, it would be stunning on her."

Gabe reached out and touched the ring. Despite the cold day, the ring was warm, like it had just been taken off a finger. "I haven't seen this ring in decades."

"I'm always grateful for Mom, especially at times like this." He snapped the box shut and tucked it back in his pocket. "She also said you don't call her enough and wanted to know if you'd found anyone special yet."

Gabe rolled his eyes, their brotherly bonding moment broken. Even though he and Greyson were the only children, he was the baby of the family and still, on a rare occasion, he was treated like it. Their mom couldn't understand why he hadn't found a nice girl to settle down with. Greyson had always gotten a pass on things like that. Being a big Hollywood actor, he was supposed to be a playboy and not get serious. "I own a bar, Grey. I can find someone special every night."

"I don't believe that, you don't have it in you. And this town's too small."

"Well, I'm not alone."

"There's a difference between being alone and being lonely."

Gabe slammed the hood of the Jeep down. "Jesus, what movie did that line come from?"

"*A Good Day to Die*, the last Ben Stone movie," Greyson said.

"Let's keep cheesy quotes like that in the movies, shall we?" Gabe put his gloves back on and rubbed his hands together to warm them.

"No problem, bro. You want a ride back to the bar?" Greyson looked at his watch. "It's only three."

"I'll walk, you're going the opposite direction. I could use the fresh air anyway, since I won't get outside tonight until well after two a.m." He waved at Greyson and turned to go. "Wait! When are you proposing tonight? Will I see you at the bar?"

"I'm going to bring her to the new house then we'll be over."

"If you don't make it that's okay, this is a big night for you."

"We'll be there, I promise."

Gabe threw out a salute then turned to walk back to Finnegan's.

He was happy for his brother. He knew Hollywood hadn't been easy on him and was thankful he was back in Amber Falls. Prudence was Greyson's perfect fit and they'd both realized it. It didn't stop a pang from hitting him square in the chest. He didn't think he was feeling jealousy, envy or even resentment. He wanted nothing but the best for them. A laugh burst out of him as he thought of the line from Greyson's movie. Maybe he *was* lonely. He'd been working long hours and, despite his big talk earlier, he hadn't had time for a relationship of any sort in over a year. He used to drop Greyson's name to get some action when he was younger, but those days were long behind him. He could be looking for something more serious he realized, surprised that a thought like that would cross his bachelor's mind.

He was almost back to the bar when the strong aroma of coffee hit him as he passed by the neighboring coffee shop.

He glanced through the window and caught a glimpse of a woman he swore he'd seen before. It took him a moment to process this information before he could turn back to the door, trying to pull it open. *Locked, dammit.* He was sure he'd just seen the same strange woman that had watched him through Finnegan's window before disappearing. She hadn't come into the bar and had backed away like she'd seen a ghost. He'd gone to the door to see if he could catch her, but she was nowhere in sight up or down the sidewalk. Maybe *she* had been the ghost.

The inside of the shop was dark, and a closed sign hung on the door. Still, he gave one more tug on the handle before he turned and left. *Please don't let me be haunted by a ghost.* He was sure he'd seen a woman inside the shop. Her profile was familiar — the curve of her cheek, the shape of her eyes. His memory flashed back to that night, and he squinted, trying to bring the faded memory of her into view, hoping they'd overlap, matching like a fingerprint test. His mind kept the details in the dark, but his body tensed in response to his beckoning memory, one that frayed his nerves and set him on fire. He was haunted, he realized, just not by a ghost.

* * * *

"Where have you been now?" Annabelle asked, clearly frustrated as Devlin slipped back into the booth. "He didn't come over here this time. Why are you acting like you don't want him to know you exist?"

Devlin knew Gabe was friends with Annabelle, but she hadn't expected him to be at their table every damn half hour. She'd been making up excuses to leave whenever she'd spied Gabe winding his way to them. "I'm going to drive you to Dr. Simmons tomorrow if you say you've gone to the bathroom one more time. That's not normal."

"Oh." Devlin gestured to no one spot in particular. "I saw one of my regulars and went to say hi." She didn't want to go to the doctor's office and had already spent more time than she ever wanted to in a bar bathroom.

Annabelle narrowed her eyes at the comment but was distracted when Sebastian walked into the bar, a beautiful brunette following behind. Devlin assessed the couple, noting how attractive they both were. Both were very tall, taller than her, with the same shade of sable hair. The night just got a lot more interesting.

"That bastard. He'd better not come over here." Annabelle pretended not to look then downed the rest of her amaretto sour. Devlin *was* looking and saw Sebastian's face light up with a smile that could only be described as devilish when he spotted Annabelle after scanning the room. The woman he was with was dressed in a short, black flapper costume and Sebastian, well, Sebastian appeared like he belonged in the 1920's. He was dapper in his form-fitting three-piece suit, a watch chain glinting against his buttoned-up vest. His black overcoat had velvet lapels that were dusted with snow. He brushed off the snow and leaned down to say something to his companion, shrugged and gestured to the bar as she left, leaving Sebastian standing alone before he walked in the direction of their table.

"Dammit, he is. I'm going to need another drink if I'm going to be expected to talk with him all night." Annabelle looked in her glass as if she could wish it to fill back up.

"I'll go get you a refill," Devlin offered.

"Let me guess," Annabelle stated when Sebastian reached them. "Either she's already bored with you, or you didn't pay her enough to stay with you the whole night."

"At least I'm here with someone, Winters." He smirked, sliding into the seat across from them. "I'm sorry you are ringing in the new year all by yourself. Alone."

"I'm not alone. I'm with Devlin and my date is..." She pointed to the bar where her date, a fellow reporter from The Bee, was talking to the brunette Sebastian had brought, their heads bent very close together. "Well, fuck."

Devlin scanned the bar once again and she saw Gabe spot Sebastian and start walking over. "I'll get us drinks." She ducked out of the booth. *Close call, Watkins.*

"Two amaretto sours and a rum and diet, please," she asked the bartender when he stopped in front of her. Gabe's visit to their table was brief, and she had plenty of time to follow him with covert eyes as he slipped through the crowd with practiced skill, greeting customers as he went. *He is so handsome tonight.* While most of the other men were dressed to the nines in three-piece suits and glossy shoes, Gabe's outfit was more subtle — a pinstriped shirt rolled to his elbows and brown corduroy pants with suspenders. With worn work boots completing the outfit he looked effortless, strong and capable, like someone who would've embodied the hard work ethic of the late 1920's laborers. She was broken out of her reverie when the bartender set the drinks in front of her.

She made her way back to the booth just in time to hear Annabelle say, "and that's a fucking fact." She paused. A feather from her headband was now in her hand, an inch away from Sebastian's nose. She lowered it onto the table and finished with a voice of steel, "Sir."

Devlin looked between the two. Annabelle's face showed pure contempt while Sebastian's was full of mirth.

"I just wanted to know if you thought it was going to snow all night, Winters."

"Drinks!" Annabelle and Sebastian started at her voice, clearly unaware that she'd been standing next to the table. She shook her head as she set the drinks down, hoping she wasn't as obtuse about Gabe as these two were about each other. Their situations were different, but still. "I brought drinks!"

Sebastian slid over when Annabelle didn't and motioned her to sit down. "Thanks, Devlin. I wasn't planning on drinking anything until midnight, but it seems like a good idea now." He shot a pointed look at Annabelle.

Annabelle scowled and took a long sip of her drink but was saved from having to come up with a retort when Chuck Charleson and his girlfriend stopped at their booth. Chuck was Prudence's ex-boyfriend and had been dating the local *EyeWitness* news reporter, Kinsley, since before Halloween. Devlin glanced at her watch as the conversation turned to what it always had as of late — the weather. She half listened thinking about tomorrow, about getting out of this bar, about anything other than Gabe, so of course she flicked her eyes to him against her will. The night was going to be long.

As it neared midnight, she'd been able to go back to pretending to be unaware of the man who owned the bar. She just had to keep it together for a few more minutes. She gave herself a shake, wondering if she shouldn't finish her drink. Her mind was getting a little cloudy and now was not the time to get careless.

"It's almost midnight, let's go get the champagne, Devlin," Annabelle suggested, breaking into her thoughts. "I think I need another drink with my champagne anyway."

Sebastian, who had stood to talk with Chuck and Kinsley, turned to Annabelle, giving away the fact that he'd been listening to their conversation. "Double fisting it, Ace?" he asked, and Devlin saw his gaze bob down to the gap in Annabelle's neckline.

Annabelle scooted out of the booth and stood, brushing against his chest, unsteady on her feet to all appearances from her drinks, but most likely to screw with him. "Wouldn't you like to know," she said with a low, sultry purr in her voice.

Sebastian's nostrils flared as he breathed in with a sharp inhale.

Chuck tugged on Kinsley's arm and moved away. "We're gonna go. Happy New Year, everyone."

Annabelle smiled and tugged Devlin to the bar as Sebastian sat back in their booth. She giggled, "Messing with him is so easy. A man is a man is a man, they don't stand a chance."

"Is that all that was, AB? Messing with him?"

"Of course. What a silly question."

Devlin surveyed the bar, not seeing Gabe anywhere. "I hope Greyson and Prudence make it," she said, knowing it was possible they wouldn't.

The bartender had just handed them drinks when someone jostled them, reaching in between them, trying to pick up Devlin's glass.

"Excuse me, ladies," the person connected to the hand said.

"Hey, get your own—the hell?" Annabelle asked. "What the fuck is that?" She pointed to a large ring.

"Oh this?" The person was Prudence. She raised her hand, admiring the beautiful ring, and smiled. "Grey proposed tonight."

"Oh my God, Pru! Congratulations!" Devlin reached out and hugged her.

"About damn time." Annabelle threw her arms around her already hugging friends. "Give us the details, this is Page Six stuff."

"Of course. Greyson wants only you to do the write-up, AB."

"Associated Press, here I come." Annabelle threw a look back at the booth. "Eat that, your royal pain in my ass."

"Speaking of." Prudence tried to follow Annabelle's line of sight. "Did Sebastian grace us with his presence tonight?" she asked as she raised her hand to get the bartender's attention, her ring sparkling in the light, nodding and flashing two fingers when the bartender indicated a champagne bottle.

"Oh yes." Annabelle jerked her head to the far side of the bar then finished her whiskey in one gulp. "He's here, and he brought a date."

Devlin and Prudence exchanged quick looks.

"Why does that matter?" Prudence asked in her sweetest, most nonchalant voice.

"It. Doesn't. Matter," Annabelle ground out and glared at the other two. "I'm just stating the facts." She noticed the second glance between the two as they grabbed their drinks. "What? It doesn't!"

"Methinks you doth protest too much, AB." Devlin steered them toward the booth their friends were gathered at.

"If by doth protesting, you mean I don't care what that abhorrent man does, then you're right." Annabelle rolled her eyes as they neared the table. "Besides, I don't want to talk about me. You got engaged tonight, Pru!"

"I hear congratulations are in order." Sebastian stood and placed a light kiss on Prudence's cheek.

Devlin once again tuned out the conversation around her, feeling like a bad friend, especially after the news of Prudence and Greyson's engagement, but she was tired. Her stomach was also starting to growl with hunger. She noticed that Greyson and Prudence had wandered on to the dance floor and Sebastian and

Annabelle had started arguing again. She slipped away from them, hoping not to be noticed. *I just needed a few bar nuts and I'll be fine.* She walked to the bar, the combination of hunger and tiredness had hit her like a wall. She was careless and didn't even look to see where Gabe was.

Chapter Three

Gabe looked at the clock for what seemed like the hundredth time. He loved New Year's Eve, being a part of everyone's night, and because of his business he was able to bring everyone together in one place, but tonight felt different. Annabelle was with a mystery woman. A woman who vanished every time he got near their booth. He swore that if he so much as *thought* about going over there, he'd look over to see she was already gone. He couldn't pin down why she was so familiar to him. He'd had brief sightings of her over the last year or so. Tonight, he caught flashes of silver and the twirl of a dress out of the corner of his eye, but she was never there. The universe had more concrete proof that bigfoot existed than his mystery woman.

He sighed and tried to shake it off. It would die down after midnight, and he'd get to sleep in tomorrow. Maybe that was all he needed, a good night's sleep. A quick zip of silver beading caught his eye and he turned. "Hey, what can I get you?" He locked eyes with the woman who had eluded him. He *did* know her; he had no doubt now. The bleach blonde from Boston now had short, brown hair — but those eyes. Now that he was mere feet away from her, he knew. He couldn't mistake those eyes, so green, the color of moss in a rolling river on a spring day after the winter snow had melted.

They stood suspended in time as the clock started its inevitable countdown to midnight.

"Happy New Year!" The sound of the crowd cheering broke them out of their daze, but now the woman looked stricken. She put her hand to her mouth with a gasp, turned, and dashed out of the door.

Gabe was propelled into movement, running around the bar, dodging a kissing Greyson and Prudence as he ran to the door, but he was too late. She was too fast and had disappeared into the cold night. He closed the door behind him, leaning against it for support. *It's her.*

"What the hell was that?" Annabelle asked as she walked up to Gabe. "What did you say to Devlin? Where did she go?" She shook his arm "Gabe? Where did Devlin go?"

Gabe snapped back to reality. "*That's* the Devlin you've been talking about?" he asked, although he now knew the answer.

"We should talk," Prudence offered as she and Greyson joined them, the sounds of the midnight ballad fading.

"I have a plan!" Annabelle exclaimed, pushing her shoulder into Sebastian's chest to move him back as he'd come to stand with the group.

"No, not one of your schemes, Annabelle." Gabe ran his hand through his hair in frustration. He sighed. "All right, I'm listening."

"First," Annabelle demanded, "tell us everything. If I'm going to come up with a plan I need to know all the details."

Gabe was uncomfortable with all the attention. He decided they weren't going to leave him alone and motioned for them to follow him to the back room, shutting the door once they'd all filed in. "Listen, the details aren't important. The last time I was in Boston I met her in a bar, and we spent one night together, I didn't know her name."

"Nice, man," Sebastian said, then yelped as Annabelle pinched his arm.

Gabe continued, "I thought what we had was special, not just a one-night stand, but she was gone the next morning. No note, no clues to her identity, so I moved on."

"What about when she moved here last year?" Prudence questioned.

"What?" Gabe noted the lack of surprise on his friends' faces. "What the hell is going on?"

Annabelle shot a quick look at Prudence, who nodded. "Devlin moved here last year and opened Books and Beans. She told us that she ran into you one day, you guys talked and decided what happened between you was in the past and you'd just move on from it."

"I haven't seen or spoken to her since Boston," Gabe insisted.

"How have you not noticed her around town?" Prudence asked.

"She's literally two doors down from you, Gabe," Annabelle added.

Gabe hung his head, letting out a sigh. "I guess I have, now that I think back on it. She was familiar, I got this weird sense of déjà vu one day when I saw a woman outside the bar, but by the time I got to the door to see who she was, she was gone. Was I supposed to track her down and say, 'hey, was it you I had mind-blowing, life-altering sex with one night a year and a half ago in Boston?' How well do you think that would've gone over? I'd end up looking like a shallow asshole no matter what. So, I just left it. I figured our paths would cross one day and I'd know, but that never happened."

"By never happened, do you mean you've been avoiding her on purpose so you wouldn't have to know?" Annabelle asked.

"Why would I *not* want to know, Annabelle?" Gabe snapped.

"Hey, I'm just saying," Annabelle placated, "sometimes it's easier to leave the unknown alone and live in blissful ignorance."

"The person I was with never told me her name and was gone by the time I woke the next morning. And *that* girl" — he pointed to the office door — "looks nothing like who I was with in Boston. She had long blonde hair and…her eyes. I didn't know for sure she was the same person until I saw her eyes." Prudence started to say something, but Gabe cut her off, holding up his hand. "And by the way, she was the one who ended up outside my window. If she wanted to say something, she could have. Plus, she lied to you both."

"I get it," Greyson soothed. "Either way, you don't come out looking great in this situation and that sucks."

"Okay," Annabelle said. "So, Devlin knows you live here, but she's been avoiding you and we don't know why."

"We?" Gabe asked the group. "Who exactly is *we*?"

Prudence and Annabelle raised their hands.

"Wait, you knew, Pru?" Greyson asked.

"The story wasn't mine to tell, Grey," she sighed. "But it's out in the open now. We've only known since the Fall Festival. She didn't go into the whole story with us, she just filled us in on the barest of details before asking us not to say anything. We didn't push her, we figured she'd tell us more if she needed to."

Annabelle nodded. "Everyone has a past, and some people want to leave theirs behind. But" she added, looking around at the group, "that doesn't mean we can't do something about it now. I really do have a plan."

"Are you being serious, Winters?" asked Sebastian, who had been silent since Annabelle had pinched him.

Annabelle turned to look at Sebastian. "What on earth are you still doing here? What happened to your date? Shouldn't you be in a sex dungeon somewhere tying her up right now?"

"Jealous?" he asked, clearly oblivious to the eyes widening in the room. He took a fraction of a step back from the force of Annabelle's glare. "She's my sister, Winters, and that's low, even for you. Besides, she already left with *your* date."

"One," Annabelle retorted without missing a beat, "you felt the need to go all night without telling me she's your sister? And two, you let your sister leave with one of your subordinates?"

Sebastian's smirk fell right off his face. "Oh, shit."

"Back on topic, guys." Prudence motioned for them to cut it out.

Gabe was both happy his friends wanted to help and frustrated they thought he needed help. "I'm serious." He decided he wanted them to stay out of it. "I'm a grown man who can take care of his own life. I'll deal with this in my own way." He walked over and opened the office door, gesturing for them to start moving out.

"Now let's get back out there and finish off the night. I have a business to run."

He turned and headed back out to the bar first when they didn't move fast enough, glimpsing the look that passed between Greyson and Prudence and the little shove Annabelle gave Sebastian to get him moving.

* * * *

Devlin was shattered. All her memories from Boston, all the memories she'd tried to run away from, that she'd wanted to bury, were ricocheting through her head. She'd only had a panic attack once and this felt the same. One minute she was gasping for breath and the next she heard the soothing voice of Annabelle, her hands running over her back. She was so grateful at this moment that they were good enough friends to have exchanged keys.

"I'm sorry, Dev," she heard her say, and focused on Annabelle's hand making circles on her back. "I rang three times and when you didn't answer I had to come up."

Devlin's breathing was returning to normal, and she sat, leaning her head against the back of her couch, her eyes closed. "Thank you, Annabelle. I didn't hear the buzzer."

Annabelle stood from her crouch and sat in the chair across from Devlin. "I figured that." She appeared thoughtful for a moment. "Well, I figured *something*. I told Prudence to go home. Getting engaged is a big deal and I didn't want her to be away from Greyson tonight."

"Oh God, no!" Devlin exclaimed. "Thank you for doing that. She would've been here otherwise. Tonight should've been a celebration of their engagement."

Annabelle grinned. "I don't think anything will stop them from celebrating." Her phone pinged multiple times in a row. "Her ears must be burning, that's her now." She was quiet for a few minutes while she typed, then set her phone down and looked at Devlin. "She wanted to come over, but I said we've got this covered. She'll bring Chinese food for lunch tomorrow, though."

"I'm glad to hear that." She lapsed into silence for a few moments before asking, "What did he say, AB?"

"He told us what happened in Boston."

"Us?"

"Prudence, Greyson and Sebastian."

"Sebastian, no!"

Annabelle grimaced. "I know, I'm sorry. He's so nosy."

"What was his version of what happened?"

"If I tell you his version, will you please tell me yours? The real one this time?"

Devlin nodded.

"He said he met you at a bar in Boston one night. You went back to his hotel and had mind-blowing sex, then you disappeared by the next morning, and he never knew your name."

"That's it?"

"Should there be more?" Annabelle questioned, ever the reporter.

"Not in Boston, that's pretty much what happened."

"He said he might've seen you here. He saw a woman through Finnegan's window who had a passing resemblance to you, but your hair was too short and not the right color, so he blew it off as a weird déjà vu."

"I remember that day. That's when I knew he was here."

"He wasn't one hundred percent sure until tonight."

Devlin nodded. Everything she'd held back felt like it needed to get out of her, and it had to happen right now.

"There was a guy." She looked at Annabelle, who nodded at her to continue. "My boyfriend. Ex-boyfriend. He wasn't very nice to me. He wasn't very nice to anyone."

"I'm so sorry, Devlin."

"Don't be. I left him right before I met Gabe. I found Amber Falls a few weeks later and have never looked back."

"Damn right you did, sister." Annabelle sat straight in her chair, nodding. "But it must've been so strange to see Gabe, right?"

"Oh yes. I had a weird feeling like being sucked into a void, like a sinkhole or something. It lasted for only a few minutes until I realized he didn't recognize me, and if he didn't recognize me then I didn't need to be around him. I came here for a fresh start. I'd finally gotten the courage to get out of a bad relationship and I didn't want anything to do with Boston, including Gabe. I could live my life, he could live his, and we'd never have to cross paths." She sighed. "Then Greyson came home."

"Yes, he did," Annabelle agreed.

"Once Greyson and Prudence got together, it felt like we started to be forced into each other's company. That's why I told you Gabe and I had spoken and to please not say anything. I didn't want you two to do anything. I was able to make excuses not to be around when I knew he'd be there until tonight." She shook her head. "Was he upset when he found out I knew?"

"I think surprised, more than upset. You guys need to talk this out."

"What a mess I've turned this into."

"You could've stayed home, Devlin. I would've been fine on my own."

"No, I decided I wasn't going to hide tonight." She shrugged. "I take that back; I wasn't going to hide out of sight the whole night."

"You don't have a bladder problem, do you?"

Devlin laughed at how ridiculous this all was. "I don't. I just left the table every time Gabe started walking in our direction."

"Thank goodness. I just want to sleep until the afternoon and not run you to Dr. Simmons.

"Are you still staying here tonight?"

"I don't think I could drag my tired ass home if I tried. Besides, why let this ruin our slumber party? I'm sleeping on your couch." She pointed to the overnight bag Devlin had grabbed earlier. "I'm ready for pjs."

"That sounds like heaven right now. I've been up for" — Devlin looked at her watch — "twenty hours and I could drop."

They sat in silence, both too exhausted to move, but Devlin needed to know what happened with Annabelle and Sebastian.

"Where did Sebastian end up tonight after you all had a heart to heart with Gabe?"

"That was his sister he was with, not a date." She stopped talking long enough that Devlin thought she'd fallen asleep. "He walked me here."

"Really?" Devlin asked, surprised both by the comment and the fact that Annabelle was still awake.

Annabelle nodded. "He said I was a pain in the ass, but I was his pain in the ass, and he wasn't going to let me get kidnapped despite me letting him know how close you lived." She closed her eyes, the combination of the whiskey, long hours and emotional conversation overtaking her. "Isn't that nice?"

Devlin watched her friend about to doze off on the couch, not sure if Annabelle knew she was letting her softening feelings toward Sebastian show. She stood and grabbed Annabelle's hand and led her toward the bathroom.

"That was very gentlemanly of him, I'll give him that. Now let's get you into your pajamas. We've got some hardcore sleeping to do and I'm not going to let you pass out in a flapper dress, no matter how tired you are."

"You're a good friend, Dev. I'll see you in the morning." Annabelle entered the bathroom, closing the door.

Devlin pulled out the hide-a-bed and dimmed the lights before entering her room. After changing her clothes she sat on her bed, drained, thinking over the last few hours. Then, she did what she hadn't been able to do for years. She let go of her past misery, giving her body a shake. Everyone had a history. She wasn't going to let hers define her and would be damned if she was going to spend another second wallowing in it. She was stronger than that.

Chapter Four

A week had passed since the New Year's Eve debacle, and Gabe still hadn't seen Devlin. *Devlin.* Sometimes he said her name out loud, in the quiet of his car, in the office of the bar, while lying awake late at night in his bed. It seemed so foreign to him, to have a name to put to the face that had haunted him. *There it is again, a haunting.* What else would you call it? For the last year her blurred countenance had inhabited his mind, unbidden and unwelcome. Now that he knew she was mere feet away from him all day long, he'd become clumsy and distracted, over-pouring beer, knocking over bowls of pretzels, forgetting orders. Even now, with his good friend Annabelle seated across from him, he couldn't seem to hold on to the thread of their conversation. In his defense, both Annabelle and Sebastian had come in separately for lunch and sat at opposite ends of the bar pretending the other person wasn't there but butting into each other's conversation. Everything was getting confusing.

"...seriously can't believe you haven't gone over there yet, Gabe," Annabelle was in the middle of saying. "How can you not go and talk to her?"

"I—" Gabe tried to answer.

"She doesn't want to see him, Winters," Sebastian cut him off. "In fact, she went so far as to lie to you about the whole thing. Like I said before—"

"Before?" Gabe asked, doing the interrupting this time. "I gather you've both talked about this at length?"

"I wouldn't call it talking." Annabelle sounded sheepish. "But yes, we've gone over the facts a few times."

"I don't know if this has escaped your notice"— Gabe looked at each of them in turn—"but she hasn't been knocking down my door to have a heart to heart."

"It hasn't escaped mine," Sebastian muttered into his beer.

"Now listen here—" Annabelle started.

Gabe held up his hand to cut her off. "Don't push this, Annabelle. In fact, both of you listen to me. I need to come to terms with her living in my city in my own time, and you need to let me approach her when I'm ready. It will happen. We will talk, I promise you both, although I owe nothing to either of you regarding this."

"She's my friend, Gabe." Annabelle's tone softened, showing a side of her that he knew came out only on rare occasions. "She opened up a little bit and I think you should hear her out. A simple conversation will take care of the whole thing."

Gabe opened his mouth to answer when the door chimed and Prudence and Greyson walked in, hand in hand. They took in the separation between Annabelle and Sebastian and the frustration on Gabe's face, looked at each other and headed to opposite corners,

Prudence to Annabelle's side and Greyson to Sebastian's.

"We're having The Talk," Annabelle explained to Prudence as she sat.

"Ah," Greyson responded. "How's it going, little brother?"

"About as well as it can with these two offering sage advice I didn't ask for."

"Hey, my advice is rock solid," Sebastian insisted. "As for Winters, I wouldn't listen to a word she has to say."

Greyson elbowed Sebastian and took a handful of fries from his plate. "We haven't said anything since New Year's but you and Devlin ignoring each other is starting to get a little weird, I have to admit."

Gabe scowled and put a pint in front of Greyson. "As I was just telling Woodward and Bernstein here, she hasn't exactly been knocking down my door to have a heart to heart. I don't understand why I'm the one who needs to make the first move. So far, she's admitted to knowing about me for over a year and not doing anything about it. She lied to AB and Pru about the whole thing."

He turned around to the till, opened it and started organizing the bills, a habit he had when he needed a moment. He could still see the look of surprise turned horror on Devlin's face, a comical change of expression that would be funny in any other circumstance but in this case, it just made him sick. He'd replayed the moment, over and over, so many times that he was sure the outcome would be different. In his mind, instead of freezing, he'd put his hand on hers to still her, stopping her from running away. She'd entwine her fingers with his and squeeze, understanding what he wanted to say without him having to speak any words.

He slammed the till shut. That shit only happened in romance novels. Telepathy was an underused form of communication in real life. In real life you had to talk and argue, be right or be wrong. Then, when you figure out what side you fall on, be willing to be the bigger person by either forgiving or groveling. He'd lain in bed for so many nights thinking about her that he had a hard time processing how close they'd been to each other. He felt like he should have sensed her, a disturbance, her life force connected to his in such a powerful manner after one night that they should've been drawn together as soon as they were in the same zip code.

In the last week, he'd started second-guessing what had happened in Boston. Had it meant so little to her that she was unfazed by his presence? How could she know they were neighbors and not want to bust his door down to shout that it was her—she was here! — and they could reconnect like no time had passed? It stung to know that not only this wasn't the case, but she'd lied to her friends about it. They'd never talked, no Amber Falls Accord had been drawn up so they could peacefully coexist in the same place.

"Gabe, we're not passing any judgment on you," Prudence called from behind him when he didn't turn back around. "We just want everyone to get along, and that can only happen if you guys talk."

He turned, all eyes focused on him, waiting for what, he didn't know. He'd said all he needed to, so he'd say it again. "I *will* talk to her."

Silence settled over everyone. Even Sebastian and Annabelle appeared to have nothing to say to each other, the quiet only broken when Leo, the chef for the bar, came out from the kitchen.

"Woah." Leo saw the somber group. "Who died?"

Annabelle laughed, breaking the tension that had taken over the room. "No one, Leo. We're just having a discussion."

"Ooh, is it about Devlin?" he asked.

Gabe turned to him with his hands up. "What the hell, Leo?"

"You've been moping about her for longer than you realize, man. I'm just pointing out the facts." He looked at Greyson and Prudence. "You guys want any lunch? I just took some ribs out of the smoker." They both agreed that it sounded perfect, and Leo left to plate it.

"In fact," Gabe decided with a suddenness that gave him whiplash, ready for it all to be over so they could go back to their regularly scheduled lives, "I'll be the bigger person here and talk to her today."

He ignored the surprise on their faces at his words. He could do it. He was an adult. He'd pull his big boy pants up, go over there and talk to her.

Long after his friends had left and he was bundling up to go and shovel the sidewalk, the thought crept into his head that when he went to Devlin, they'd once again be sharing the same space. *The same air*. But a promise was a promise, and he told them he'd talk to her today. Why did he think he needed more than courage to approach her?

* * * *

It had been over a week of blistering wind and seemingly endless flurries. Devlin shoveled a fresh blanket of snow from the sidewalk in front of her shop.

She hadn't expected him to come running the next day to proclaim his undying love for her, but some sort of acknowledgment would've been nice. She supposed she could've gone over there too, but...well...she hadn't.

She heard a jangle from the doorbell two doors down and out walked the man she was trying so hard not to think about. He emerged from the bar door, a shovel in one hand and a bag of sidewalk salt in the other. Turning in her direction, his eyes widened just a fraction when he saw her. Devlin tried not to look; she tried not to pay attention as he started to shovel, his movements graceful as he heaved the snow into an increasing pile. She couldn't stop staring and had stepped an inch toward him when her movement was broken by a group of men carrying items out of the building between theirs. She resumed her shoveling, the movers creating an invisible line that couldn't be broached as long they were there, watching each other with wary eyes.

The middle shop had indeed gone for sale like Annabelle had told her it would, but the way the township bylaws were written, the town council had to approve the sale. Tonight was the town council meeting where she'd present her bank approval and put in her official offer. When she'd bought Books and Beans, she'd given a quick informal presentation in front of the council, and they'd approved her purchase right away. She had no reason to see why tonight would be any different.

She was excited, with so many ideas and plans, and seeing the movers empty the space out made everything seem real. She'd been able to view it a few times with her realtor but couldn't help wanting to know what it looked like empty.

Devlin approached the men. She could sense Gabe's attention was on them despite him being turned away from her. "Hey, guys, do you mind if I take a quick peek inside?"

Gabe's head turned to the side, a sharp movement as if a noise had startled him. She saw his perfect profile come into stark relief against the low winter sun that shone down the street, his breath white puffs, sharp and heavy.

"We're done here, I'm just locking it up," one of the men said.

Devlin batted her eyes at the helpless duo. "What if I promised to lock the door behind me?" At their hesitation, she explained, "I own Books and Beans, right there." She pointed next door. "You know where to find me if anything is amiss. And your next cup of coffee is on me."

"All right, but double check to make sure the place is locked tight when you leave."

Her sexy pout turned into a large grin that fell off her face and she jumped when she heard Finnegan's door open with a loud bang. Gabe walked inside with an inscrutable expression on his face, but the hard line of his mouth gave away his displeasure.

She shrugged and turned to enter the old art gallery. The winter day was dreary despite the sun hanging on at the horizon, so she flipped on all the overhead lights and let out a sigh of pleasure as she looked on to the bare walls. The brick along one wall was the same as in her shop and she imagined the extension into this room — seamless and perfect.

No more than thirty feet across, the space was smaller than her store. She ran her fingers along the rough brick of the wall and walked the length of one side, planning where she could take down a partial wall. An arched entry, maybe two, would open it up. She pictured bookshelves lining the walls, leather couches and overstuffed chairs welcoming customers to stay and drink coffee while they browsed and sampled books. Long farmhouse tables for the writers to hit their deadlines or students to finish papers. Prudence would be the perfect decorator — her design aesthetic was the ideal fusion of youth and elegance — a tricky blend to pull off, but Prudence did it with an ease Devlin envied.

I can do this. It would be another marker of her journey to Amber Falls, to become successful enough that she'd be able to expand. Getting pre-approval had been easy with the way business was going right now at Books and Beans. She was going to finalize her proposal after work. She picked up a roll of packing tape off the floor left behind by the movers and fiddled with it as she walked to the front of the store, her fingers dancing over the leaded glass detail of the window, then door. What would she do with this entrance? She couldn't imagine needing two.

"It's you." A soft voice broke her from her thoughts. She shrieked and spun around, blindly throwing the packing tape in the direction of the voice. The voice of Gabriel Atwood.

She raised her hand to steady her thumping heart. He'd ducked, and the tape had hit the wall and landed on the floor at his feet.

"It's you," she repeated, not knowing what else to state other than the obvious.

They stood there for a long moment, staring at each other. She blinked, her throat tight, and tears pricked at the corners of her eyes. He was there, in front of her, arms motionless at his side except for one finger on his right hand tapping the side of his leg.

"It isn't polite to sneak up on people like that," Devlin accused.

"Sorry, I thought you would've heard me come in."

All thoughts fled Devlin's mind, wiped out by a panic that started to rise from her stomach. If her heart was beating fast a moment ago, it had nothing on the Formula One race now speeding around her chest. Her nostrils flared as she took deep breaths, trying not to betray her state of disquiet. *How can he not hear the beating?* She turned around to look at the wall behind her, taking the moment she needed to compose herself.

"What are you doing here?"

"I'm going to put an offer in on this place and when I saw you come in here, I decided I'd come take a look."

She spun around and her panic rose again. "You're putting an offer in, too?"

"Too?" Gabe looked confused. "Who else is?"

Devlin raised her eyebrows, waiting for understanding to hit him.

"Shit," he said. "That's why you're in here."

Devlin didn't know what to say. She didn't need to confirm what they both now knew.

"Who are you?" she asked.

Gabe wasn't sure what had propelled him to walk to Devlin, he only knew his feet moved of their own accord and within seconds he was close enough to touch her. He reached his hand out to ease the tension in her shoulders but let it drop back to his side. Taking a deep breath he inhaled her scent. *Vanilla*. The same scent that had plagued him, a scent he could breathe in again after so long.

"I'm sorry, what?" he asked, not having heard her question.

"Who *are* you?" she repeated.

Her earnest look, and quiet voice took Gabe by surprise. For all he knew, his life and his secrets had already been divulged to her by Prudence and Annabelle, and probably Greyson. She'd had plenty of time to find out everything about him and he'd only known who she was for a week. He tamped down his rising frustration, remembering his promise to the group, and did the only thing he could think of. He reached out his hand. "I'm Gabriel Atwood. Nice to meet you."

"Gabriel," she sighed out his name and his frustration at the situation was having a hard time competing with how delightful his name sounded coming from her delectable mouth.

"And you are?" he prompted, hoping to prolong this time with her.

"Devlin. Devlin Watkins."

She'd left his hand hovering in midair and just as he thought she was going to withdraw, she reached out and grasped his hand. Her palm was warm and soft and the jolt of electricity he felt at the contact startled him. He had no explanation for what came next. He pulled her into his arms and brought his mouth to her lips. She sank into him, just as she had that night. They felt so right, matched like two pieces of a puzzle.

He walked Devlin back until she was against the roughness of the brick. He braced one of his hands on the wall and moved his other to run through her short hair. He remembered doing the same when she was a blonde, but the softness he felt now begged him to use both hands this time, to let the silken strands slip through his fingers.

She made a sound, low in her throat, and hiked one leg, pulling him closer. He grabbed her by the ass and lifted her, her legs wrapping around him, held up by his body and the brick wall. Breaking the kiss, he ran his mouth down the side of her neck, inhaling the smell of vanilla that radiated off her, and could feel his day-old scruff scraping on her soft skin.

Gabe staggered when Devlin pulled away, dropping her feet to the ground and ducking out of his embrace.

"I can't." She turned to the wall, still breathing hard.

Gabe stood for a moment, surprised at both of their actions.

"I'm so sorry, Devlin," he apologized. "I don't know what came over me."

When she didn't reply, he went to the door, risking one last look at her. Their eyes met until she dropped her gaze and he turned and walked out.

* * * *

Devlin walked down the street later that day, her feet dragging, and a gust of wind kicked up and blew her skirt into a tangle. She was weighed down by the reality of what was happening tonight. She'd felt light as air since deciding she wanted to buy the old art gallery but her excitement for the town council meeting had been dampened by Gabe's revelation that he, too, wanted to buy the building in between them. She brought her hand to her mouth, a finger tracing ever so lightly where Gabe's lips had been mere hours before.

After over a year of remembering and wanting—aching—for him she'd not only seen him but had had a hot make-out session that had been moments away from turning into full-on sex if she hadn't come to her senses. *Why did I come to my senses?*

Because this was her fresh start. It had become her mantra that needed repeating. She couldn't let anyone get in the way of her dream, no matter how scorching his kisses were. There could be no more kisses. No more searing gazes. Just…no more.

Her pace slowed as she approached the community center where the township meetings were held. Her hair had become tousled in the wind, so she smoothed it down and ran her hands over her skirt.

"You look good."

Startled for a second time today, she whirled around, clutching her saddle bag tight to her. Gabe stood behind her, a slight smile on his lips.

"You've got a habit of startling me," Devlin pointed out.

"Sorry, I thought you heard me this time. I said your name."

"We're repeating our conversation from this afternoon." She felt her face heat, thinking about what else they could repeat from that afternoon.

Gabe coughed. "Yes, well…"

They stood there, looking at each other, the wind carrying away the lightness she felt, then stopping as it did when it changed directions, so it seemed like no wind was blowing. The skirt that had been whipping around Devlin's legs dropped. She felt this shift and squared her shoulders. There would be no pleasant conversation tonight. Her life and her business were on the line, and she was going to fight for them

Gabe seemed to sense the change in her demeanor. He brushed by her, close enough that she could see the stubble on his face, and a wave of lust rolled over her, remembering that stubble scratching her in much more intimate places. She snapped back to attention when she noticed he was still standing at the door. He motioned her forward with a sweep of his hand.

"After you."

She walked into the community center, shook the snow from her coat, and stamped her feet, the motion more a habit to shake off the cold. Gabe strode past her and sat in the back row.

Devlin went to the front of the room and looked around. The seats were almost full — there were more people than she'd expected. She hadn't thought that a small place like Amber Falls needed to accomplish that much business at its township meetings, but she sure was wrong. Finalizing the Winter Wonderland schedule, permits for various winter related activities and an open comment session for the townspeople were all on the agenda.

She sat, letting her mind wander to listening to one resident ask for a permit to build a small skating rink in their yard. She twitched as an awareness almost like anticipation rushed over her and she slowly turned her head, her eyes meeting Gabe's, and she couldn't look away. Her lips tingled and she pursed them together.

"...and I understand we have some new business tonight, is that right, Council President Reardon?"

Devlin snapped to attention, gathering her composure. *Stop it, Watkins!*

"Yes, thank you, Mr. Campbell." Janet Reardon continued, "As you know, township bylaws require council approval before any downtown properties are purchased. What we do is issue permits to the winning party then they can go forward with the purchase of the property. We have one property that housed the former Silver Creek Art Gallery that just went for sale. Two parties have expressed interest in the property. Devlin Watkins and Gabriel Atwood. Both own properties downtown already, on either side of the building in question, so they have been approved before. We haven't had multiple offers on a property since the township law went into effect."

"Yes, this is an interesting case. What is your recommendation?" the first council person asked.

President Reardon pondered for a moment. "Following Robert's Rule of Order. we should hear from both of the parties tonight, for a start." She nodded to Devlin. "Ms. Watkins, would you please come to the microphone and state your reason for wanting to buy the property?"

Devlin stood and walked to the microphone. She cleared her throat before starting. "President Reardon, we live in a college town. College kids need a place to go where they can work on papers and hang out. My coffee shop had brought a space much like this to the Amber Falls downtown, but being able to expand into the new building will give them an additional place to gather and study. Someplace other than their dorm or the college library. My proposal will offer them a place just like this." She took a breath; confident she'd gotten her vision across.

"Thank you, Ms. Watkins. Mr. Atwood, if you please?"

Devlin sat as Gabe walked to the microphone. He shot a glance at Devlin before starting. "Downtowns are what make a city. You can have as many tree-lined streets, parks or festivals as you want, but the heart is always downtown. We can't deny that college kids want a place to be themselves. Expanding Finnegan's Bar to include an all-ages eatery will benefit not only the college crowd, but it'll bring in families with young children downtown where the hope is they will visit more shops. This is the growth we're looking for. Thank you."

Gabe avoided her eyes as he walked back to his seat. Devlin focused on the council people, who were talking in hushed voices, occasionally looking at Devlin and Gabe before President Reardon once again addressed them. "Since this is the first time we've had multiple people interested in the same property, we've decided that we'd like written proposals from both of you. We'll adjourn today's meeting and have a special session four weeks from now. The proposals will be due to us no later than the Friday before this session. Thank you."

The meeting was over. Devlin stood and turned to see Gabe already walking out of the door, and Annabelle making her way toward her.

"Annabelle, I didn't see you here."

"I was in the back, I got here late. His Highness told me to cover the meeting then kept me late at the office. I had to run here, and I do *not* wear footwear that's made for running."

"You heard the end at least?" Devlin asked.

"I did. What you said was good, but your proposal's gotta be great. You're going up against a longtime business owner and one of the town's darling sons."

"Don't remind me. He made some damn good points." Devlin grimaced. "Don't tell him I said that!"

Annabelle laughed. "I won't. At least four weeks is long enough to make your proposal perfect."

"I can't believe you're on my side in this."

"Of course I am, Dev, but I'm not taking sides. A local coffee shop is always on the top of my list."

"I hope it's on the top of the town council's list, too."

"It will be, I guarantee it. Oh! Pru mentioned having a ladies' night on Friday, can you make it?"

Emma was going to be opening the shop on Saturday morning and Devlin could think of no better way to spend her Friday night than with her best friends. "You can count me in."

Chapter Five

It had been days since the meeting. *The meeting*? No, it had been days since he'd gotten to kiss Devlin again. Gabe was at Finnegan's, and he wasn't paying attention to the conversation around him. Greyson, Sebastian and Chuck were at a table with him, but he was thinking only of Devlin. The roughness of the brick wall in contrast to the softness of her body. The way her hair had slid through his fingers, the short length making him come back to run them through that silk again. Devlin wrapping her legs around him and cradling his erection as he pushed her against the wall —

"I hope you concentrate on your game as much as you're concentrating on whatever's going through your head right now, since we're partners this week." Sebastian clinked his glass against Gabe's to get his attention.

They were gathered for their Thursday night Finnegan's Gentleman's Ye Olde Dart League, named late one night after quite a few drinks. They didn't meet every Thursday, but rather when their schedules allowed. Gabe took a sip of his whiskey and composed his thoughts. As if that afternoon hadn't been in the front of his mind all week. "I've got the proposal on my mind," Gabe lied.

"Proposal?" Chuck leaned in conspiratorially. "I didn't know you were dating anyone."

"No, I'm talking about a proposal for the town council." Gabe rolled his eyes. "The owner of Books and Beans and I both want to buy the old Silver Creek Art Gallery building to expand into. We had the meeting on Monday"—he swallowed, the feeling of Devlin's hands on his ass still imprinted in his mind—"and they want both of us to put together a written proposal before they decide."

"The town council getting involved in sales is ridiculous. One thing happened a hundred years ago, and they just can't forget it," Greyson complained.

"Oh, now I'm interested," Sebastian broke in. "What happened?"

The three locals looked at each other before Chuck explained, "Just under one hundred years ago, right in the middle of Prohibition, when Howard Crenshaw—"

"A relative of the current Mrs. Crenshaw?" Sebastian groaned. "I hate myself for knowing enough about this town that I'd ask that."

Chuck nodded. "One and the same. Well, old Mr. Crenshaw purchased the exact property in question today under the guise of it being a haberdashery, when in fact he turned it into a speakeasy. The mayor was beside himself when the place was raided and introduced a bylaw that the town council would need to approve any downtown business sales."

Sebastian looked confused. "But it wouldn't matter what or who they approved, the person who buys it will do whatever they want anyway, right?"

Greyson laughed. "Don't bring your big city logic into this. It is what it is, and the business owners just live with it."

"We live with it," Gabe took over, "but I guess it's only an issue if two people want the same space. The council said they hadn't seen this before, so they told us we both needed to submit written proposals. When I got this place, they gave me verbal approval at the meeting before the paperwork was signed, but I wasn't competing with anyone. I gave my best pitch for expanding at the meeting, and I don't know what more they want." He looked at Greyson. "You knew Devlin was going to offer for the place the whole time, didn't you, Grey?"

"Nope, not going to let you bait me, little brother. She's one of Prudence's best friends and I won't get in between you on this. You and Devlin can work this out but leave me out of it."

Gabe turned to Sebastian. "Did you know anything about this?"

Sebastian shook his head. "I'm not dating, nor have I ever slept with, any of the women in our friend group. I have no reason to know anything that goes on, and I'm more than happy to keep it that way."

"Well, AB and Pru will be rooting for Devlin, I know that much. Can you at least help me with the proposal?" Gabe asked Greyson, verging on begging.

"I'm just an actor, I wouldn't know where to begin writing any kind of proposal. Unless it's for the female audience." Greyson winked at no one. "In fact, my marriage proposal in—"

Gabe groaned over Greyson's words then turned to Sebastian and Chuck with a hopeful expression.

"Sorry, buddy," Chuck said. "I was no good at the business end of business."

"I'll help," Sebastian offered. "I've got plenty of experience writing proposals. Plus, if I can piss Winters off in the process, I'd consider that a win-win."

Greyson had been silent for a moment, then added, "I did play a real estate developer as one of Ben Stone's aliases. I might be able to remember some lines." Now everyone groaned. "What? I did a good job with that one."

After a moment, Gabe exclaimed, "Hey, I have an idea!"

"Why do those words scare me?" Greyson narrowed his eyes.

"Why don't we go to Mom and Dad's cabin? I'm ready for a break and you can get away from the renovations, and Pru said she's had her normal slow start to the year. The timing is perfect. I can buckle down and work on the proposal uninterrupted."

"That might be the best idea you've had in a long time." Greyson looked at Sebastian and Chuck. "You guys in? The cabin has plenty of room."

Chuck shook his head. "That sounds like fun, but I don't have the time for a vacation right now."

"C'mon, Sebastian," Greyson goaded, turning his attention to Sebastian. "You can perfect your mountain man persona."

"I can swing a mean ax, but I'm no mountain man. Besides, I'm with Chuck, I don't have time for a vacation. I've got too much to do at the newspaper. This Winter Wonderland crap is worse than the Fall Festival.

At least with the Fall Festival it wasn't an ungodly shade of cold out."

"You own the newspaper," Gabe said, "so I relate as a fellow business owner, but can't you just delegate for a weekend?"

"The newspaper business doesn't work that way. Plus, if I took time off, I'd never hear the end of it from Winters, and it's a good day when she doesn't have something to yell at me about."

"I'm guessing Annabelle would come with, though." Greyson fidgeted with his darts as he spoke, lining them up on the table.

"Not if I don't give her the time off." Sebastian smirked.

"You'll give her the time off," Gabe stated. "I don't think you can deny her anything."

Sebastian was somehow able to appear both affronted and guilty at the same time and he took a quick sip of his drink. "I can deny her whatever I want."

"Whatever you say." Greyson rolled his eyes. "Anyway, before we get started, I have something to ask you."

"Now I'm the one who feels like he should be scared."

"Pru and I are setting a date for our wedding. We're thinking late August. Would you be a groomsman?"

A smile lit Sebastian's face. "Of course!" He looked at Chuck and Gabe. "You guys, too?"

Gabe nodded his affirmative. "I'll be Grey's best man."

Chuck, however, shook his head. "Not me. Considering Pru and I dated for a while, we decided it might be too awkward. I'll just be attending."

Sebastian raised a suspicious eyebrow. "I'm not paired with Winters, am I? 'Cause if I am, I might have to re-think this."

"Don't worry," Greyson said. "Pru hasn't asked the girls yet, but Annabelle would be the maid of honor. Devlin is the other bridesmaid."

Gabe pictured Devlin, walking down the aisle of a church, a beam of sunlight shining through a stained-glass window making her short hair look like a halo. He shook his head to get that image out of there.

Sebastian went on, clearly not noticing Gabe's face. "Thank God. Working with her is bad enough, let alone being paired up at a wedding."

"Well," Greyson cautioned, "just because you're not walking down the aisle with her doesn't mean you won't have other things to do together."

"As long as the things don't include lovey-dovey wedding stuff, then I'm in." Sebastian clapped Greyson on the back. "Thanks for asking, man. It'll be an honor to stand up with you on your wedding day."

"We're not sure of all the details yet, but I wanted to get this part all squared away."

Sebastian nudged Gabe with his elbow. "Looks like you're in charge of corralling Winters and I get to waltz with your girl, I think I got the better part of this bargain."

Gabe pictured Devlin walking down the aisle again, but this time she was with Sebastian. Irritation bloomed in his chest.

Sebastian did notice Gabe's face this time. "I'm just joking, Gabe. I have no interest in playing kissy face with any of the ladies in our group. You guys have cornered the market on that."

Gabe forced out a laugh. "I know," he lied. "I was just thinking about how much press this wedding is going to get. Nadia must be livid she's not getting the payoff from this publicity." Gabe referenced Greyson's ex-agent, who had tried to break him and Prudence up during the Fall Festival. The story of Greyson retiring from acting right at the height of his fame to come home and win the love of his longtime friend was absolute gossip magazine fodder. Hollywood and its fans were enamored of their story.

"Oh, she is," Greyson confirmed. "But she's down to calling me only once a day trying to get me back as a client. Her latest pitch was to just be on retainer in case I decided I wanted some role. The Passel nomination renewed her fascination with me." Greyson had been nominated for a Passel award, his industry's highest accolade, and Greyson and Prudence would be leaving sometime this summer to go to L.A. for awards season.

"I can't believe you haven't blocked her number already," Chuck said.

"I did at first, but she has her ways. Besides, I have more fun this way." Greyson stood. "And speaking of fun, let's get this dart game started, shall we, boys? I've got a fiancée to get home to."

Gabe finished the rest of his whiskey then picked up the empty glasses. "I'll grab refills first. You get started." He walked toward the bar, past the spot where he'd first seen Devlin on New Year's Eve and ran his fingers over where her hand had lain on the bar top, a habit he now had whenever he walked by the spot. It felt like they were being thrown together at every turn, everything in their lives intertwining. Talking to her should've cleared the air, but now they were competing for the shop, and they'd be in Greyson and Prudence's wedding together this summer. He filled a pitcher of beer from the tap and poured another whiskey before walking back to the guys. He reached the table just as Chuck threw a triple twenty. "Nice, man!"

"Thanks." Chuck flexed his hand. "It's all in the wrist."

Sebastian snickered. "You said it's all in the wrist."

"Don't be gross, Seb," Greyson cringed.

"I was talking about darts!" Sebastian squared up and took a shot, barely hitting a single. "Dang. Well, what are you guys doing tomorrow? You all have early mornings? Except for you, Grey. We know you don't do anything important."

"I keep Prudence satisfied, that's the most important job I can have."

"You said you wanted us not to be gross." Chuck pointed out.

"Whatever, it keeps me happy, too." Greyson shrugged then gestured at Gabe and Chuck. What about you two?"

"Just work," Chuck said.

Gabe picked up the darts, ready for his turn. "I'm meeting Pru at the store to pick out furnishings for the basement." He threw a bullseye.

"Oh yes, now that you say that she did mention something about you needing to get some finishing touches." Greyson gave a slight cough.

Gabe turned, Greyson's tone alerting him that something was up. "What are you not telling me, Grey?"

"I don't know what you're talking about. You're meeting at the store to pick out stuff for your house. That's all I know." The look on Greyson's face was one of pure innocence.

Gabe eyed Greyson for a moment longer, then let it go. Greyson had no reason to lie to him about a shopping trip, right?

Chapter Six

Devlin pulled her car into the home store parking lot. She'd texted Prudence that she was on her way and only got a smiley face emoji as a reply, which seemed a little odd. Prudence prided herself on being on time, so an emoji rather than written confirmation was out of character.

She noted how busy the store was as she found a spot at the far side of the lot. She squinted into the sun and swore she saw Gabe Atwood standing at the front entrance. Slamming her car door shut, she sidled around a large SUV, not seeing any sign of Prudence or her car.

"Oh, Pru, you didn't," she muttered.

Gabe looked perfect. His hands tucked into the front pockets of his jeans; he bounced on the balls of his feet while looking around. The spring in his step stopped when he spotted Devlin, and he lifted his hand in a wave. As she glanced back at her car, a longing voice whispered *it's not too late, just turn around and leave*. He couldn't know she was there for him, or whether she was coming or going. He didn't know Prudence had oh so casually said that she could use some company when she was going to pick out furnishings for a client the next day. Gabe squinted and repeated his wave, and he seemed so unsure of himself in that moment that Devlin had no choice but to head over to him.

"Out doing some early morning shopping?" Gabe asked as she approached.

Well. He obviously didn't know she was going to be there. "I'm supposed to meet Prudence to help her shop for a client."

Gabe's eyes narrowed. "I'm Pru's client."

"I think we've been set up." Devlin sighed.

Gabe glanced around one more time before settling his gaze on Devlin.

"Okay, what are you here for?" Devlin asked after a prolonged silence. "We might as well shop. I'll deal with Prudence later."

"She was going to help me pick out some things for my house. I've been renovating it over the last few years."

Devlin wasn't going to say that she knew this — Prudence had mentioned sparse details of the renovations before — and asked instead, "Oh really? What kind of renovations?"

"My parents' old house." Gabe shifted, rubbing his hands together like he was warding off a chill. "I don't suppose you want to help, since Prudence isn't here?" When Devlin hesitated, he added, "Even just to warm up, it's cold out here."

She accepted with a nod and went through the door as he ushered her in. They stood for a moment and took in the size of the store. She'd been here a few times before but preferred to shop at smaller boutiques rather than big box stores.

"I come here when I know I'm going to be ordering in bulk for a large project, otherwise I like the shops downtown for everything else," he said, as if reading her mind.

"Cutting costs is always a good idea, then you can spend a little more on the finishing touches. All right, if I'm going to be of any help, I need to know more about what you're looking at getting done today. I don't have an expert eye like Pru, but I'm here and I'll do what I can. What do you need?" They started wandering through an aisle.

"I'm working on the basement. Most of the rest of the house is done, but I hadn't decided on what to do downstairs until the last few months."

She raised her eyebrows in question.

"I'm going to have a wet bar and game room."

"How very *bacheloresque* of you." Devlin stopped herself. She had no right to offer any critique of what he was doing with his house. "I'm sorry, I didn't mean it that way. Have you started on anything down there?"

Gabe shook his head. "Nothing, it's a blank slate. Insulation and sheetrock is all that's down there. And the bathroom, but just the toilet and sink so far."

"So, let's start with the tile then." She guided him to the right section. "What kind are you thinking?"

Gabe pointed to a busy mosaic pattern. "I like this one."

"What tile do you have upstairs?"

"It looks more like this." He pointed to a classic subway tile found in many old farmhouses in Massachusetts.

"Will there be a guest room?"

"No, I have four bedrooms upstairs, that's enough."

"But what if you have a family?" she asked without thinking, then could feel her face heat in a deep flush. "I mean...you know, they might not always be guest rooms."

Gabe studied her for a long moment, his expression inscrutable, before replying, "I hadn't thought about it like that."

If the silence before was long, it had nothing on the current lonely stretch of highway they were cruising down, the traitorous image of mini-Gabe Atwoods running around a renovated farmhouse filling her mind.

"Back to the tile." She redirected them to the original subject, pushing out the picture of little boys with wheat-colored hair — and her nose — out of her mind.

"You want to keep as much of the original style as possible. The house has a history, and it would be such a waste to think that history didn't mean anything anymore, but I'm sure you know all that." Gabe wondered if she was alluding to their history, as little as they had. "You seem like the kind of guy that would try to hold on to that — isn't that why you started remodeling the house?

Gabe was surprised by the question. He'd never looked beyond the aesthetics of the project, about why he felt the need to remodel other than the basic fact that the place had to be updated. He wasn't ready to think about the why, so he kept it to the basics. "The stairs had a runner carpet that was so threadbare it had to come off. I never paid attention to it when my parents lived there — the house wasn't mine and besides, doesn't every kid think their childhood home is perfect?"

"Not every kid." Devlin seemed like she was avoiding Gabe's searching gaze, answering the question he didn't have to ask. "My childhood was fine, just not the picture of suburban paradise. So, what about the carpet?"

Gabe hesitated and Devlin moved away, touching another sample. She clearly didn't want to talk about her childhood right now. "The kitchen has a door that leads to the driveway that I use, but one sunny day after Greyson and I bought it from our parents, I went in the front door and when the light hit the stairs, I couldn't believe I hadn't noticed how worn the runner was before."

Devlin laughed. "It just took a little sunshine for you to see all the imperfections?"

"I find that sunlight is the best light to see anything, imperfections and all."

He hesitated and Devlin must've picked up on the pause. She continued, asking a neutral question. "What did you do then?"

"I spent the rest of the day going through the house just looking and observing, and I saw so many things I'd never noticed. I called Greyson and told him we needed to renovate the house and he wanted nothing to do with it. He was too busy with his career and gave me his half of the house."

"He just gave it to you?" Devlin seemed skeptical.

"He wouldn't let me buy him out and said the money I saved would be his contribution to the remodel. He also added that this way I wouldn't be calling him anymore with boring questions about what crown molding would look best in the foyer and to just make the damned decisions myself. That's where Pru came in. I didn't want to second-guess anything."

"What did your parents say?"

"They said the house looked fine, but that's what everyone who did a remodel in the eighties thinks. Ultimately, they said the house was ours—mine—and whatever changes I made was my decision."

Devlin stopped at a thick carpet and ran her fingers through it, giving it a slight scrape with her fingernails. *Just like she did to my hair.* And there it was—their kiss back in the forefront of his thoughts once again.

"This is the one," she declared.

Gabe ran his fingers through it also, just brushing hers, and electricity between them ignited. She snatched her hand away, cradling it.

"I'm sorry." Gabe reached out but she stepped back.

"I'm fine, just a shock. You should get this kind. It's nice and thick, and with a good pad underneath the cold from the floor won't seep through. Unless you get water in the basement, then no carpet."

"No, no water. One of the good upgrades my parents did was drain tile and a sump pump."

"That's good," she murmured, walking over to look at paint colors. "Our basement got water. That's where my room was, so I could never have carpet. The place was always so cold."

He knew she was hesitant to share anything of her past, or talk about any of *their* past, so he kept on going with the most mundane topics, just to keep their conversation alive and to not lapse into yet another silence, awkward or otherwise. He wasn't sure if he wanted to thank or throttle Prudence for this stunt.

"Where did you live growing up?"

Devlin turned a corner to walk down another aisle and he lost sight of her until her voice came from across the shelf. Most of her was obscured by paint cans but she continued, almost as if not being face-to-face helped her to keep talking.

"Just a neighborhood in South Boston. It doesn't matter."

"It matters to me," Gabe remarked.

Her eyes popped up meeting his through the gap in shades of yellow, then she continued down the aisle, and her voice floated from a few rows over. "I like this color."

He followed the path she had taken around the corner of the shelf to a section where darker paints were shown on a wall display in different settings.

"Which one do you like?" he asked, coming to stand next to her, his shoulder almost brushing hers.

"That one." She pointed to a dark blue. "Everyone wants to brighten a basement, but I say let it be." She looked at the color again then pointed to a deep green. "This one is nice, too. Dark doesn't mean a cave. It can be warm, and with the right fixtures around it, very cozy."

He watched her smooth her short hair, much like she had outside the community center a few days ago, and realized she was designing what she'd wanted her room to be as a kid. He felt his heart squeeze in his chest and ached to reach out and pull her into a bear hug and never let her go. He stepped away from her, shaking himself out of this impulse to save her. She didn't need saving. Whatever had happened, she'd already saved herself — he recognized that strength in her.

"I like the forest green," Gabe decided, looking at Devlin.

Her face bloomed into a smile. "Me too."

"So, we have carpet and paint, what's next?"

"I'd wait until you get those done. After that, you can tell what the character of the room will be, and you can pick out furniture and everything else later." She pivoted her head, her eyes meeting his. He was startled to realize for the first time that she was almost as tall as him. "If you have the time, that is."

Gabe studied her face, the arch of her brow, the curve of her cheeks and the tiny slope of her nose. "I have nothing but time," he said with the most truthfulness he'd used in quite a while. He felt like time was irrelevant when he was with Devlin. A year ago, a minute ago, a second ago. It all rolled up into a timeless capsule that would be forever theirs.

The sound of an announcement crackling on a speaker snapped Gabe out of his reverie and he noticed Devlin move away from him. *Damn whoever needs a manager in aisle seven.* But he was thankful for it at the same time. He had no right to have these thoughts about her. Or them.

"All right, that should do it for now," Devlin stated, hiking her bag higher on her shoulder and turning to the front of the store. "I think five gallons of paint should do just fine, maybe an extra gallon for touch ups later. You know the square footage for the carpet order?"

They checked out and walked to his car to unload the purchases they were able to take today. He slammed the trunk and turned to Devlin.

There was that long, questioning silence again. Gabe lifted his hand, trailing it along the fringe of her short bangs. Her breath was coming out in small puffs into the cold air, dancing across his cheek. She moved her hand to the front of his jacket, quick, then stepped back. He could sense something in her, a softening that hadn't been there a mere hour ago, but the feeling was gone before he could catch it and he wasn't ready to chase after it just yet.

"Well, thank you for helping me shop. The vintage tile will look much better than anything I would've picked." He was surprised to realize that he didn't want this time with Devlin to end. "Did you want to grab an early lunch? I know a little place just up the road."

Devlin lifted her eyes to his, her expression unreadable.

"No," she responded after a moment, and Gabe's hopes deflated. "Thank you, though, for offering. I have plans for the rest of my day."

"Okay. Well…"

Devlin reached around him and grabbed his phone that was tucked into his back pocket. Her fleeting touch on his ass set him aflame and his jeans became an uncomfortable level of tight. *Damn.*

She held the phone in front of his shocked face, the phone unlocked, and she tapped in a quick staccato then held it out to him, seeming reluctant to let it go when he took it back. "Here's my number. I know Prudence is your designer, but if she's busy and you need help, let me know." Devlin turned and walked to her car before he could say anything, her skirt whipping around her legs in the wind.

He was bewitched by the fact that in addition to her jeans and blue Chucks, she also wore skirts in winter. The more time they spent together the more details he noticed, and the more his attraction grew. He watched her get into her car and realized they hadn't talked about the one thing that was both binding them together and pushing them apart—the shop between them—but figured they'd get to talk about it at some point before the next meeting. They'd seen each other enough times this last week that he was expecting to be thrown together for yet another random reason. At least he'd get a chance to re-group his emotions when he went to the cabin without her there. Out of sight, out of mind.

Chapter Seven

"Devlin, you have to come with." Prudence stood at Annabelle's kitchen island having just poured two glasses of wine. "You sure you don't need anything, AB?"

Annabelle held up her whiskey in reply. "I'm good for now, thanks."

"I can't go," Devlin insisted again. Prudence had been trying to steer the conversation into going to the Atwood family compound for the better part of an hour and Devlin was recycling all her excuses, trying to think of a new way to say no. "Now that I know Gabe and I will be competing for the building, I need to stay here and get everything in order."

"Grey's family's cabin is beautiful. It would be worth it to go just to see it." Prudence tried a different tactic.

"It is," Annabelle agreed.

"I'm telling you, though, the cabin is the best place for you to be to get everything done. Just think of it, an entire week dedicated to getting this sale." Prudence handed her one of the wine glasses then sat in a chair that matched the mid-century modern leather sofa that Devlin and Annabelle occupied in the living room of Annabelle's condo. "No work, no distractions."

"Now you're distracting me!" Devlin exclaimed. "You can't keep ignoring my question of why you set me up like that at the store with Gabe this morning. I was supposed to be meeting *you*."

"Oh, Dev, it wasn't a set up. Not really, I mean." Prudence looked sheepish. "Okay, it kinda was."

"I knew it!"

"Hear me out, though. I was just trying to get you both to a neutral place where you could talk."

"We already talked on Monday. What else was there to talk about?"

Annabelle leaned in, the ice in her tumbler clinking. "But what did you talk about then? You didn't turn and hightail it, did you?"

"No, he needed help, so I helped him. I wasn't going to leave him stranded." She didn't mention that her first instinct had been to do just that. "We talked about his house and the remodel."

"You had to have talked about more than that," Annabelle said.

"Nope, nothing but business." Devlin flicked her eyes between the two women. "I don't know what you're playing at, but I made it clear that I didn't want anything to do with Gabe. I'm a grown woman and I don't need or want you two interfering with my love life."

Prudence reached out and laid her hand over Devlin's. "I don't know why I did it. I heard you loud and clear this fall when you said you wanted to let it go, but then New Year's happened, and we found out that you didn't tell us the whole truth. That's been weighing on me all these months later, that you didn't trust us. Or don't trust us."

"Oh, Pru, I do trust you." She grabbed Prudence and Annabelle's hands. "I trust both of you. I shouldn't have lied, and I wish I hadn't, but you must know how much I've come to rely on you both." She pulled away and grinned to soften the tone of the conversation as she added, "Then you go and pull a stunt like that."

"I don't know what came over me." Prudence shook her head. "I'd just gotten done planning the shopping trip with Gabe and you called right after, and I did it without thinking."

Annabelle stood and went to the kitchen to refill her whiskey. "We may have known Gabe since we were all in diapers but—and I'm a broken record because I say it so much—friendships don't come around like ours and I value them more every day. Pulling stunts like this notwithstanding."

"You didn't know Pru was going to do this?" Devlin held up her wine glass and Annabelle brought the bottle back to the living room.

"No, I would've either talked her out of the harebrained scheme or made it one thousand times better."

"I'd like to know what would've been better, believe it or not," Devlin admitted.

"Well—"

"Anyway," Prudence interrupted, pulling out her phone and showing the screen to Annabelle. "He sent me pictures of what you picked out. You have a good eye. You might not need me when you renovate the new space."

"*If* I can renovate the new space. And yes, I'll need you, Pru. I just helped pick out the flooring and paint. Your expertise is what makes it all come together."

"Well, it won't be an if, especially if you come to the cabin and we can have some solid time to prepare your proposal. It's just for a few days."

Annabelle sighed. "If I go, will you go? I wasn't planning on it, but I could use a break from Sebastian and if this helps you out, it'll be worth missing work."

Devlin's eyes filled with tears as she looked at her two friends who were willing to drop everything to help her out.

"Do I need to kick someone's ass?" Annabelle asked.

Devlin wiped her eyes. "No, I'm just touched that you'd both help me like this."

Prudence displayed genuine confusion at this statement. "Of course we would, Dev. We just got done saying all of this! I couldn't imagine not doing whatever I could to get this done for you."

"Gabe has been your friend for a very long time — neither of you knew he was going to, or wanted to, expand?"

Prudence and Annabelle exchanged looks before Prudence took the lead. "Gabe doesn't clue people into his plans until they're in motion or already done. Take Finnegan's, for example. I was surprised when he wanted to open the bar, I figured he would do woodworking or something with more manual labor."

Devlin had always thought Gabe had the look of someone who worked hard physically but was surprised by this last comment. "Manual labor and woodworking? He mentioned that he did his house renovations himself, but I didn't know he was that into it."

"Yeah, he rebuilt the stairs at the house, he did the bar top at Finnegan's, and a bunch of other little projects."

Prudence added to this list. "He made my kitchen table and let me tell you, he makes sturdy furniture."

Annabelle gave Prudence a small shove. "I don't want to know how you know that Pru."

"You already know because we've talked about it."

Devlin scrunched her nose. "We did already get all the details of that one, AB."

"Anyway, that leads me to my next topic I want to talk to you two about," Prudence said.

"You and Grey fucking on a table leads us into our next topic?" Annabelle questioned.

Devlin started to laugh, needing to set her glass of wine down. "I do love you two. Okay, Pru, I'll bite. What does your next topic have to do with, as AB put so delicately, you and Grey getting handsy in the kitchen?"

"Well, I realized I never asked either of you, I just assumed, but would you please be in our wedding?"

Annabelle squealed and Devlin was glad she wasn't holding her wine because she jumped at the sound. "Yes!"

"Me too," Devlin said.

"Oh good, I'm glad it's official. Annabelle, if you could be my maid of honor and Devlin my bridesmaid?"

A flash ran through Devlin's mind about the opposite wedding party and Annabelle must've thought the same because she asked, "Who did Grey choose?"

"Don't worry, AB. Gabe is the Best Man."

Clearly not assuaged by Prudence's words, she asked again, "But who is his other groomsman?"

Prudence's eyes shifted. "He asked Sebastian."

"Are you serious? He's weaseled his way into *my* friend group and now I must deal with him at your wedding, too?"

"I'll be the one dealing with him," Devlin broke in. "I promise you won't have to worry about it."

Devlin's mind went to who she *would* be worrying about. The image of Gabe dressed in a tuxedo and reaching under her dress to pull down a garter came unbidden into her mind. The fact that she was wearing white in her vision was not lost on her. *What the actual fuck, Watkins?*

"It'll be fine," Prudence was saying. "I don't think the wedding will be until later in the summer and I'm hoping it'll be outdoors, so you should be able to keep as much distance between you and Sebastian as you want."

"Is me on a beach in Fiji enough distance?"

"C'mon, Annabelle," Devlin started, needing to break away from her daydreams of Gabe. "This is verging on ridiculous. You and Sebastian need to do it and get it out of your systems. Just give into it."

Annabelle almost dropped her tumbler. "You have got to be kidding me right now, Devlin. I might throw up at the…the…*thought* of touching that man. He's wholly incapable of love or any other emotion other than pure selfishness."

Prudence raised her eyebrows. "She never said anything about love. Just a quick fuck so you can both move on."

"You've both gone absolutely mental. There's no way in hell we could function if we…" Annabelle faked a gag and stood. "I need to use the bathroom."

Devlin smirked at Annabelle muttering "Off your fucking rockers" as she walked out of the room.

She knew Annabelle and Sebastain had history from before they worked together at the paper. "I know those two had at least one run in when you guys lived in Atlanta, but I feel like she's not telling us the whole story."

"Me neither. She won't even talk about some things when I ask." Prudence turned their conversation back to the subject from earlier. "Is everything really okay? I don't want my dumb stunt to come between us."

"Believe it or not, I didn't have a bad time and if anything, it may have helped us get over being awkward together when we see each other next time, which will probably be for wedding preparations."

"Really?"

"He was funny and thoughtful and—"

Annabelle walked back into the room, interrupting the apologies. "Okay, Pru. I'll do everything I can—minus fornicating with that devil—to make sure your wedding is as beautiful as it should be."

"You're always the picture of grace," Prudence told Annabelle, "and I knew this wouldn't be any different. I'll let you both know when I'm ready to start planning. I don't have any idea what I want our wedding to look like."

The image of Gabe reaching under her dress popped back into her head. *Gabe's calloused hand was rough on her thigh. They were hot from dancing and a bead of sweat showed on his brow as he locked his eyes with hers and inched his hand higher and higher, well past where the garter was.* "I don't believe it," she almost shouted, trying to erase the picture from her mind. "You've never imagined what your wedding would look like?"

"When I was younger, I wanted a big princess dress, a long veil and a whole lot of lace. But now? None of it seems important as long as I'm getting married to Grey. Nothing else matters until those papers are signed. I don't care about chicken or fish, or fonts, or table assignments."

"That's what we're here for," Annabelle said. "You're Hollywood's darling—the only woman who could snag the most sought-after actor and get him to give up being a bachelor, not to mention all his fame, for his small-town love." She paused. "At least that's how the stories go. They want a fairytale wedding to rival Grace Kelly or Princess Di."

"I guess there's that." Prudence looked overwhelmed.

"Don't worry, we'll help you plan the whole thing, so nothing gets out of control," Devlin promised. "A nice wedding doesn't mean an elaborate affair, and we'll make sure you get what you want."

"Thanks, guys. The pressure of his decision is starting to affect me. I didn't expect there would still be so much publicity."

"Try not to let it bug you, Pru. Besides, Wyatt Reed has a new movie coming out and it's supposed to be the big summer blockbuster. They'll turn their attention back to him in no time." Annabelle waved away Prudence's worry.

"I know Grey doesn't want the spotlight anymore but that's going to piss him off."

"They don't get along?" Devlin asked. "I always thought that was for show."

"I guess I wouldn't say they don't get along," Prudence explained, "but they both started around the same time and the press just loves Wyatt and seems to be more critical of Greyson."

"Wyatt is so handsome." Annabelle's face took on a dreamlike stare.

"Grey is handsome," Prudence corrected her. "Wyatt is acceptable."

"Whatever you say, dear. So, what are we doing about this cabin vacation?" Annabelle changed the subject.

Devlin pondered the idea of the cabin once again. She'd heard worse ideas and the more she thought about it, the better it sounded. "I guess it could work. Emma can handle the shop for a few days and her sister who helped at Christmas will be visiting then, and I know she'd help if she's needed."

Prudence almost jumped for joy. "Yes! We can get so much done in those two days."

"I'll be more than happy to take a full weekend off work. The cell reception is spotty, if I remember from the last time I was there?" Annabelle asked.

"Yep," Prudence confirmed.

"Then his royal headache can't get ahold of me for two days. This is sounding better by the minute," Annabelle agreed.

"We won't spend the whole-time writing." Prudence nudged Annabelle. "You should have some time to work on your next novel."

"Yes, how's that going?" Devlin asked. "Have you submitted the last one to any publishers?"

"No, I haven't," Annabelle admitted. "I'm just enjoying writing now; I'll deal with everything else when I'm ready. For now, I'm happy with a mini vacation."

"I could use a girl's weekend," Devlin added, "but it's not a girl's weekend if we're getting in between you and Grey's alone time."

"That's okay, Ga—" Prudence's eyes widened, a panicked look crossing her face. "Don't hate me, Dev, I forgot!"

Devlin's eyes narrowed. "What do you mean?"

Prudence looked chagrined. "It didn't occur to me to tell you that Gabe will be there, too."

"It didn't *occur* to you?" Devlin asked, suspicion filling her voice. "We just got done talking about how you set me up this morning and you're telling me you just *forgot*?"

Annabelle's eyes darted between the two. "Hey, ladies, we have plenty of room at the cabin. C'mon, Dev, you know she wouldn't do that"—she raised her eyebrows— "again."

Devlin sighed and, seeing no hint of deception on Prudence's face, relented. "All right, I believe you."

"It'll be perfect, I promise, no distractions." Prudence echoed her words from earlier.

Devlin could think of one major distraction. Gabe.

Chapter Eight

Gabe never hated Mondays. He hadn't worked a traditional Monday through Friday job, so it was just as likely that he'd have that day off as he was to work it. It so happened that he'd had this weekend off, and after his Friday shopping date with Devlin he'd spent the last few days working in his basement or on various projects all the while trying not to be consumed with visions of Devlin.

He felt like his phone was burning a hole in his pocket since she'd grabbed it and put her number in. He'd pulled it out at least a hundred times and had placed it back in his pocket just as many, alternating between typing out witty texts like 'hey' and making up reasons why he'd need to call her. He even flirted with the idea of pretending to butt dial her just to hear her voice.

In fact, right now, his phone was sitting on the bar, next to a freshly washed set of highball glasses that were now air drying with unsightly water marks. Gabe stared at his phone as he wrung the unused drying towel in his hands. The glasses were eventually forgotten about when Greyson walked in and bellied up to the bar, pausing a moment as a group of customers moved to a table.

"What'll it be?" Gabe threw a sidelong glance at Greyson, although he already knew the answer, and covertly pocketed his phone once again.

"You know, Gabe, I've always wondered why you didn't go with a wild west theme in here. A saloon with rowdy chorus girls and cowboys doubling down on bets at the poker table."

"Greyson, I'm only going to say this one more time, I'm concerned with you not working," Gabe said, sliding a low ball of Jameson Reserve the short distance across the gleaming wood top bar.

Greyson sighed. "I know. I was thinking about asking the university if I could start this spring instead of in the summer, that way I could get ramped up before summer stock."

"I like that idea. I know I throw shade around, but you'll have a big project once the remodel is in full swing."

"I thought about that too, but other than what you and I decided to work on together, I think that hiring out the rest of the work is what I'll do."

"You don't want to get those smooth hands too dirty?"

"Pru likes my smooth hands." Greyson smirked. "Besides, one of the perks of being obscenely rich is that I can afford to hire a crew."

"What are you trying to say, big brother?"

"Hey, I offered to send the best when you were working on Mom and Dad's house, but you said no."

Gabe reminisced on the years it had taken him to do the work on their parent's house himself, but every second of the renovation was worth it. If he'd completed the work any sooner, he wouldn't have been at the store with Devlin yesterday, and he couldn't regret that. "I loved doing it all. The house was Mom and Dad's, I'm sure that's the reason why. I know it took me years longer to finish it by myself, but everything was worth it."

"And now we get to go to the family cabin. You think you'll want to renovate that?"

"You know, I'm not sure. A caretaker looks in on it every so often, usually before and after winter, and they haven't reported anything major wrong with the place, but that doesn't mean it isn't out of date. An outdated cabin can be charming, though, being rustic and all that. I guess we'll know soon enough. So, what do you think we'll need for the trip?"

"I'm thinking some Johnnie Walker, and maybe a couple bottles of Grey Goose, and a bottle of Macallan…"

"One, I'm talking about food and supplies, and two, that sounds suspiciously like my private collection."

"Bro, the liquor *is* supplies. If we've got that everything else will take care of itself. Plus, I kind of figured that Pru or AB would deal with the food."

Gabe waved his hand toward his kitchen. "Really, Grey?"

"She likes to cook, not for any other reason."

The response was lost on Gabe, as mumbles and grumbles could be heard coming through the door. He watched as Sebastian and Annabelle came in along with a swirl of cold air. *An alcove, why did I not build the door in an alcove?* He added that to his mental list of renovation ideas for his plans for the expansion.

Annabelle gave a quick wave and a smile as Sebastian tried to guide Annabelle to one of the few empty booths, reaching his hand to settle at the small of her back. Annabelle smacked Sebastian's hand away.

"Do you know what you want for lunch?" Gabe asked Greyson, who was now looking at the menu.

"Steak sandwich and fries."

"I don't know why I ask, or why you bother with a menu." Gabe punched in the usual order then moved to fill two glasses of water for the newcomers.

The lunch rush was light, the weather tending to keep people inside on days like this. Gabe reached the booth and placed the water in front of the grimacing occupants.

"You've got to be kidding me, a snowman decorating contest, hot cocoa bar, snowball toss —" The look of horror on Sebastian's face made Gabe chuckle.

"It amazes me that these things still surprise you," Annabelle interrupted. "In fact, all that's followed by ice skating and a chili cook off."

"This just keeps getting worse," Sebastian groused.

Annabelle rolled her eyes.

"It amazes me, Winters, that you can't seem to keep it professional. Rolling your eyes at your boss could be seen as an act of insubordination."

Annabelle let out a belly laugh. "Please." She looked to see Gabe next to their table. "Hello, dear."

"Hi, AB. What can I get you?"

"I'll have the lunch portion Chicken Alfredo, and a Jameson, please."

"This is a working lunch, Winters," Sebastian pointed out.

A little smile tilted Annabelle's lips. "Make that a double, Gabe." She turned her attention back to Sebastian who was still looking at the menu. "Also, I won't be here to report on the Polar Plunge. I'll be with *my* friends this weekend."

"And who am I supposed to have cover that in your absence?" Sebastian asked, his head still buried in the menu.

"I don't care who you make do it. Maybe you should write the story yourself, then you could participate, and no one will be around to witness your shrinkage."

Gabe's eyes widened at these words and he swung his gaze to Sebastian waiting for him to return the verbal volley. Sebastian's head slowly rose from the menu, and he took a visible long, slow breath. He waited a beat, his eyes on Annabelle before he turned to Gabe.

"I'll just have a whiskey for now."

Gabe nodded and backed away from the table, walking around the bar just as Leo set Greyson's lunch in front of him.

"Did I hear them say they were having a working lunch?" Greyson asked as Gabe poured two doubles back at the bar.

"That's what Seb said."

"I wonder what they're working toward?"

"I'm sure we'll all know once they figure it out." He turned back into the lion's den, saying a little prayer, having not yet acquired the same skills as Prudence and Greyson with disarming these little spats. It seemed like he walked back in on another doozy of an argument.

"I know I'm the boss and all, but even I get to take some personal time," Sebastian was saying.

"You're not invited," Annabelle spat back. "Besides, you might have to do something that requires survival skills, like in a place like that and I'm not sure you're capable of starting a fire."

"I'll have you know I was a Boy Scout, Winters." He held up one of his hands in the Boy Scouts honor sign then, at her guffaw, turned his hand and lowered his two outside fingers, leaving the middle finger up.

Gabe didn't want to intervene, so he set down their drinks and got the hell out of there, but that didn't stop him from hearing the last of the argument.

"I can't believe you!" Annabelle all but shouted. She stood, slipped her arms into her coat and was out of the door in a flash.

Sebastian slid from the booth, a look of defeat and exhaustion on his face as he walked over and sat next to Greyson, his glass trembling just a little in his hand as he set it down.

"I have to ask, what do you say to her, to get her so riled up?" Greyson moved over his plate of fries for Sebastian to share.

"I just told her that she had to submit a request for time off through our HR portal and I needed it before today was over or she couldn't have the time off."

"Why would that make her so mad? Isn't that protocol the same pretty much anywhere?" Gabe asked.

The side of Sebastian's mouth ticked up in a devilish smile. "We don't have an HR portal."

"Man, you just can't wait to rile her up, can you?" Gabe said.

"Riling her up is so easy—you can't blame me."

Leo came out from the kitchen with Annabelle's lunch.

Rachael Heinan & Kimberly Metcalf

"Just box it up, Leo. The least you can do is take this to her, Sebastian."

"Yeah, I will." He downed the rest of his whiskey. "Anyways, I'm in for the cabin this weekend if there's still room."

Greyson slapped Sebastian on his shoulder. "There's always room for you."

"What brought on the change of heart?" Gabe asked. "It wouldn't have anything to do with a certain tiny reporter that's also going?"

"Nah, man. I was going to go before I knew Winters was." He saw the doubt on the brothers' faces. "I'm serious. We can work on the proposal for the building purchase. But do me a favor and don't tell Winters? I want to see the look on her face when I show up."

"How awkward is this weekend going to get?" Gabe wondered aloud.

Sebastian turned a speculative eye to Gabe. "Is Devlin going as well?"

Gabe's heart skittered at the thought of spending the weekend in complete seclusion with Devlin. And four other people. But...Devlin.

Leo came back out with the to go box and handed it to Sebastian then took one look at Gabe's face. "Were you guys talking about Devlin again?"

"Leo, you're fired." Gabe wasn't sure if he was joking or not.

"Hey, man, no harm no foul." Leo looked to the other two men. "You were though, weren't you?"

Gabe pushed Leo back toward the kitchen then motioned for Sebastian to go. "No lunch for you, but that'll get cold if you don't get it to AB soon."

Sebastian put on his coat and walked to the door, snagging a fork on the way. "It won't have time to get cold if I eat it all on the way back." A cheeky smile crossed his face as he pushed out of the door.

"I think we should bring more whiskey," Greyson stated.

"All of the whiskey," Gabe agreed.

A regular in the corner held up a glass, indicating a refill was needed. Gabe poured a beer and motioned to Greyson that he'd be right back. Greyson nodded, his mouth full of a bite of steak sandwich. It gave Gabe a few much needed moments to consider the possibility of Devlin being at the cabin this weekend. It had been just a day since they'd gone shopping and he'd hoped he'd have a break from his senses being inundated by her until at least after the proposal to town council was due.

"Never mix business with pleasure," Greyson prophesized as Gabe got back to the bar.

"How on earth do you know what I'm thinking about?"

"You get this dreamy expression, like you're having a waking daydream."

"I do not get dreamy."

"Well, no wonder Leo knows when you've got Devlin on your mind."

"I hadn't seen her in so long and it seems like we're together all the time now. I didn't get to ask you. Did you know that Pru set me up?"

"She make you take the fall for the bank heist? You know, that was a plot in my movie—"

"Be serious, Grey. Did you know she was going to send Devlin in her place when we went shopping the other morning?"

"I one hundred percent did," Greyson said, without a hint of remorse. "She told me after you talked that she was going to somehow get Devlin there, that way you'd have to see each other."

"Why are you two meddling in my personal life? If I want to see Devlin I will." Gabe pushed aside the contentment he'd felt being with Devlin yesterday, more annoyed now that Greyson and Prudence thought they had the right to interfere like this.

"I don't think Pru saw it as meddling. She knows both of you will be in the wedding party and she just wants to make sure things are the least amount of awkward."

A flash of Devlin in a flowy white dress pinged through Gabe's mind once again.

"I think we're going to have to worry about Sebastian and Annabelle more than anything," Gabe pointed out. "Those two can't be in the same room without combusting. I can see either of them sabotaging the other while they're walking down the aisle, oblivious to the havoc they'd be wreaking."

"I'll take care of that, don't you worry. No one is going to ruin that day for Prudence. I won't sit around and let it happen, I'll act. You know what they say about idle hands?" Greyson asked.

They said in unison, "They're the devil's playground—"

Gabe continued, "And I'm ready to climb all over you. From *The Night You Didn't Want to Die*, I know."

"My third Ben Stone movie. A classic. I'm glad you have my lines memorized. It means a lot to me."

"You repeat them so often I can't help it."

"Just so you know, Prudence invited Devlin to the cabin. When I told her I was going to help you with your proposal—"

"Sebastian is going to help me." Gabe tried to ignore the flutter in his stomach now that he knew for sure Devlin would be there.

"Whatever. *We're* going to help you. But when she heard that, she decided her and AB would help Devlin with her proposal this weekend. She would've invited her, anyway, though."

"Now that Sebastian is coming with, it'll be a working weekend for all of us, it sounds like."

Greyson grimaced. "I'll have to plan another time to take Pru, just the two of us, before winter is over."

"Does Devlin know I'm going also?" Gabe asked casually.

"I'd assume that they had a very similar conversation to the one we're having right now."

"Minus the Ben Stone quotes, I hope."

"Nah, there's a Ben Stone quote for any situation. Pru does me proud."

All right. He knew she'd be there for sure, and he wasn't...disappointed by the fact. It sounded like they'd be together but separate, each working on their own proposal.

Chapter Nine

Gabe lay in his bed the morning they were leaving for the cabin, reliving the past few days. Devlin was a whirlwind, just as she'd been the night they'd met. He needed this time away, even though he knew he'd be spending most of the weekend tempering his feelings. He knew he was hard to read, just like his brother. They were often told they'd gotten that from their father — told so by their mother.

A shock of cold air rushed in, as he prepared to get out of bed, so he drew the covers back over himself and snuggled in, hoping for a few more minutes of warmth. Grabbing his phone from the nightstand, he opened his thermostat app, upping the temperature in the master bedroom a few degrees. Five more minutes wouldn't hurt, so he let his mind drift back to Devlin and her pretty face. Her features, though sharp and angular, were strong and bold. Her style was so different from when they'd first met. She was still bold, but she'd softened. He pictured her rounded hips, felt the swell of her breasts against him when he'd pulled her close in the old art gallery. She just *fit*. Gabe felt himself starting to throb as he grew hard.

He glanced at the clock. Greyson and Prudence would be there to pick him up within the hour, and he still needed to shower, but the air was so cold and his skin was so warm, so he slid his boxer briefs to his mid thighs, turning onto his back. He thought back to their last kiss, he ran his hand up and down his inner thighs, growing harder as he thought of her soft lips. He gripped his shaft—*those lips soft on his head, fuck*—already the bead of pre-cum was forming on the tip. His thumb swiped over it and letting a groan build in the base of his throat, he used the moisture to stroke his cock now erect and throbbing. His mind drifted back to that night, how in control she'd been, his pace still slow. He had yet to taste her, and he imagined the bliss that might await him, he pictured her body hovering over his, her legs spread over his face as she took him in her mouth. He would lick her clit, and lap up her wetness, driving her wild. He stroked harder and faster, mimicking what she might be doing with her mouth as she tried to stay focused during his ministrations. He would go back to her clit, sucking with just the right amount of pressure, licking back up then in circles over and over, sucking a little harder with each pass. Her motions would become erratic as her thighs started to tremble. He gripped his cock tighter and stroked harder. Would she give in or try to fight it? He remembered that she'd given in to the sensation while he'd been fucking her, and he had no doubt her orgasm would be on his lips with little coaxing, sliding a finger in as he focused on her clit, she'd clench and the warmth would spread, just as his ejaculate spread now into his hand. He relaxed back into his pillows. Good lord he needed to taste her. He was desperate for her.

If he'd thought getting out of his warm bed into the cold room had been hard before, it was unbearable now. Sprinting into the shower, he blasted the water, toying with the idea of masturbating once more. As tempted as he was, he was running late enough. Sporting a dark flannel and warm vest, he trotted down the stairs, his hair still wet, as he heard Greyson let himself into the house.

"Morning, little brother," Greyson offered in a cheerful voice. "Ready to go?"

"Yes, just these few boxes and my bag at the door are going. You want any coffee to go?"

"Devlin is bringing the caffeine this morning." Greyson smiled like the cat that ate the canary.

"What's with the weird smirk, Grey?"

"Let's just say Prudence is almost as good at planning as Annabelle. We're meeting at The Bee in about five minutes."

Gabe's look grew more confused. "I don't want to know. Let's go."

Greyson and Gabe carried the boxes down the front steps, navigating the small patches of ice on the walkway leading to Greyson's black SUV idling in the driveway. He could see Prudence through the windshield, bobbing with excitement.

"Hi, Gabe." She beamed, getting out of the car to help with the boxes of wine and spirits.

"Mornin', Pru," Gabe greeted, stacking the boxes and his bag in the already full back end then securing the hatch.

"Take the front and sit by Greyson, you'll have more leg room." Prudence slid into the back seat. "I'm so excited, I love the mountains and it seems like forever since I've been there. The pine trees lined up like toy soldiers, marching to battle."

Gabe rolled his eyes as he climbed in the front seat, knowing full well she had something up her sleeve, since she only chattered on like this when she was nervous or a plan was in action—and she wasn't nervous.

"Do you know if we still have fishing poles at the cabin?" Gabe asked in a quiet voice, letting Prudence keep hyping the virtues of mountains. "I looked for mine, but I must've misplaced them somewhere."

Greyson backed out of the driveway and started in the direction of The Bee. "I think so. Remember when Dad left ours at home and just bought a bunch to keep at the cabin?"

Gabe laughed at the long-lost memory. "I don't believe for one second that he forgot them. He hated packing those things with a passion and forgetting them was the only way Mom would let him have two sets."

"You think we'll have time for ice fishing?" Prudence leaned forward between the two seats. "I love ice fishing."

The drive to The Bee was as brief as her list of reasons why she loved ice fishing, which consisted only of getting to wear her cute winter gear to not having to use live worms as bait, with a long pause in between.

As they pulled into the parking lot, he could see Devlin getting out of her car. Greyson parked beside her, hitting the button to lift the rear gate.

Prudence and Gabe got out of the SUV at the same time. "Good morning, Devlin!" Prudence chirped, going to help Devlin with the coffee.

"Devlin, where are your bags?" Gabe questioned. "I can grab them for you."

"I just have the one in the back seat, thank you." Devlin smiled at Gabe.

"You continue to amaze me," Gabe quipped.

He made quick work of the small bag and had just gotten back into the car when Sebastian pulled into the parking lot, followed by Annabelle. She parked and hustled around to the back door where Devlin and Prudence were already settled in the back seat of the warm SUV.

"Move over, ladies," she commanded, reaching for the door handle. The telltale sound of the locks engaging was her only response. Annabelle reached out and tugged on the door handle. "Prudence Marie, you would not do this to your best friend since grade school. Open this door right now!"

Gabe realized what was happening when he spotted Sebastian leaning against the back end of his SUV, the lift gate open. Prudence rolled down her window. "Sorry, friend, full here. Good thing Seb decided to come too. It would've been too tight of a squeeze."

Annabelle growled low in her throat. "Did you just call him Seb?"

Prudence extended her arm, handing Annabelle a coffee. "Here, you may need this."

"No way, Prudence." She grabbed the coffee then pleaded with Gabe. "You have to ride with him."

"Bye." Prudence smiled. "See you guys at the cabin!" As Greyson backed out and shifted into drive, Prudence smirked. "And the student has become the master."

"You did that on purpose?" Gabe asked.

"I sure did. Annabelle meddles in everyone else's affairs, it's time she got a taste of her own medicine."

"You know there's a good chance she goes back home," Devlin chuckled.

"You know as much as I do that she's been looking forward to time off and out of town. She'll forgive me as soon as she gets out of the car there and breathes in the mountain air."

"We're not in the mountain air yet and the wind is already picking up," Gabe commented. "I wonder if the forecast for snow might be right this time."

"It should clear up when we get out of town," Greyson advised. "I hope," he added with a grimace.

With that they fell into comfortable chatter as they drove the two and half hours out of town through the snow-covered countryside of Massachusetts. Gabe kept his mind off Devlin, following the conversation, nodding and chiming in in all the right places. As they pulled up to the cabin, he was brought back to his youth and the time spent there with their parents. Gabe took in a lungful of cool fresh air when he stepped out of the car. Not that they lived in a big city or anything, but mountain air just hit different out here, and he did believe Annabelle would forgive all once she got there.

"Will you ladies please go in, turn up the heat and start uncovering the furniture?" Greyson asked. "No need for all of us to bear the cold, we'll bring all the stuff in."

"You bet, babe." Prudence kissed his cheek.

Greyson and Gabe were making quick work of the boxes and bags when Sebastian and Annabelle pulled in. Sebastian had just stopped when Annabelle jumped out of the car.

"Never again, Sebastian!" Annabelle slammed the car door shut. "Argh!" She let out a melodramatic yell, then opened the door, grabbed her bag, and slammed it again for apparent good measure before storming up the walkway to the cabin. "Prudence! Friendship off!" she bellowed as she opened the door.

"I have no words." Sebastian made his way to the door to where Devlin was peeking out.

"Need more help?" Devlin asked. "We're all set up inside."

"Last box here," Gabe responded, and the three of them followed Sebastian inside to the kitchen where Annabelle was unpacking the food. She was slamming items on the counter when she did a double take at Sebastian. He noticed Greyson and Prudence were already missing.

"You do have some actual outerwear, don't you?" Annabelle asked, clearly unimpressed by Sebastian's hiking boots and windbreaker. "These winters are no joke, and the wind outside isn't letting up—that tells me a storm's coming."

"I *am* always prepared," Sebastian promised. "Besides, the last two months of forecasted snowstorms, other than the little bit we had this morning, haven't happened. I have no faith the weatherman is right about this one."

"Let's get the rooms situated," Gabe interrupted. "The cabin has five bedrooms, plenty of space. I'm going to assume Grey and Pru are already in the master, and you two"—Gabe pointed at Annabelle and Sebastian—"can have the other rooms on the second floor, I'll take one of the downstairs rooms."

Annabelle looked thoughtful for a minute then gasped. "Like hell we will!" she exclaimed. "Those upstairs rooms have a connecting bathroom. We already had to share the car ride here, I'm not sharing a bathroom with that man!" She looked at Sebastian with clear disgust and shuddered. "He looks like he'd be…hairy."

"Hey, man," Sebastian addressed Gabe. "She doesn't need to have access to my room, who knows what she'd do to me. I wouldn't get any sleep, wondering when she'd bust through the door to ravish me."

Greyson entered the kitchen, keeping a safe distance from the commotion. Prudence slid past him while shaking her head, moved to rejoin the girls and began to open the first bottle of wine she saw.

"Oh, you wish—" Annabelle started.

"Okay! I'll stay upstairs with Sebastian and you two ladies can be downstairs."

Devlin searched the cupboard pulling out two large baking sheets.

"Listen, Sebastian." Greyson leaned in closing the distance between them. "Sorry about the reception. I'm sure it'll improve once she gets some food in her."

"Or something else," Gabe joked.

"It'll be a long two days if she's expecting that." Sebastian stood. "I need to burn off some steam, didn't you mention a bonfire tonight?"

"Yeah, we're pretty sheltered off the back patio. Want to chop some wood?" Greyson asked.

Gabe poured the guys all two fingers of Glenlivet then propped his hip against the kitchen island.

"Really? The Boy Scout couldn't chop pre-split wood," Annabelle teased, making it apparent she was listening to their conversation then taking her glass of wine and sitting on the bar stool at the kitchen island. "That smells amazing, Dev."

"Thank you, chicken and artichoke pizza."

Sebastian downed the remainder of his drink. "Winters, you are on my last nerve. Don't you have some matron of honor things to be planning?"

"*Matron* of honor? The title is maid of honor, since I'm not married," Annabelle corrected, walking right into his apparent trap.

"Surprise, surprise." Sebastian threw over his shoulder but was already out of the side door before Annabelle could reply. They all watched him walk across the patio to the wood pile. He unwedged the ax and stacked the log to be split, widened his stance then swung the ax over his head, his other hand coming up to grip the handle, bringing it down on the log with a powerful blow.

"Well, shit," Annabelle mumbled, almost missing the island when setting down her glass of wine.

"Careful there, AB. You seem distracted." Gabe chuckled and winked at Devlin. "Marshmallows for toasting tonight?"

"I'm in." Devlin smiled back, sprinkling the last of the cheese on the pizza.

* * * *

After dinner, the group moved outdoors to toast the marshmallows as promised.

"I'm glad Mom talked Dad into putting this patio in." Gabe removed the cover from the fire pit, turned on the propane and ignited the fire.

"What was here before?" Devlin looked over to Gabe, who was sitting next to her on a bench.

"Well, this has always been a patio," Greyson answered, "but Mom wanted more privacy, and a fence wasn't good enough, so Dad decided to rebuild it from the bottom up, adding the wind breaks. We're so high up that the wind can get nasty, but there's almost nothing, even when the wind is blowing as hard as it is now."

"I can't imagine needing more privacy. No other houses are around for miles," Devlin pointed out.

"That wasn't always the case." Prudence skewered two marshmallows. "I recall a house fire led to the nearest house being torn down, right?"

"Yep." Gabe motioned to a space behind the tree line. "That house was the reason Mom wanted more privacy in the first place, but then they decided not to rebuild after the fire and my parents bought the land from them."

Gabe watched Devlin's face as she took in this information and realized he was happy to share this all with her. She appeared so content bundled in her fur-lined parka, white boots and matching hat and mitten set. A half smile played on her lips while the group talked, interjecting only at a few points but seeming satisfied to just be a part of the group. The family.

He found himself quieting and letting the rest get louder as the hot toddies and spiked cocoa kicked in. His Irish coffee was landing just right but he felt mellow rather than boisterous. Soon midnight neared and yawns were taking over the frequency of the conversation.

"Brrr." Annabelle shivered. "I'm gonna turn in, guys. I think I'm starting to get a chill."

"And you thought I'd be the one in improper dress." Sebastian gestured to her high-heeled winter boots.

"Please. These boots have seen me through many Massachusetts winters, and they'll last many more." She stood and turned to leave.

Sebastian followed, opening the door for her, their conversation fading out as it softly clicked shut behind them.

Prudence stood as well. "You ready, Grey?" she asked, reaching out her hand.

Greyson took her hand and winked at Gabe and Devlin. "Always. Night, guys."

Gabe and Devlin watched the second pair go in, then they were alone.

"I think I'll stay out for a little while more." Devlin reached into the bag for another marshmallow. They'd been seated next to each other all night and with slow, unintentional movements, had eased themselves so they were so close but barely touching now, a hint of pressure with each almost made contact.

"I'll keep you company." Gabe second-guessed himself. "Unless you wanted to be alone?"

"No, I'd like for you to stay."

"Thank goodness, my room is right next to the master, and whatever Grey and Pru are doing, I don't want to hear it."

Devlin laughed, a sweet peal of sound that washed over Gabe like a security blanket. "I'm glad I'm sleeping downstairs."

"I might end up on the couch. They just can't get enough of each other."

"I wonder what that's like," Devlin murmured, so quiet he wasn't sure he'd heard her. His blood thickened and he pushed down a wave of desire. Swallowing hard, he cleared his throat enough to ask the question he wasn't sure he could handle the answer to right now.

"What do you mean?"

"I wonder what that kind of love is like. So in love that nothing else matters. Not fame or fortune. So wrapped up with another person that they're the air you need to breathe, or you need them otherwise your body just doesn't function."

Gabe's body was functioning fine right now, and it took this opportunity to remind him that he was a red-blooded male with a stunning woman sitting inches from him, looking at him now, her eyes wide and searching. He lowered his head, giving her time to retreat. It seemed like she was going to, pulling back a fraction before stopping. His lips touched hers with the lightness of flower petals brushing against each other in the breeze.

A gust of wind blew in so fast and harsh that it almost extinguished the fire's flames, and the blast was so icy that it startled them apart. Devlin stood and backed toward the door.

"I'm sorry, Gabe. I don't know why I let this keep happening. I meant it when I said I didn't want any entanglements right now. I want to focus on Books and Beans with nothing else to distract me." She didn't give him the chance to respond before pulling open the door and retreating inside.

Gabe knew she was right. They were competitors now, both needing the building between them to expand their businesses. Only one reason existed for them to be here at this cabin — to put together proposals good enough to knock the other one out of the competition. He stood and turned off the fire pit's propane and replaced the cover. He moved through the patio door, turning to lock it behind him. Divesting himself of his winter gear, he turned off the downstairs lights and trudged up the stairs.

"Gabe, wait!" He was halfway up when he heard Devlin's loud whisper. His heart stuttered then soared when he saw Devlin stop at the base of the staircase. *This is it, we're going to happen.* All thoughts he'd had moments ago about how correct she was to back away jumped right out of the window.

"There's a man in my room."

His soaring heart plummeted. "What?"

"A man. I'm assuming Sebastian, since Grey and Pru wouldn't spend the night apart." She motioned with her hand for him to follow.

When he got to Devlin's room, he indeed saw a man on her bed. He walked over and shook Sebastian's shoulder, getting a muffled, "Not now, Winters," in reply.

Gabe bent over Sebastian's prone figure, lying face down, quiet snores escaping his nose. "Dreaming about AB, huh?"

He jumped in startlement when Sebastian replied, "Fine, just put it on my desk you infernal woman."

Devlin snickered under her breath, still standing in the doorway.

He shook him again, to complete silence this time. "He's out." Gabe looked around the room, then sighed. "It seems wrong to wake him, you might as well just sleep upstairs in his room, we'll figure it out tomorrow."

"Hold on, let me grab my pajamas." He heard a muffled oath as she almost tripped on Sebastian's coat and shoes that he'd left in the middle of the floor. "I should turn the light on, that'll teach him."

"I don't think he'd notice."

Devlin struggled in the dark then picked up her suitcase. "I might as well just take the whole thing, I never unpacked anything." She stopped and threw a blanket over before they left, pulling the door shut.

"You old softie," Gabe joked, taking her suitcase to carry upstairs.

"I'd like to think he'd do the same for me."

As they ascended to the second floor their fingers brushed once, twice. He showed her to Sebastian's room, opened the door and turned on the light, depositing the suitcase by the door. "A bathroom connects the rooms. You can go first, I'll use it after you." He waited for her to go in. *Please, you have to be the one to leave first.*

Devlin gave him a small smile, slipped through the door and closed it. He heard the click of the lock that signaled the definitive end to the evening.

Chapter Ten

Devlin awoke the next morning to the gray light of winter straining to break through the clouds. One look at the nightstand clock told her it was far too early for her to be awake. Her usual wake-up time was four a.m. and she was grateful that hour had long passed, but she could stand to catch a few more hours of sleep. She needed her wits about her for the long day ahead so she closed her eyes, willing herself to fall back asleep when the image of Gabe underneath her while she straddled him came unbidden into her mind.

Her eyes popped open, her skin flushing as she could almost feel the smoothness of his chest, his hands running up her sides to her breasts. Maybe she just needed a release then she could sleep. Her body had been strung tight like a bow since they'd made out in the old art gallery and last night's sweet kiss hadn't helped matters any.

She ran her hand down the smooth planes of her body, reliving what it had felt like, that night with

Gabe, drawing on memories of him since they'd reconnected. Back then she'd felt frantic, not wanting to think about anything else in that moment. He'd tried to calm her, putting his hands on her hips to slow her movement, but her pace wouldn't abate. She touched her clit in a lazy circle—he'd done this once he'd realized she wasn't going to do anything but ride him hard and he'd used his fingers where they'd joined to give her the friction she'd strived for. It felt so good—a long moan escaped her lips—that night had been so good. She came in a long shudder, her fingers stilling.

She heard the faucet turn on in the bathroom and bolted upright. Her heart had been beating fast from her orgasm, but now it stopped. *How long has he been in there?* She hadn't been loud, but she hadn't been quiet either. Throwing off her covers, she slid out of bed and tip-toed to the bathroom, putting her ear to the door. The water shut off and silence permeated until the loud flush of the toilet made her squeak and jump back. She stood motionless, believing that standing still would erase the noise that just came out of her mouth, hoping he wouldn't open the door while at the same time praying that he would. For a long moment she heard nothing, then the shower turned on.

She breathed a sigh of relief, glad he hadn't come through the door, vulnerable after her release. She was going to work with Annabelle and Prudence today to go over her proposal and Gabe was going to do the same with Sebastian and Greyson. She had no more time for dalliances or make-outs or masturbating while dreaming of Gabe's touch. The time to get down to business was now.

Devlin was making her bed when she heard the bathroom door open and close on the other side. She waited a few minutes before going in herself. The room was still steamy from Gabe's shower, and she could smell his aftershave. She took a deep breath and noted his toiletries in a neat line on his side of the sink, feeling an intimacy with him that came with sharing this personal space. She felt her face heat, wondering again if he'd heard anything.

* * * *

Gabe turned on the shower, not paying attention to the temperature, and was doused with a spray of ice cold water. At this point he didn't care, and let the water run over his body hoping to cool his burgeoning erection. He'd woken this morning already thinking about Devlin. He wasn't sure he'd ever stopped — the night before, his dreams had been filled with her. They weren't always erotic, but dreams of mundane daily life. From domestic tasks like making dinner or folding the laundry together while watching television, to her being in charge of her life, behind the counter of her shop, or in her office, on the computer, reading glasses perched on her nose while she did the books.

I've never been inside her shop.

He was puzzled at the nature of the dreams. The domesticity turned him on. The in charge boss lady turned him on. He was coming to realize that everything about her turned him on, even the parts of her he didn't know, or that she'd tried so hard to keep hidden from him. He'd lain in bed until long past sunrise, the milky light of impending snow hiding the sun. When he decided he needed to get going for the day, he was sure that he had himself under control, that he'd get through the day seeing and being with Devlin without throwing himself prostrate at her feet, begging her to tell him all her secrets.

The simple act of entering the bathroom shattered his calm determination. At first he wasn't sure what he was hearing. A low moan then a rustle of movement coming from Devlin's room. Approaching the adjoining door, he put his ear to it and heard the unmistakable keen of a woman having an orgasm. A good one at that. He knew that sound — he'd been on the giving end of that sound.

Standing now under the shower, the sound of her coming pinged around him like a symphony. The cold water was doing next to nothing to deflate his libido, so he turned the faucet to hot. How the fuck was he supposed to get through the day now? His intimate knowledge of her was so far in the distant past that he was able to disconnect from it, but now? Now he wanted to knock down her door and continue whatever journey Devlin had just been on. *This is pure foolishness. You don't mix business with pleasure, no matter what.* He finished in the shower, his anger at himself giving him just enough edge to get through the rest of his morning's preparations without losing it.

Gabe followed the smell of freshly brewed coffee into the kitchen where Sebastian was sitting at the island, his back to him, looking like he was nursing a mug of the stuff. The open space was separated by the kitchen island with a large sectional and fireplace in the living room. Gabe wasn't a big fan of the open concept layout, but it suited the cabin, since the fireplace helped to heat the main floor.

"Did the infernal woman make the pot, or were you able to figure it out?" Gabe asked, grabbing a winter-themed mug and pouring out a steaming coffee.

"What?" A perplexed look crossed Sebastian's face.

"You called Annabelle an 'infernal woman' in your sleep last night after you told her to leave you alone."

"How on earth would you know that I was talking in my sleep? And to piggyback off that question—I talk in my sleep?"

"You were passed out in Devlin's room last night. I think you startled her."

Sebastian ran his hand over his face, a yawn splitting his features. "I swear, last night was the first night since smartphones were invented that I wasn't up until all hours going through emails or texts."

Gabe grabbed a bottle of creamer out of the fridge and offered it to Sebastian. "You don't seem like you take a lot of vacations."

"No, running a company is a full time job and then some. Even when I'm not at work, I'm at an event or someplace with Wi-Fi so I'm always connected."

"Spotty reception can have its perks."

They turned when they heard voices approaching. Devlin and Annabelle walked in, Annabelle looking perfect as usual and Devlin freshly washed with mussed-up, damp hair. Gabe could smell her shampoo, hear the echoes of her orgasm.

"Morning, ladies. We're talking about vacations and bad cell reception," he informed them, moving away from the coffee pot so they could pour some for themselves.

Annabelle shot a pointed look at Sebastian. "You'd better not be complaining. I told you we had no reception here."

"I'm not complaining, Winters. In fact, I was just telling Gabe how nice it was not to have to answer a bunch of emails before I could go to bed. I slept like a baby."

"In my bed," Devlin pointed out.

"What?" Annabelle asked in a voice that was too loud for the situation.

"He passed out in my bed last night," Devlin explained. "Imagine my surprise when I almost sat on him when I got to my room."

Gabe's mouth went dry at the imagery.

"Where did you sleep, then, Dev?" Annabelle looked between Sebastian and Devlin.

"It wasn't worth waking him, so I just grabbed my stuff and went upstairs."

Now Annabelle looked between Gabe and Devlin. "Really?" she asked, one eyebrow raised.

"Two rooms, AB," Gabe stated. "Devlin stayed in the other room."

Annabelle shrugged and propped one hip against the counter. "I'm just saying."

"I'll change the sheets before you go into the room, Devlin," Sebastian said.

Devlin waved away his concern. "Don't worry about it. Why bother with changing two sets of sheets? My luggage is already upstairs and toiletries in the bathroom. We've got enough to do today working on the proposals without room switching for just one more night."

"Sounds good to me. I'll grab my stuff later." Sebastian stood and refilled his mug.

Annabelle sighed. "Seems like I'm going to end up sharing a bathroom with you anyways. At least I got in there first this morning." She jumped as the rattle of the wind blowing at the sliding door stopped Sebastian from responding. "I know Grey keeps saying no storm is coming, but this wind is telling me otherwise." She pulled her cell out of her back pocket and walked around the kitchen, holding it up in various locations. "Do you still have that old weather radio here?"

Gabe tried to picture various locations in the cabin and where the radio would've been stored. "I don't remember the last time I saw it, or if it would still work."

Devlin walked to the sliding door, peering out at the still gray sky. "The sun's not coming out any time soon."

Gabe moved to stand behind her, close enough that the warmth of her skin radiated to him, and reached around her to point to a group of pines about fifty feet from the house. "When we were kids, my dad would tell us that you can base the weather on how those trees move."

Devlin moved back, almost leaning into Gabe's chest.

"If the tips of the trees whip like a trebuchet, bad weather is on the way."

Devlin's laughter vibrated through Gabe and the impulse to wrap his arms around her was almost too much to bear. "A trebuchet, huh? That's very specific imagery."

"Dad likes all things medieval, what can I say?"

She leaned a fraction more into Gabe just as he shuffled his feet closer to her.

"I don't think they're quite at that level yet. Maybe a slingshot." She lifted her head and her hair brushed against Gabe's morning stubble. He breathed in the fresh scent of her, and was starting to lift his arms to embrace her when Annabelle's voice broke in.

"I don't know why I'm bothering." Lowering her phone, she glanced to where Devlin and Gabe were standing and appeared startled. "All right, you two. We should focus on breakfast then proposals. We're only going to be here one more night, I can live that long without cell reception."

Gabe stepped back from Devlin and a chill seeped into him at the loss of contact. *I'm getting moony over trebuchets and shampoo.* Devlin had walked to the fridge and was bent over searching for something, her ass doing a delectable wiggle. *Now this I can get moony over.*

"Breakfast sandwiches are in the freezer," he called out to Devlin. "Leo whipped up a batch and I figured that would be good enough for this morning."

Devlin grabbed the sandwiches as Annabelle turned the oven on. "Works for me. If I get to eat I'm happy. Coffee isn't enough for me in the morning."

Annabelle pulled out cut fruit from the fridge and set the container on the table. "I'm good with just a cup or ten of coffee until lunch. Then more coffee."

"That doesn't surprise me," Sebastian said as he grabbed plates. "No wonder you love Devlin so much, you were stuck with office coffee until Devlin opened up shop."

"Really?" Devlin asked, surprised. "I can't be the first coffee shop that's been in Amber Falls."

"The first good one," Annabelle deadpanned.

"You and Pru always say that, but I figured you were joking." Devlin spoke over her shoulder as she slid the pan into the oven. He wasn't ashamed to be looking at her ass, but when it wiggled again, his eyes darted up to meet her gaze, a smile lighting her eyes, and he swallowed hard.

"I never joke about my coffee." Annabelle refilled her cup, sitting next to Sebastian at the table.

"She's telling the truth," Gabe interjected, needing to think about something other than what he could do with that ass of Devlin's. "I think AB and Pru started drinking coffee in grade school."

"I had my first espresso shot in fifth grade," Annabelle stated.

Sebastian gave her a look of obvious appall. "Please tell me you're kidding."

"Of course I'm kidding. I wasn't raised by over-caffeinated wolves." Annabelle appeared thoughtful. "Okay, I guess I do joke about my coffee."

Devlin laughed and walked over to where Gabe had ended up by the sink and reached around him to grab the oven timer.

"What do you think," she asked, her hip touching his. "Fifteen minutes?"

Gabe's mouth went dry, and he gulped his too-hot coffee. He could do so much with her in fifteen minutes. He'd start with that ass. Then he'd make her touch herself, recreate the noises he heard through the bathroom door this morning. The moans, the —

"Gabe. Does that sound about right?" Devlin repeated.

"Oh yeah, fifteen should do it."

The sound of laughter coming from the stairs grabbed everyone's attention. Greyson and Prudence stopped at the bottom landing, smiles wiped off their faces as they saw the group staring, then they broke out into giggles once again.

"Did you already forget other people exist in the world?" Sebastian asked.

Greyson sauntered over to the kitchen island and pulled out a chair for Prudence, gesturing for her to sit. "When I'm with her, there really isn't anyone else in the world."

"Oh, Grey," Prudence said, "you're embarrassing me. But thank you."

Greyson walked around the island to the kitchen counter, pulling a container of cleaning wipes from the cabinet. "I'm just gonna give this a good clean," he said under his breath to Gabe, as he wiped off the surface and Gabe's eyes widened in horror.

"You didn't."

"Well, I didn't, but Pru did."

"Is there any place else I need to avoid?"

Greyson glanced around the living area. "The couch should be dry by now, I won't tell you where, and the staircase, we didn't have enough time to make a mess there."

"We haven't been here for twenty-four hours. When did you get the time to do all that?"

"That woman has amazing stamina."

"Grey, I didn't need to know that. Too much information is a real thing."

"Nothing about Pru is too much. Hey, here she is." Greyson moved aside so Prudence could grab a cup for coffee.

"Whatcha talking about?" she asked.

Gabe evaded her eyes and she punched Greyson's arm. "What did I tell you about oversharing?"

"That's what I said!" Gabe exclaimed. "And he overshared just a tad too much. I'll take it to the grave."

"Thanks, Gabe." Prudence gave Greyson another light punch as she walked away with her mug.

"Worth it," Greyson explained. "Now she'll have to punish me later."

"For fuck's sake, you don't learn, do you?"

Greyson winked. "I never have."

The kitchen timer went off and Annabelle called out, "All right, guys, butts in seats please."

"Here." Gabe opened the cabinet drawer and handed silverware to Greyson.

"So, what's everyone's plan for today?" Greyson asked as he set the table.

As the group dug in Sebastian said, "Guys call the living room."

"You call it?" Annabelle sneered. "Can I call dibs on our bathroom later?"

"Yeah, you can't call a room, Sebastian," Devlin agreed. "The living room is the brightest, with the best setup for the flow of ideas. Plus" — she gestured to the kitchen — "coffee proximity."

"I *was* kidding, but now I want the living room." Sebastian speared a pineapple chunk with this statement.

"The den upstairs has just as much light," Gabe pointed out. "I don't care where we work, the guys can be up there." He shot a small smile to Devlin, who nodded back.

"I was joking too, but I appreciate it," Devlin acknowledged. "We can switch this afternoon if it makes a difference."

"No need. Good ideas will come no matter where we are." Greyson glanced at Devlin. He must have seen her shift in her seat as he added, "Sorry, Dev. It's not personal."

"It's not," Sebastian insisted. "I could just as easily join with you and give you all my expert advice."

"None of this is personal," Devlin acknowledged. "You've all become my friends and whatever happens here won't change that. Now, if we're all done, I'm ready to get started."

Chapter Eleven

"So, what you're saying is that statute fifty-two, bylaw four states that you guys can resolve this with a dance off?" Sebastian's eyebrows rose almost to his hairline as he said this.

"Not in the typical sense," Gabe tried to explain to Sebastian once again. Of all the things he could've forgotten to bring, he hadn't grabbed his copy of the township bylaws which outlined the convoluted codes for buying a downtown property. "Think more of a 1920's dance-a-thon."

Sebastian sat in silence for a moment. "Okay, I am thinking of that, and it still doesn't help me understand why that would be a legal way to solve a property dispute."

Greyson, who was lying on the leather sofa, moved his arm off his eyes. "No one knows why."

"And this is the same building that was the speakeasy?"

"Yes," Greyson and Gabe answered in unison.

The planning part of the morning so far had had little actual planning. Sebastian, in an apparent attempt to understand the town and its laws better before offering his advice, had been asking question after question, and his frustration increased with each brother's reply.

Sebastian sat thoughtful for a moment before asking, "Do you think you can out dance Devlin?"

Gabe laughed at the reality of his situation. He'd gone from putting an offer in on the building, to being told he needed to put together a proposal that would beat out the woman he was scared he was falling for, to seriously considering having a dance competition to win.

"This thing is going to drive me nuts," he said. "It doesn't help that I forgot to bring a copy of the city codes so I could try to find some sort of loophole that would make me a slam dunk."

"You shouldn't need loopholes, Gabe. You've got a strong proposal, plus your business has been established for many more years than Devlin's." Greyson put his hand back over his eyes and groaned. "I hate talking like this. I *like* Devlin!"

Gabe swallowed past the lump in his throat that popped up every time he started to think about winning. He'd been able to peek behind the curtain that Devlin had kept shut when they shopped for his house and no matter what voice was telling him to be cutthroat about business, a louder, more insistent voice stated that whatever this woman had to show him was far more important than a business expansion. The problem was, he didn't know which voice to listen to.

Sebastian pulled out his phone. "The city codes have to be on the township website." He tapped the screen a few times before cursing. "Fuck! I forgot about this whole no reception thing."

"I can't be upset with anyone but myself," Gabe admitted. "I had it all saved to my thumb drive" — he tapped at his computer's keyboard — "but that's no good if I forget the thumb drive."

"I can't think of a single place within a two hundred mile radius from Atlanta that doesn't have cell reception," Sebastian complained.

"Same for L.A.," Greyson added, sitting up on the couch, a yawn escaping.

"C'mon, guys," Gabe implored. "Isn't there something to be said about the solitude of knowing there's no point in picking up your phone just to check if anything needs your attention? That the world will continue to function without your input. You can focus on the here and now, whoever you're with and whatever you're doing."

"I have trouble with the here and now," Sebastian admitted. "Something always needs my attention."

Greyson pointed at Sebastian holding his phone. "Why do you still have it with you? You know your phone isn't gonna work, just throw it in your bag until we leave."

Sebastian gave a rueful grin. "I still think a hundred emails and texts will all start coming in at once."

"They won't," Greyson assured him. "You'll be about halfway down the mountain when that happens and since you're driving, you'll have to wait until you're home."

"I'll just have Winters read them all to me, get some business done on the drive back."

"You're not going to have anything coming through that you don't want her to see?" Gabe asked.

"Nah, I've been so busy since I moved here that I haven't had any time for fun. Having Sofia here at New Years didn't help, either. That was my last chunk of time not sitting at my desk and I spent it doing sibling bonding."

Greyson got up to stoke the fire while saying, "I find it hard to believe that you've been celibate since October."

"Longer than that, if you must know," Sebastian admitted. "I'm serious when I say that buying The Bee and the move has taken up every ounce of my energy. And no offense to Amber Falls, but there's not exactly a swinging singles scene here. It's a college town and the older I get, I just don't have the patience for twenty year olds."

Gabe laughed. "And I'm sure they're just as thankful that Old Man Locke isn't as lecherous as media moguls are portrayed. Besides, you don't need a group of ladies, just one. In fact, I know that Annab —"

"Enough about me," Sebastian broke in. "Since we're at a standstill with work, who else wants to talk about their feelings?" He gave Gabe a pointed look.

"Hey, man, I don't have feelings," Gabe insisted, lying through his front teeth. "In fact, I'm completely dead inside."

"I have so many feelings," Greyson said.

"We know, Grey. We know," Sebastian deadpanned. "I'm serious, Gabe. I got some...vibes between you and Devlin. You wouldn't stop looking at her at breakfast this morning."

"No vibes whatsoever. We're competitors, that's the whole reason we're here — to take business away from the other person. She wouldn't be here if you didn't invite her, since this trip was supposed to be just us, but

Grey couldn't bear to be apart from Prudence for two days."

"You'll get it someday, bro," Greyson promised.

They sat in silence for a few minutes until Sebastian spoke. "You know the ladies are having this exact same conversation downstairs, don't you?"

* * * *

"You're here because you want to be, Devlin," Prudence insisted. "Being here with Gabe is the only reason why."

"While I don't *quite* agree with that," Annabelle broke in, "I'd like to think that our company is stellar, I do agree that Gabe was a big draw for you coming along."

"I don't think it matters what you two think. Don't forget that I agreed to this before I knew Gabe would be here."

"But you didn't back out of it," Prudence explained. "Besides, I saw you wiggle that cute little butt of yours when he was looking."

Devlin felt her face flame. "I was just having a little fun."

"Fun is putting together a charcuterie board for dinner, not wagging your ass at a dumbstruck Gabe," Annabelle said.

"I was not *wagging* it. I just gave a little shimmy, and I only did it because it was so obvious he was staring."

"Did something happen at the shopping trip that you're not telling us? Because it seems like you're not telling us something." Prudence went to the kitchen to grab the pot of coffee, snagging a snack tray from the fridge on her way back.

"Nope, nothing happened at the shopping trip," Devlin insisted.

Annabelle narrowed her eyes. "Hmm. Did something happen at a time, say, other than the shopping trip?"

Devlin knew she hadn't told them about the kiss, and she justified her silence by a nagging feeling that they'd meddle more if she said anything, and she needed meddling friends right now less than a Scooby Doo villain did.

"Okay, don't be mad," Devlin started.

Annabelle stopped midway through opening a package of crackers. "I knew you were holding out on us!"

"Last week I was looking at the art gallery. The movers had just finished emptying the place and they let me look around after I promised them I'd lock up." She saw the wide eyes of her friends and realized that she might shock the unflappable duo with this next admission. "Gabe came in after me and I don't remember who started it, but all of a sudden I was against the wall, and we were making out."

"All of a sudden?" Prudence asked. "A deer jumps out at you all of a sudden. You don't shove your tongue down someone's throat all of a sudden."

"You know what I mean, Pru! I wasn't expecting it to happen. I was a ball of nerves on the day of the town council meeting, and I guess it just took the edge off." Devlin looked over at Annabelle, who had been silent so far. Suspicion filled her — Annabelle was up to no good when she was quiet like this.

"Oh," Annabelle said when the attention was directed at her. "I'm sure it did. Take the edge off, I mean." She continued to nibble on a cracker. Devlin wasn't fooled by her lack of reaction.

"C'mon, AB. What do you want to say?" she asked.

"Well." Annabelle took her sweet time finishing her bite. "You and Gabe already have a history. I know that you both want the same shop, but why should that stop you from having some fun with him in the meantime?"

"Having some fun with him?" Devlin wasn't sure she understood what Annabelle was getting at.

"You know," Annabelle started to explain, "get your frustrations out. There has to be something cathartic about absolutely fucking his brains out knowing that he's the source of your frustration."

Prudence guffawed at this, then appeared to reconsider. "That's a pretty good point."

"That's a terrible point!" Devlin exclaimed. "What happens when the city makes their decision and one of us loses? Who do you guys pick then? I meant it this morning when I said I don't want my need to buy this building to come between any of you guys."

"Who says we have to choose?" Prudence pointed out. "Life goes on. You guys make it work, or you don't work, and were just fuck buddies for a while. We're all adults."

"You don't believe that." Devlin was shocked at what they were saying. "You're telling me that if you and Grey don't work out, we'll all continue to sing kumbaya together as one big happy group?"

Prudence had the courtesy to appear abashed. "That's different."

"Pru, you know it wouldn't end up any different." Devlin needed to calm down. She felt like she was getting upset with her best friends every time they had a conversation about Gabe. She was better than that. They were better than that.

"I appreciate your advice, but like I said before, and what seems to be the theme of this weekend, none of this is personal."

Even as she said so, she knew she was lying because every single thing with Gabe seemed *very* personal. As much as she tried not to think about her ex-boyfriend, she was thrown off guard whenever he popped into her head like he did now. He had been controlling, and she couldn't help to bring him into the equation. She tried to tell him to leave, that it had been over a year and she was tired of putting him into her situations, still making decisions based on what she thought he'd do, or how he'd react. Like now, she knew he'd expect her to put him first, to put everything she wanted on the back burner in order to make him happy. She didn't know how to stop this.

Get the fuck out of my head, you asshole.

Annabelle, who had the knack of knowing when a change of subject was needed, laid her hand on Devlin's arm, indicating a cease fire. "What do you think they guys are doing? They should be coming down for lunch anytime now."

As if manifested out of thin air, they heard footsteps on the stairs.

"Ah, here come the three wise men now," Annabelle deadpanned.

Greyson made his way to Prudence, pulling her into a hug and a deep kiss. "I missed you, Pru."

Prudence returned the kiss and sighed. "We're ready to take a break for some lunch, what about you?"

"I'm famished," Sebastian exaggerated. "What did you ladies make for lunch?"

"We're very important businesswomen, Sebastian. We've been waiting for house husband Greyson to come and make us some food," Devlin teased.

"House husband. I like the sound of that, believe it or not." Greyson nodded his assent.

"You would," Gabe said. "I'll grab stuff for sandwiches. Don't let us bother you, keep your planning session going." He leaned over Devlin's shoulder, obviously pretending to look at her notes.

"Hey! Eyes off, mister," Devlin admonished, surprised but pleased at his playfulness.

Gabe winked and went to the fridge to gather supplies for lunch.

Chapter Twelve

A late lunch turned into a later evening of more planning. Gabe was tapped out. He'd given his all to finalizing the proposal all while trying to keep Devlin off his preoccupied mind. It was exhausting. Dinner had been an easy frozen lasagna that Leo had prepared, and they'd adjourned to the cozy living room with its built-up fire to unwind and have some drinks.

"I'm serious," Annabelle insisted. "I know I sound like a broken record, but this wind has been picking up all day and now the snow is starting to fall hard."

"Sorry, Grey," Prudence added. "I know you think you have a sixth sense for when storms are coming in, but I think you're wrong on this one."

Sebastian scoffed and shifted in his seat, ice cubes clinking in his tumbler. "It's just some fluff, you guys."

Gabe noticed that Devlin had wandered into the kitchen and was busy pouring a glass of wine. The invisible force that guided him to her that very first night in Boston pulled at him again and he was helpless but to follow it. She shot him a weary glance as he grabbed what he needed to make another drink and he kept his distance, leaving her plenty of room to navigate around him to look out of the window.

"Snow globe snow." Devlin's voice was low, blending in with the crackling of the fire.

"What does that mean?" Gabe asked, leaning closer to hear her.

"So light and fluffy that you can imagine we were all turned upside down, shaken up a bit, then righted." She continued to look out at the winter scene. "I could fall forever like this."

Gabe's heart squeezed and all he wanted to do was to reach out to her and wrap himself in the serenity she was so clearly feeling. He turned as well and they stood, quiet, the conversation behind them providing a comforting hum. The peace was shattered when she spoke again.

"When I moved to Amber Falls, this was the kind of snow that fell early in the season. Boston snow always seemed so heavy and wet, but this — this was so light that it had a silence to it like it could absorb sound and you could just be...whoever you wanted to or didn't want to be. Everything stilled and the world stopped."

A gust of wind took the snow and whipped it in a ferocious circle and Devlin turned to look at Gabe, her tongue mesmerizing him as it darted out to wet her lips.

"I think this is the part of the snow globe's journey where we're upside down." She sighed and turned back to the kitchen island, leaning over and propping her chin on her hand.

Gabe's last ounce of sanity shattered at this innocent image of Devlin's backside. Everything he'd been enduring since this morning simmered to the surface and broke free. "I heard you this morning." He came up behind her and trailed his fingers over her backside, the same one that had been tantalizing him all day. "I heard you in your room."

Devlin gasped then quieted, not wanting to alert the others to what was going on. Gabe moved his hand to the front of her pants and ran a finger over her covered slit. She felt a rush of wetness at the touch and moved her backside until it pushed against him. He cupped her mound and flicked his tongue against her earlobe, his words sending shivers through her. All anyone had to do was turn around and they'd know what was going on. Another rush went through her, excitement this time.

"I wanted to open the door and take you slow and hard, until you begged me for release. Until *I* had to beg you for my release."

At his words, she moved back against him, needing more friction.

"I never realized I was an ass man until you. I can't stop thinking about it. What I'd do, where I'd start." He had unbuttoned her pants while he was speaking and one of his hands delved inside, under her panties, finding her slit again. He ran his middle finger up and down before sliding it inside her. Her legs buckled at the contact, and he reached his arm around to brace her. "I'd take you right here if I could —"

Do it she implored silently.

" —but I want to take my time." He withdrew his hand.

She felt a loss so intense that if she could have mustered up any emotion other than blinding lust she would have wept.

He stood there a moment before stepping away. "If you want this as much as I do, leave your bathroom door unlocked tonight. I'll come to you. One night and that's all. We're back to normal once we're back in Amber Falls."

She stared at him, his gaze intense, then nodded her assent. "One night."

Gabe looked out into the room, the occupants unaware of the agreement that had just transpired. "I'm going to go grab some more firewood, guys," he called to the group. "I'll be right back." Then he was gone.

Her face felt as hot as the fire burning across the room. She filled a cup with cold water from the sink, holding it to her forehead before gulping it down. After taking a few calming breaths, she returned to the living room against all her instincts to follow Gabe. She couldn't leave now but the need she felt to follow him was alarming.

"Where's your drink?" Prudence asked.

"Oh, I just needed some water. The altitude must have me dehydrated."

Prudence nodded and Devlin noticed the quick glance between Prudence and Annabelle. She was thankful that, since this morning, the planning of Gabe and Devlin's future was off the table. *For now.* She expected the ceasefire from Annabelle and Prudence would be over once they were back in town, especially if they were picking up on the tension that was ready to snap between her and Gabe.

She looked around at the rest of the group assembled and, except for Sebastian, saw a close group of friends who had known each other for decades. She felt a surge of emotion that she was lucky enough to be included with these wonderful people. She didn't want anything to jeopardize these friendships that had become as important to her as any familial connection. Gabe's body left an imprint behind her from moments ago and she tried to shake it off, but she made the fatal mistake of looking out of the sliding door to the backyard where she could see him chopping wood. As he lifted and heaved the blade back down, she was conscious of every rhythmic strike as if he was pounding into her.

I'm going to leave my door open tonight.

She didn't have time to second-guess herself, she knew this to be an indisputable fact that she wouldn't deny herself any longer. She just needed to hold on to any thread of sanity until he came to her. She stood, picking up her glass. The conversation around her had come to a lull, everyone else just as tired as her from the long day. "I'm going to turn in. What time are we planning to leave in the morning?"

"I was thinking around noon?" Greyson offered. "Give us one last chance to sleep in, have some brunch then hit the road."

She looked around the group, at the satisfied Prudence, the mellow Annabelle and the half asleep Sebastian. "I think that sounds perfect. Have a good night." She cast one last look outside before leaving the room.

* * * *

Gabe was nervous. *I'm a grown man that's nervous to go to a woman's bedroom.* He stood outside Devlin's bathroom door and hesitated, his hand hovering over the handle. He couldn't turn back after this, business and pleasure would be forever intertwined. Whatever he thought—

The door swung open, and Devlin stood in front of him wearing just a shirt. "Are you just going to stand there and keep me waiting?"

Gabe smiled at her forthrightness. Now this was the Devlin he knew. "I was giving myself a pep talk."

"Really?" Devlin moved aside and gestured him into the room, closing the door behind him. "You didn't seem like you needed a pep talk earlier tonight. Are you going to leave your jacket on?"

Surprised, Gabe realized he was still wearing his jacket and shoes. Letting out a laugh, he toed off his shoes and threw his jacket over a chair. "I came back inside, and everyone was gone. It felt for a minute like I imagined the whole day and I'd been here by myself, but then I saw all the glasses still on the table and knew I wasn't alone. I didn't stop and came right here."

Devlin padded over to him and ran her hand up his chest, toying with the top button of his flannel shirt. "I'm glad you did. If you can't tell, I was getting a little impatient."

They were almost eye to eye. Gabe held her gaze for a moment before lowering his head to capture her lips. He raised his hands to frame her face, running his thumbs over her cheeks as they had the most chaste, tender kiss he'd experienced. Then he ran his hands down her back and realized she wore nothing under her shirt. The silk of her ass, a perfect handful, would forever be a sensory memory of his.

Devlin reached down and pulled her shirt off, tossing it to the floor. She backed up as Gabe removed his clothes and he got his first look at her. His first, *I've been waiting years to see this*, look. *I've been waiting my whole life*. Every memory he had of her was so underwhelming compared to what he saw in front of him now. When she had long hair she'd used it almost like armor, to cover her breasts and hide part of herself from him, but her short hair gave her a vulnerability that he didn't think she realized she was exuding.

The lust he saw in her eyes when he was naked moved him forward and they tumbled to the bed as their mouths clashed together, ferocious in their need to touch each other everywhere all at once. It reminded him of their first time together and his promise to her earlier tonight that if they repeated it, they'd go slow. He stilled his movements, holding on to her, enjoying her body nestled against his, how they fit just right, every dip and hollow meeting its perfect counterpart.

She nipped his chin and tried to move on top of him, but he took her mouth in a languorous open-mouthed kiss before flipping her to her back and moving downward.

"I told you we'd go so slow you'd beg me for your release." Gabe's voice was muffled by her breast, and he flicked a tongue out, teasing her nipple.

"I don't want it slow," Devlin growled. "I want you now."

Gabe smiled at her and continued his descent. "Why do you want it so fast?" He dipped his tongue into her belly button, swirling around as she let out a purr.

"Why slow?" She gasped as he ran light fingers up the inside of her thighs to tease her.

"I asked you first." The heat in her eyes was almost his undoing, his cock so swollen that he felt like he was going to explode, but when he looked at her, spread open before him, he knew he was going to taste her tonight and that was all he needed to know to continue to take it slow.

He didn't wait for her answer, preferring to show her why taking it slow had its benefits, and lapping up everything her body wanted to give him. The pleasure he felt when he heard her moan as he first touched her clit almost made him pass out, her fingers scraping on his scalp the only thing keeping him going. He alternated between dipping his tongue into her and circling then sucking her clit until she tensed and trembled, then he eased away. She yelped and bucked her hips upward, almost knocking him off the bed.

"Easy there, Devlin. I promise I'll give you what you want."

She scrabbled her hands back to his head, guiding him down. "Don't stop, Gabe, please."

"I won't deny you anything." And he didn't. He refused to go fast, wanting to prolong this moment in case this was the only one they had. Finally, he held his tongue over her clit and let her ride his mouth until she came in a shuddering orgasm.

He pulled himself to his knees, holding his body sway over hers, the tip of his cock teasing her entrance, the wetness of her sending shivers over his body. He leaned down and took her mouth in a kiss, then lifted her and helped her to position herself on her knees. Kneeling behind her, he fondled her ass, parting her cheeks and running his cock up and down, searching for her wetness once again.

"I told you, you made me an ass man." He grabbed each cheek and dipped the tip of his cock into her. "I always thought I was a breast man until you." He grabbed a condom that she'd lain on the bed and rolled it on, then inched inside her, the still rocking pulse of her orgasm pulling him deeper inside with each thrust.

Every atom of his being was screaming at him to take her hard and fast, to pound into her until his world shattered. He picked up his rhythm until he heard Devlin laugh, her striking eyes watching him over her shoulder. "No going slow for you?"

Gabe halted in mid thrust and bent over Devlin. He was able to take her at a different angle and she gasped at the change. He could hear her starting to pant as the pressure built inside her once again. Leaning her elbows on the bed, she gave him complete access, allowing that vulnerability he knew didn't come easy to her show. He draped over her to cover her, like he was shielding her, protecting her, and only started to slide back in when she reached behind her, twining the fingers of one of her hands with his.

"Please," she whispered.

He had never gone so slow in his life. They set a rhythm and every time he felt he was building up to release, the pace held him back. He wanted to just let go and take everything he could from her, but this was not about taking, it was about giving, and he was going to give Devlin everything. Reaching around her, he touched her clit and she orgasmed almost instantly, but he didn't change his pace, he let her orgasm squeeze his cock until he came, a blinding white light flashing before his eyes.

Devlin collapsed on her stomach and Gabe lowered himself next to her on his back. "Fuck," he said, laying an arm over his eyes, then lifted it, giving a covert sniff, but she'd turned and was watching him. "I think I should've showered."

"You smell like cold and wood and fire and sex." She snuggled closer. "There should be a fragrance that smells just like you do now."

He shrugged and reached his arm around her to pull her closer, grabbing a blanket with his free hand to cover them. "I'm glad you approve."

Chapter Thirteen

The sound of distant knocking startled Gabe from his sleep. He was disoriented and a weight, like a heavy blanket, was over him. He blinked, surprised to see Devlin sprawled over him, a slight snore coming from her mouth. His face bloomed into a smile as he remembered the night before. Well, he assumed it was the night before — the clock had toppled to the floor at some point in the evening.

A more insistent staccato alerted him that someone was indeed knocking, but not at Devlin's door — his door — which propelled him into action, disentangling himself from Devlin's tight grasp. He slipped through the bathroom, grabbing and throwing on his robe, tying it as he cracked his door.

"What the hell, I've been knocking for like five minutes," Greyson accused, trying to peer around Gabe into the room. "You have a girl in there?"

Gabe opened the door to let him in, thankful that he'd thought to close his side of the bathroom door on his way into the room. Now he hoped that Greyson didn't notice the untouched bed.

"Sorry, Mom, just a heavy sleeper."

Greyson did indeed eye the bed but didn't say anything.

"Have you looked outside yet?" he asked instead.

"I just got up, Grey."

"Yes, that's clear."

Gabe walked to the window and pulled back the shade, a low whistle escaping him. "What the hell happened out there?"

"I think that's the Nor'easter we've been promised all season. It hit overnight."

Gabe looked out again to a winter wonderland. Heavy snow was falling and all signs of life—like roads—had been erased.

"I'm gonna go outside and assess the situation."

"Okay, let me get dressed, I'll be right out."

"I'm going to let Pru know, meet you back here in a few."

Greyson slipped out of the door and Gabe gave a longing look at the adjoining bathroom before sighing and getting dressed. He went out into the hall just as Greyson returned. They started toward the stairs when he remembered his jacket and boots in Devlin's room.

"One sec, my boots and jacket." He turned the knob on Devlin's door then stopped.

"That's not your room, bro."

Gabe shot him a quick look. "I know," he stated, then slipped inside and gathered his stuff, moving quietly, not wanting to wake Devlin. He looked at her for a moment. *Fuck it.* He moved to her side and kissed her softly on the forehead, she stirred but didn't wake. He felt torn between wanting her to sleep and not wanting her to wake with him gone. Her peaceful slumber won out, and he moved back out the bedroom door. He avoided Greyson's stare as they went downstairs, but their conversation was cut off as they noticed the six foot drift piled against the sliding door.

"Wow." Greyson walked to the door and measured the drift to his height. "We're gonna need a bigger shovel."

"I need to be well caffeinated before I can deal with this."

"I'll go wake Sebastian, you start the pot." Greyson gave Gabe another side eye glance before disappearing down the hall.

It didn't matter that Greyson knew. He was an adult, and he wasn't going to act like a caught child who needed to explain himself, but explain himself is what he did when Greyson returned.

"Will you please not tell anyone?" Gabe asked as he filled two cups.

"It's none of my business."

"Not even Pru."

"Now that's my business."

"You know that all she'll want to do is get in the middle and try to make this into more than what it is."

"And what is it?"

Gabe was silent for a moment before answering. "I don't know. Something to take the edge off this whole thing, something we both needed."

Greyson appeared to contemplate what Gabe said. "You're mixing business with pleasure. That's never a good idea."

"I know this. I knew this. But what's done is done, can you please just not say anything?"

"I don't know how long I can keep anything from Pru. She's very intuitive and she'll know at some point that something's going on."

"Not until we get out of here, I hope."

"I don't know when that will be, though. Remember the Christmas storm of '97? We were stuck here for a week."

Gabe groaned. "We can't be here for a week, there's no way it'll take that long to get the roads opened."

"I'm not saying it'll be that long, just to plan that we won't get out of here today."

They sipped in silence. "How did it happen?" Greyson asked. "We just talked about it yesterday morning and you said there was nothing between the two of you."

"I happened," Gabe admitted. "It was all me."

Greyson nodded in understanding. "I get it. Most of it was me, too. The ladies didn't stand a chance against the Atwood charm."

Gabe laughed. "I guess you can call it that."

Sebastian walked into the room, rubbing his eyes and scowling. "What can you two find so amusing on a morning like this?"

"The old Atwood charm," Greyson explained, "is a mysterious yet powerful thing."

"Is Atwood charm going to get us out of this cabin today?" He waited until all signs of mirth were wiped off Greyson's and Gabe's faces before continuing. "Because if it's not, let's focus on coming up with a plan, shall we?"

"I don't know how to plan around Mother Nature," Gabe admitted. "She's dumped a lot of snow out there and we're not equipped to get rid of most of it."

"Have we got shovels and maybe a snowblower in the shed?" Greyson asked, looking at Gabe.

"I don't remember a snowblower, but I haven't been out here in the winter in a long time. The caretakers could've gotten one." Gabe pulled open a pantry door to take stock of the supplies. "I'm also happy they seem to keep food here. We didn't have enough for much more than a few days."

"First things first, let's see if we can get some of this cleared out," Sebastian said, "then we can plan for everything else. If we can get to the cars, we just might make it out of here." He noticed the look Gabe exchanged with Greyson. "We're not making it out of here, are we?"

"I'm not going to say we're not, but this is your first major storm, and we just happen to be in the mountains where it's always worse." Greyson started pulling on his winter gear. "I didn't think to bring snow pants."

"Those, I know we have here." Gabe added.

"I meant it when I said I was a Boy Scout," Sebastian said. "I have those and boots. I already brought them in from the truck yesterday just in case I couldn't get to it."

"When did you get snow pants? I thought you said we'd never get snow here."

"Not never, just that I didn't think any of the forecasts until now were accurate."

"Now is a good time to be prepared. I don't think any of the girls brought much in the way of survival gear."

Gabe heard shuffling on the stairs and saw a sleepy looking Devlin making her way down to them.

"What on earth do we need survival gear for?" she asked, walking over to Gabe and standing a little too close. Gabe didn't miss the glance that passed between Sebastian and Greyson.

Gabe pointed to the sliding doors, and he could feel Devlin's sharp intake of breath.

"Talk about a winter wonderland," she breathed. Gabe was mesmerized by the look of serenity on Devlin's face. She looked as though she didn't mind the inconvenience of being snowed in at all, and he understood what Greyson had said last week that he wouldn't mind being stuck with Prudence. He was certain he wouldn't mind a week snowed in at the cabin with Devlin.

"I'll get another pot started, and breakfast when Pru and AB get up." She moved over to the coffee pot then turned. "I don't suppose we have enough supplies for another few days?" she asked.

"We have the leftovers and whatever was packed for breakfast. The caretakers have some canned goods, but not much, and nothing in the way of anything fresh," Greyson replied.

"Hey, we just talked about ice fishing on the way here — do you think we can get a path to the lake so we can take a shot at some trout?" Gabe asked.

"Let's get started on making sure the roof isn't going to cave in and getting to the cars, we'll work on the food later," Sebastian said.

"Yes, sir." Greyson saluted him. "I'll go get Pru up so they can see what we can do about the food situation, and what to do if the power goes out."

"I'll go see if I can find those snow pants." Gabe walked past Devlin to the front hall and startled when he felt the brush of her hand on his, so soft, as a half-smile lit her face. At least he'd have memories of last night to keep him warm while he braved the elements.

He was sifting through the pile of things in the front hall closet when he heard Annabelle make her way into the kitchen. He wasn't eavesdropping, he swore he wasn't, but his body was halfway buried in the closet when their murmur of voices turned into a crescendo.

"Oh my God, you had sex," Annabelle exclaimed.

"I'm sorry, what?" Devlin sputtered in the way of a response.

"Sex. Doing the nasty, shagging, buttering the biscuit, doing the devil's—"

"That's far too many sex euphemisms for this early in the morning."

"But you did. I can tell."

"How can you tell, AB?"

Gabe heard a shuffling in the kitchen and decided to stay put for the moment. He didn't need to alert them to his presence. Besides, he wanted to know what was behind Annabelle's new superpower.

"It's just a thing."

Well, that was a disappointment. He'd hoped Devlin had the look of someone who had been fucked well and good, the glow of multiple mind-blowing orgasms showing on her radiant face.

"You can't just say it's a thing and leave it at that," Devlin pressed.

"You have this look about you. I know it's cliché, but your face is glowing."

Okay, that's a bit better.

"Whose face is glowing?" Gabe heard a third voice enter the conversation as Prudence came into the room. He needed to make his presence known. He clamored loudly as he extracted himself from the depths of the closet, grabbing onto the two items he went in there for, the snow pants.

"Ah!" Annabelle shrieked at his emergence. "The hell, Gabe!"

"Sorry, I didn't know anyone was in here." Prudence had made her way into the kitchen along with Greyson. He held up the snow pants, trying to disguise that he'd heard their conversation. "I was in the back of the closet looking for these. We're going to start trying to clear some paths outside and see what got piled on the roof."

"Woah," Prudence said in awe. "I haven't seen this much snow in a long time. Remember the Christmas of '97?"

"Oh, yes," Gabe answered, walking behind the kitchen island. "All the Atwoods were here, remember?"

Prudence's eyes widened. "That's right! You didn't make it home until New Year!"

At the mention of New Year, Gabe's eyes went to Devlin, wanting to see what her reaction was, but she'd turned herself away from the group.

"1997 was a much different time, though," Gabe reminded her.

"I can't even call Emma to tell her we can't get out. You don't think it will be a week, do you?" Devlin asked, her voice quiet. She turned around and sought out Gabe's face. She started to take a step toward him then stopped.

He stood for a moment, not answering Devlin's question, the silence broken by the sound of polyester rubbing against itself as Sebastian walked into the room dressed from head to toe in his winter gear.

Prudence let out a snort of laughter and Annabelle walked over to Sebastian, reaching out her hand, apparently trying to test out the puffiness of his very oversized jacket.

"You look like a marshmallow," she said as she gave him a small shove. "I could knock you over and you'd bounce right back."

"Hey, I'm going to be toasty warm if we have to walk anywhere." He eyed her. "You, however, won't make it any farther than the driveway. I've seen what you call winter clothes."

"I just have to get as far as your overcompensating truck."

"I'm not overcompensating for anything, thank you very much, but I'm not sure even that'll get us home at this point."

"Let's not be all gloom and doom, at least not yet." Greyson grabbed a pair of snow pants. "If we can get to the main road, we have a good chance of getting out of here still today, or tomorrow, depending on when the main road gets plowed."

Greyson kept talking but Gabe tuned him out, instead focusing on Devlin, who had made a slow meander until she was close to him. While the others were now gathered around Sebastian toward the living room, just Gabe and Devlin were in the kitchen and his mind flashed back to the previous night. She set a mug of coffee in front of him. He started to thank her but went rigid when he felt Devlin's hand on his back side, caressing his ass.

"Don't get too cold out there," she whispered. Her breath was warm, and it tickled his ear as she leaned closer to him, her hand now running up his back under his shirt, her nails scoring his skin, all while he tried not to react in front of the others.

One tilt and his lips were right at her temple, and he fought every urge to place a kiss *just there*. At this point, he both cursed and thanked the weather. It seemed more likely that they'd get to spend at least one more night together and he couldn't wait until they were alone again, but that meant he wasn't able to let this just be what they agreed on—one night—then they'd be back in reality, back in Amber Falls and able to keep their distance from each other.

I'm not ready to let her go.

The unbidden thought appeared, and he realized it wasn't an unwelcome one.

"Hey, Gabe," Sebastian called from the front door. Startled out of his reverie, he fumbled the coffee cup and it clattered onto the countertop, spilling hot liquid over his hand. He hissed in pain, waving his hand through the air. Gabe saw that the rest of the group had made their way to the door, with Greyson now all dressed for snow removal.

"Oh no!" Devlin moved him to the sink and started to run cold water over where the coffee had landed. "Here, hold it under the water, it'll stop the burning from getting any worse." She gave him a rueful smile. "I know a thing or two about hot coffee burns."

"Sorry, man," Sebastian apologized, "but I'm roasting in this getup. We're going to go out and see if we can get to the driveway."

"I'll meet you out there in a few minutes," Gabe called over his shoulder. The burn wasn't that bad. It seemed like the coffee had been in the cup for a while and was lukewarm at best. He didn't tell this to Devlin, however, and reveled in her holding his hand, feeling foolish that he was this content with just being near her, the simple touch of her hand on his skin grounded him in a way he'd never felt before.

"The trick is to keep it under the water until your finger is almost too cold. That'll stop the skin from getting any worse." A smile crossed her face. "I remember the worst burn I had."

"Now, why would you be smiling so much at the memory of your worst burn?"

"Because it was the dumbest way to get burned and I laugh every time I think about it. I was working in this restaurant, and I'd bent over to plug something in next to the fryers." She'd turned the water off at this point but kept his hand in hers as she continued the story. "I was wearing a high ponytail and when I bent over I didn't realize that the tip of it dipped into the hot grease. When I stood my hair whipped across my face and left a Nike Swoosh symbol on my forehead."

He stared at her, speechless for a moment. "You have got to be kidding me."

"Hand to my heart I'm serious. That's how it happened."

"No offense, but that's the dumbest story of getting a burn that I've heard."

"Believe me, you're not the first person to react like that. Can you see why I laugh every time I think about it? I either laugh or cry at my own ridiculousness."

Gabe chuckled at the imagery. "I can see why you chose to laugh about it."

They both jumped at the sound of a clearing throat behind them and turned to see Prudence and Annabelle standing and staring.

"Oh, sorry," Devlin said. "You've got to go." She let go of his hand and he felt bereft of her presence already.

"That's okay." He shot a look at the other two ladies. "They're fine without me for a few minutes."

"Don't mind us," Prudence breezed. "We were just discussing how fortunate we were that the pipes didn't freeze overnight, but I can see that there's plenty of heat in those old pipes, uh, flowing."

Annabelle snickered at this as she started clearing away the mess on the counter.

Gabe was not amused. "My hand is fine, by the way, thanks for asking."

"I'm sure it is, dear," Annabelle said.

He rolled his eyes. "Thanks for your help, I should be fine to go and shovel."

They all turned toward the front of the house when they heard the unmistakable sound of a snowblower turning on.

"Thank the sweet lord," Annabelle praised. "I won't have to be stuck here with Sebastian for much longer."

As Gabe started to get dressed to go outside, he felt a pang and wished that he'd have more time with Devlin.

Chapter Fourteen

"I never want to see snow again," Sebastian groaned, propping his feet on the coffee table.

Devlin walked back into the living room carrying three bottles of beer for the men who had just come in from outside. She and Prudence had tried to clear off the patio while the guys were working on the driveway. They'd spent a fraction of the time outside and were sore, so she could only imagine what they felt like.

"Tell me again why you don't think we'll be out of here for a few more days," she asked, handing out the bottles before sitting next to Gabe on the couch. She was close enough that she could low-key lean into him, but not so close as to cause any suspicion.

Gabe laid his head against the back of the sofa and took a long sip of beer. "We got as far as the main road, but that hadn't been plowed yet. In my experience, if the main road isn't done by now it means, it'll still be a few more days before they get to us. Monday afternoon or night at the earliest, but more likely sometime on Tuesday. Even if they get to it by tomorrow evening, I wouldn't drive on the mountain roads at night."

"That is if we don't get any more snow, and we won't know that unless it happens, since we have no way to get a forecast," Prudence pointed out. "I know we talked about you having an old weather radio here—I looked for it this afternoon but didn't find it. Can you think of any place it could be?"

"I haven't had a chance to look," Greyson chimed in.

"I'll go," Gabe offered. "Just give me a few more minutes to rest."

"I still can't believe we got that much snow," Annabelle said from the kitchen where she was looking through the cabinets to find food to start dinner. "The fact that it took that long with a snowblower just to get to the road blows my mind."

Devlin leaned toward Gabe. "I'll come help you search for the radio if you'd like."

He raised his head from the couch and smiled, one corner of his mouth tilting up. "I'd like nothing more." He rolled his shoulders. "If I keep sitting I think my muscles will start to petrify."

Devlin stood and reached out her hand, a jolt running through her when Gabe touched her. She gripped his hand and pulled him up, and he emanated strength.

"We're going to take one more stab at finding this weather radio, guys," Devlin announced to the room. "Is there any place you didn't look, Prudence?"

"I didn't go into the basement. The light wouldn't work, and I couldn't find any extra bulbs. I've seen one too many horror movies to know that a lone female going into a dark basement is never a good idea," Prudence explained.

"We don't have any ghosts here, Pru," Greyson said.

"That's what every victim in a horror movie says. Besides, I heard moaning last night, and I don't think I was hearing the wind," Prudence clarified.

It took every fiber of her being to not look at Gabe right now. She was sure her face had either gone very red or very pale. *Don't look at him. Don't look at him.* She looked. He, of course, was staring right at her, his mouth quivering with apparent mirth.

"Well," Gabe got out, "if we find any moaning ghosts we'll be sure to report back to the group." Without waiting for a reaction or replies, he ushered her out of the room. She was able to hold it together for just as long as it took to get to the basement stairs and started laughing once the door closed behind them. Her sudden laughter faded as fast as it started when she noticed the pitch black. She reached for the wall switch and flicked it, with no luck.

"Pru wasn't lying about the bulb being out," she whispered, the darkness lending an intimacy to the situation.

Gabe's breath mingled with hers, his warm arms holding her steady on the much too narrow top step.

"As much as I want to kiss you right now, I'd rather not risk a broken neck." Gabe shifted and the flashlight on his cell phone illuminated the space as he took a few steps down the stairs, motioning for her to follow.

At the bottom, Devlin glanced around the basement cluttered with old furniture, boxes, trunks and totes, with an entire section labeled 'Christmas'. The basement walls were stone, almost looking like they'd been carved right into the mountain, and it was much warmer and a lot less damp than she would've guessed.

"It doesn't look half bad down here," she observed, walking around and taking in what she could see from the beam of her cell phone flashlight.

Gabe reached the far side of the room, shuffling a few things before a click sounded and a dim light illuminated the room.

"Looks like a few more bulbs are out, but this should give us enough light to search for the radio."

"Oh, we're looking for a radio?" Devlin teased as Gabe walked back over and wrapped his arms around her waist. "We're not looking for a moaning ghost?"

"I already found the moaning ghost." He nipped her bottom lip. "Not only did I find the moaning ghost, but I'm ready to make her moan again."

And moan she did as he took her mouth in a scorching kiss, his tongue plunging into her depths as he reached his arms up to lift her, but he broke away with a moan of his own.

"You're that sore?" she asked, breathing heavy from the kiss.

"Like an old man. Every part of my body hurts," he groaned, rolling his shoulders again, just like he had upstairs earlier. "I think I pulled something."

"Here, come sit," Devlin commanded as she guided him over to a couch with a loud floral pattern that had to be from the 1960s and not a decade later.

She started to massage his shoulders, neck and back, gently at first, then pushing harder at his request.

"God, that feels good." He leaned into her, the smell of him taking over her senses.

She used her thumb to work on a hard knot and he let out a deep sigh. Her mind wandered as she worked, thinking about their surreal situation, being in the basement of Gabe's family cabin when not even a month ago he didn't know she was in Amber Falls, and it wasn't even twenty-four hours ago that they'd made love.

She was startled to realize that the man she'd avoided for the better part of a year had seeped into her pores overnight. She couldn't remember experiencing this level of ease with anyone, the complete abandonment of reality and her senses, not caring what happened next, just that she was with this one person. It scared her, but the exhilaration outweighed everything else. In the deep recesses of her mind, thoughts of her coffee shop and expansion tried to wiggle out, but she fought them back, deciding to let herself enjoy the moment for the few extra days they'd have together. Her actions were mimicking her ruminations and the massage had turned from therapeutic to caressing.

She snapped out of her reverie as she sensed him getting restless. "Is that better?" she asked.

He shifted on the couch, leaning back into her. "That helped, thank you."

Devlin leaned forward, her mouth touching the side of his neck. "Does every part of you still hurt?"

He made a low noise. "Not every part."

She moved her mouth to the other side of his neck. "How about here?"

"That spot doesn't hurt at all."

"Maybe it would be easier if you showed me what parts of you didn't hurt."

Gabe took her hand in his and ran it over the front of his jeans, cupping his erection with both of their hands.

"I feel no pain here. Nothing but pleasure." He unbuttoned his pants and unzipped his fly as she reached in and released his cock, caressing it from root to tip. He turned to kiss her, undulating his hips into her grip as she captured his tongue with her teeth, then sucked it, mimicking what she'd do with his cock. He reached his hand up to tangle in her hair, fusing his mouth to hers as he pumped into her hand, then broke the kiss and straightened. Grabbing a condom from his wallet, he pushed his pants to his ankles. He quickly tore it open and rolled it on.

She stared at him, half naked with an impressive erection jutting out, and her mouth went dry, and wetness pooled below. She swung one of her legs over his and straddled him once he'd sat, her thighs quivering in anticipation. Thankful that she had on yoga pants, she lowered herself over his cock, her arousal already soaking through the fabric. Leaning slightly back, she rubbed her over him, the friction and wetness of her pants over her clit had her ready to orgasm as she ground against him, slowing only when he stopped her to pull down her pants.

His cock slid through her folds, and he teased his tip into her entrance before gliding through her lips once again. She put her hands on his shoulders for balance and was happy that he didn't wince in pain.

"No moaning this time, Devlin," he gasped.

"I wouldn't dare to."

She stood no chance to hold off coming as the entire length of him slid against her clit time and time again, and she shuddered in a powerful orgasm. He waited until she'd ridden it out before lifting her and sliding straight into her. She had no strength left in her legs, but he'd taken over, thrusting until he held her down as he pumped his release into her, the couch sliding backward at the power of his thrusts.

As she collapsed on him, she heard a thunk on the floor and the sound of radio static.

"Found the radio." He grinned at her, pulling him to her and kissing her.

"Oh fuck, you found more than the radio." She moved over him, loving that his cock was still buried inside her, a fullness that she didn't realize she'd been missing. Sex wasn't the only thing she'd been missing, but the specific feeling she got when she was with Gabe. She wasn't ready to name it, but was very aware the feeling was there.

"Devlin," Gabe whispered in her ear, sending a shiver down her spine. "I'm going to come again."

At this, one of the most erotic things anyone had said to her, she finally did moan. She brought his head to her chest and cradled it as she rocked over him, not letting him thrust. He reached his hand between them to circle her clit and within moments they were both orgasming again, almost not moving as they let it wash over them.

Once Devlin came back to her senses, she extracted herself from Gabe's arms, pulled her pants back up and plopped on the couch next to him. She grabbed his hand and twined her fingers with his, running a thumb over the delicate skin inside his wrist.

She sat there, her senses stunned and her muscles weak. She tried to get the sound of rushing water out of her ears until she realized it was the radio Gabe had knocked over, still blasting static behind the couch. She giggled at the thought that their lovemaking was so good it caused her hearing to glitch.

"I'm not sure that's the sound I want to hear after doing what we just did," Gabe said.

"I'm not laughing at that, definitely not at that." She pointed behind the couch with her free hand. "I forgot about the radio and thought for a moment that you'd knocked my senses off balance."

A satisfied smile crossed his face. "Don't believe that I couldn't."

He put himself back together while she leaned over the back of the couch and grabbed the radio.

"Here, let me see." Gabe reached out and took it from Devlin. The sound of static had grown quieter but was still there. He took the antenna and pulled it up, rotating it around the room, trying to catch a transmission. The sound sputtered then died.

"Damn, I swore this was a crank radio. We're gonna have to find batteries."

"Can we stay here for just a bit longer? I don't think they'll get suspicious—they won't notice when we come back with the one thing that we all want."

Gabe kissed the top of her head, letting her nestle into him. "The radio isn't the one thing I want."

Devlin was quiet for a while, content with the last words Gabe spoke. She was fighting this too hard. *I haven't fought a single thing since we've been here.* She hadn't tried. They had a few more days to live in this bubble before they could leave and reality would hit, and she wanted to take every advantage she could. She reveled in the rise and fall of his breathing, listening to the steady beat of his heart.

"Do you think anyone knows?" Gabe interrupted her calm.

"You heard Annabelle this morning, I'm assuming?"

"I didn't mean to."

"She thinks she knows, or suspects."

"You think we can keep it on the down low until Tuesday?"

She toyed with a button on his shirt, thinking. "I can if you can."

"Is that a challenge, Dev?"

She stood and reached out to pull him up, just like she'd done in the living room earlier, and he stood this time with more ease and less noise.

"Not a challenge," she said as he flipped the light off and she led him to the stairs. "Just a statement of fact."

Opening the door at the top of the stairs, Devlin walked out first, hoping no one would be around. What she didn't expect to see was Annabelle practically perched on Sebastian's lap as he was sitting in one of the oversized chairs. His eyes were wide as Annabelle twirled a piece of his hair at the nape of his neck around her finger. She noted Greyson and Prudence on the couch watching the whole thing happening, both still, like deer caught in the headlights.

"So, you're telling me that Gutenberg's *wasn't* the first printing press?" Annabelle asked in a sweet voice.

"It was the first moveable type press and that revolutionized the printing world," Sebastian explained.

"Just fascinating stuff." Annabelle ran her hand down Sebastian's chest and stood. "I've got to visit the ladies' room. I'll be right back."

Silence fell over the room after Annabelle walked out and Sebastian let out a slight cough.

"Sebastian, you can't be this dense," Prudence finally said. "Annabelle has worked in newspapers longer than you have. She knows how a printing press works."

"But—" Sebastian started.

Greyson gestured to the pile of notes on the coffee table. "Let me guess, you were looking over Gabe's proposal when Annabelle came in here and she just happened to all of a sudden forget how one of the most important pieces of equipment at a newspaper works." He exclaimed with obvious glee, "you've been Mata Hari'd!"

"What?" Sebastian asked, apparently flustered.

"Mata Hari, the famous spy—"

"I know who she is," Sebastian interrupted. "But that's not a *thing*."

"Oh, it's most definitely a thing. It's the exact definition of a thing. In fact, I just witnessed it happening."

"You did fall for it," Prudence pointed out, standing and taking a small step closer to the notes on the table. "I, for one, was very interested in your answers." She sat on the arm of the chair next to Sebastian, a look of rapt attention on her face while she glanced sideways at the notes.

"It's amazing how the printing press has— Hey!" Sebastian swiped the notes into a pile and flipped them over. "That's enough from the both of you."

"What happened?" Devlin asked.

"Grey and I had left the room for maybe ten minutes, and when we got back Annabelle was draped all over Sebastian asking inane questions about printing."

"She wasn't draped all over me," Sebastian said.

"Draped is a nice way of saying it," Greyson confirmed. "Neither of them noticed us coming back into the room, so we sat down and watched what was happening. It was so apparent that Annabelle was studying Gabe's proposal notes during Seb's long-winded replies."

"Hey!" Gabe exclaimed. "Those are confidential, man."

"I'm sorry, Gabe, I didn't know she was doing it. I thought we were having a real conversation about something that interested both of us."

"Do you think she could decipher your chicken scratch?" Gabe asked.

"She's the only one at work that can," Sebastian groused.

Devlin was secretly excited that Annabelle had got to see Gabe's plans, but she couldn't let him know that. "I'll talk to Annabelle," she promised. About what, she didn't say.

"That was the nicest she's ever been to me," Sebastian muttered.

"It'll happen again," Prudence promised, gesturing to the window. "Hell has officially frozen over after this storm."

Prudence stood and walked into the kitchen, passing Devlin along the. "Hey, the radio was down there!"

"Yep," Devlin confirmed, holding it up. "We tried to get reception downstairs, but all we got was static, then the batteries ran out."

"Is it a creepy basement?" Prudence asked.

"Anything is creepy without lights on," Devlin answered. "Gabe knew where the other switch was and that gave us some light. I didn't see any ghosts, though."

"I might have heard some moaning," Gabe said, his tone casual. Devlin's eyes widened at this, and Gabe continued, "But I think you're right, it's probably just the wind. It seemed to pick up while we were down there."

Greyson grabbed batteries from a kitchen drawer and handed them to Gabe. "Here, try these. I swear the radio wound up."

Devlin watched as Gabe popped the batteries in and extended the antenna. He pressed the weather button and they all waited with bated breath as the static turned to a weather signal stating that the state was in a blizzard watch until the end of the day.

"That was more than a blizzard," Gabe said, "the whole sky dumped down on us."

"Would a local station have more information on when things will clear here?" Devlin asked.

"I'm on it."

Devlin watched Gabe's strong fingers play over the radio knob and felt her face flush, knowing where those fingers had been no more than a half an hour ago. Gabe lifted his eyes as if he sensed what she was thinking and tilted a half smile at her as a local disc jockey crackled on talking about the storm. Annabelle had come back into the room by this point, and they all listened as he repeated, probably for the one hundredth time since the storm ended, that they'd received almost three feet of snow, but the wind made the drifting seem like more. Crews were out working on the roads, the mountains would be cleared by Monday evening at the latest, and no further snowfall was expected.

Prudence had made a makeshift charcuterie board by the time night had settled in, and they were all gathered around the fire still listening to the radio.

Crackers, smoked oysters, olives and pickles were being eaten and tea was poured as the group settled into a comfortable routine of conversation followed by silence as a captivating news story came on then conversation again as they discussed what they'd just listened to.

Devlin and Gabe were next to each other, and Devlin used all her willpower to not lay her head on his shoulder or grab his hand. The coziness of their surroundings made her long for what she couldn't have, at least not with Gabe. It made her want to have a brood of children running around, playing with dollies or wooden cars, the youngest one nestled in her arms, sleepy, warm and ready for bed. She felt herself listing toward Gabe, and straightened, needing to speak to stay awake from the heat of the fire.

"I feel like I should be darning socks or crocheting a sweater while the men smoke pipes," Devlin ruminated during a commercial break. "This is what our grandparents did when they only had a radio. Sit around and just listen to what was happening in the world."

"Times were simpler then," Gabe added. "I miss my phone, but not having to look at it every few minutes is nice. We have a lot of other things to do, even if it's just being here together."

Just like the night before, the group broke off, going to their own beds. Tonight, though, as Gabe and Devlin ascended the stairs, Gabe reached out and took Devlin's hand and she didn't resist.

Chapter Fifteen

The next morning was almost afternoon by the time Gabe woke. The bright sun shone through the curtains, a stark contrast to the last few days of gloom and storms. He stretched his body and his muscles protested the movement, but he persisted, his body more relaxed after.

He reached out to where Devlin should be sleeping and touched only an empty space. He sat up in bed as he heard running water in the bathroom. Throwing on a pair of boxers, he made his way to the bathroom door and when he gave a light knock, a muffled "come in" sounded from inside.

He opened the door and was pleased to find Devlin at the sink wrapped in a towel that reached the top of her thighs. She was brushing her teeth and stopped at the sight of him, finished, then flashed him a smile.

"Well good morning," she said as he came up to her, kissing her.

"Did you know it's almost afternoon?" Gabe asked as he started his own routine, not surprised in the least at how comfortable he was with Devlin's presence. In one short day he could already picture himself waking up with her on a much more permanent basis.

"I'm glad. After yesterday you needed your rest."

He grabbed a bottle of shaving cream and started lathering it on his face. "You did put me through a lot, both afternoon and last night."

Devlin punched his bare shoulder. "You know what I mean—all the time you spent outside removing the snow."

He grinned. "I only want to remember the glorious removal of other things."

She cocked her head as she looked him over, then picked up the razor off the counter. "May I?" she asked. "I've never shaved anyone before, and I've always wanted to try it."

Surprise washed over Gabe. "I've never been shaved, but if you want to, go ahead."

He put his hands on Devlin's waist and helped her to sit on the large counter, parting her knees so he could get close enough to her. He swallowed hard, arousal shooting through him at their intimate position. He stood statue still while she ran the razor over his face. He needed to move, though, needed to be connected with her body, so he braced his hands on her bare thighs, this touch apparently causing her only momentary lapse of concentration. She made adorable little huffs of breath as she focused, running the blade under a stream of water before continuing after each stroke. Occasionally her tongue would dart out to wet her lips and he stared, mesmerized by that little action.

With each stroke he became harder, as if the blade running over his face was her hands running over his cock. By the time she was wiping a cool washcloth over his face, he was readier than he'd been the last few days. He couldn't explain why this simple act was such a turn on and his mind drifted back to the thought he'd had earlier about how comfortable he was with her, that this small act of domesticity was changing him in a way he felt he was ready for, putting him on the path he needed to be on. As this realization hit him she finished and looked into his eyes with a satisfied smile.

"All done."

He cradled her face and led her mouth to his, hoping his kiss would convey everything he couldn't say right now. As she reached her arms around him, her towel loosened and fell off, baring her to him.

He broke off the kiss and took in the vision of her, running his hands over her breasts and tweaking her nipples. She hissed and opened her legs wider, pushing his boxers down and trying to guide him into her. He almost exploded from the contact, but he wanted something else from her this time.

"Do you remember— Fuck, was it only two days ago, that I heard you masturbating in your room?"

Her flush rose from her chest to her cheeks, and he was pleased that he could get this reaction out of her even after everything they'd done.

One of her hands drifted toward her center as she replied, "I can't forget that."

"Will you do it for me now?"

A sharp intake of breath was her only reply. He watched as she lifted one foot to the counter then touched herself.

"This is one of the hottest things I've seen," he stated.

After a few moments, she reached out and took him with her other hand, up and down. "Oh fuck, I take it back. This is way hotter," he stuttered out. He thrust his cock into her hand. "Do it like you did that morning," he commanded. She released him and he couldn't help himself, taking hold of his cock and stroking as he watched her.

Her tentative smile grew more confident as she watched his own ministrations, sliding a finger into her vagina then running it through her slit. He growled, low in his throat as she repeated the motion with two fingers, this time taking her time at her clit, her two fingers caressing around and over until she was rocking her hips.

He watched the display in front of him, entranced by the singular focus she was now paying to her clit. He stroked himself hard, his eyes meeting hers before looking back down to her actions. His cock must have known when she was getting close to orgasm and he slowed, wanting to enjoy the look of pleasure on her face when she made herself come. She apparently did not like this slowing, as she hooked her legs around his waist in a tight grip.

"Come, now," she demanded, and his movements became jerky and erratic as he let his orgasm build until he came on her. She dragged her finger through his cum and used it to swirl around her clit, her head knocking against the mirror as she pulsated with her own release.

Her legs went slack around his waist, dangling over the side of the counter. He braced his hands on either side of her and kissed her on the lips, smiling at the almost chaste contact after their mutual masturbation.

"I haven't showered yet," he joked.

Her eyes lit as she gestured to his ejaculate on her abdomen. "As it happens, I could use another shower. Lead the way."

They lay in bed post shower, naked and nestled together under the covers, and Gabe reflected on earlier, when he realized he had started down the path he needed to be on and that path included Devlin. Now, despite any of her earlier protestations, he needed to convince her that whatever happened with the proposal they could deal with but, damn, she was caressing him and making it very hard to concentrate on what he wanted to say to her.

"Hey, Dev." He took her hand in his, and shifted so he could see her face.

"Mhmmm?" came the unintelligible and sleepy reply.

"Can we talk?"

At these words, Devlin was awake and aware. "I shouldn't have done that in the shower without asking, but I guessed you'd like it."

Gabe laughed at this. "No, not that, you can do that whenever you want." He moved again, sitting up this time, and he felt exposed both emotionally and physically. "I've been thinking about where this is going—where this came from."

Devlin sat, pulling the sheet up to cover her body in the process. She looked so lovely that his concentration faltered for a moment.

"You see, I had this thought earlier, about how much I liked being with you, and that I don't want this to end after we leave here."

"Gabe—" Devlin started, but he had to keep going.

"I think we should still see each other when we get back to Amber Falls."

He could see the wheels turning in her head, going over what they'd already talked about, how they were supposed to have a one-night thing, but the storm had turned it into multiple blissful days. He wasn't sure what he'd do if she didn't want the same thing he did, if what they'd had these last few days had been enough for her and she would be content with going back to a lonely existence. When she nodded, he almost wept with relief.

"I'm not ready for this to end yet," she agreed, "but we have to be honest with ourselves that it will end at some point, and we can't deny the reason why."

This time he nodded, despite the little voice screaming in his mind that he would give up everything just to make her happy. She didn't need that from him. She didn't want that from him, and he had to respect that. Right now, he needed to be content with the concession she gave him.

His stomach chose this moment to give a loud rumble, reminding them both they hadn't eaten since the evening before.

"That's one way to break the tension." Devlin swung her legs off the bed and started to get dressed. "I don't think we have a prayer of hiding this from the group anymore, not after holing up in here all morning."

"I hate to break it to you, but I think everyone already knew."

Gabe made quick work of his clothes and followed Devlin downstairs where the others were setting up a game of Monopoly on the kitchen table.

"About damn time," Annabelle stated.

"Hey, guys." Gabe ignored her. "So, we have something to tell you."

"Don't bother, bro. You've been very obvious," Greyson pointed out.

"Congrats," Prudence added.

Gabe looked at the group, waiting for Sebastian to say something as well. When he stayed silent he couldn't help but ask, "What, you don't have anything to say?"

Sebastian shrugged. "Nope. I was clueless." He shot a look at Annabelle. "I guess I'm clueless about a lot of things."

"What does this mean about the proposals and the art gallery?" Prudence asked.

Gabe didn't want to say the wrong thing here, so he waited for Devlin to answer.

"I think we'll worry about that when the time comes. For now, we're just going to be casual."

They sat silent at this, and it stretched until it verged on becoming uncomfortable when Sebastian chimed in. "We're just setting up Monopoly, do you guys want to play?"

Gabe sighed at the reprieve. There would be more questions later and he hoped they'd come when he didn't have an empty stomach. "Sure, we'll play. I'm going to grab something to eat first."

"We found enough food for sandwiches and there's a bag of chips on the counter." Annabelle gestured. "Fix yourself something and come on. I've got all your souls to crush."

A few hours later, the game was down to three players—Annabelle, Devlin and Gabe. True to her word, Annabelle had crushed the other players with her skill. Greyson and Prudence were out of the game early, but Gabe was sure they'd folded on purpose so they could go to their bedroom. Sebastian was harder to defeat, his Monopoly prowess being on par with Annabelle's. She'd finally bested him with a whoop, and he'd retired to the living room with a tumbler of scotch and a newspaper he'd found.

Gabe and Devlin had been staying under the radar as Annabelle had focused all her attention on beating Sebastian, and once he was out she went in for the kill. She'd made the critical error, however, of trading Boardwalk and was getting destroyed by rent on that hotel.

"You never trade Boardwalk or Park Place," Sebastian commented from the living room after Annabelle had landed on that monopoly and had to mortgage almost all her properties.

"Oh, be quiet," Annabelle called out to him, then muttered, "I *never* trade Boardwalk. What was I thinking?"

One turn and one unfortunate roll of the dice later, Annabelle was out. She stood and held out her hand, shaking both Devlin's and Gabe's. "Well done, you two. I haven't lost this game since the late nineties. Well done."

"That long?" Devlin asked.

"No one has wanted to play with me since then. But still, my streak is over. I must be tired." She yawned. "I think I'll go nap before dinner."

She walked past Sebastian on her way to the room. "Good game. I'm sorry I called you a pillock. It was all in good fun, *sir*."

Sebastian stood and followed Annabelle out of the room. "Apology accepted. I think I'll lay down, too. Yesterday did me in."

The sound of their voices drifted down the hall and Gabe and Devlin were alone once again.

"Did you want to keep playing?" Gabe asked.

"Of course. I may not have anything to prove like Annabelle, but I still think I can win this game." She picked up the dice and rolled, landing right on Free Parking.

"You're cheating, I know it! Are these weighted dice?"

"We're not playing craps in Vegas. I'll have you know that I've never cheated at anything in my life."

"Seriously?"

"Nope, I'm honest to a fault."

"Honest you say, like when you lived in Amber Falls for over a year and never let anyone know that we'd...met before?" Gabe was joking, but the words held a question of truth in them.

Devlin looked chagrined. "We haven't talked about this yet, have we."

"That wasn't my intention." He rolled the dice as he spoke and moved his piece. "But no, we never have."

Play continued for a while until Devlin spoke again. "Amber Falls was—" She paused as if searching for words. "Unexpected. I'd already decided to leave Boston before we met that night. I scoured the classifieds for months for the perfect place to open my shop, not planning to go much farther away than a suburb, but I wasn't finding anything in my price range in a location I knew would work. I kept searching farther and farther out until I found my shop."

"Life can play out in the most fascinating way," Gabe mused. "When I woke that next morning and you weren't there, I thought that for the rest of my life you'd be a vague memory that popped into my mind from time to time, the woman I'd always wonder about."

"You were the same for me. Imagine how I felt when I saw you months after I moved to town. Seeing you was such a shock, I could've convinced myself that I conjured you up."

Gabe gave a rueful laugh. "I was sure you were haunting me."

"What?"

"That day you stood outside Finnegan's window — you were ethereal to me — through the etched glass you were like a watercolor painting. I remember I was serving a customer when I saw you, but by the time I got to the door you weren't on the street. I figured the only way you could've gotten away so fast was if you just disappeared. Then months later, on New Year's Eve, I saw you through your shop window, but I didn't know the shop was yours then. The only rational explanation in my mind was that you were haunting me."

"I thought something cosmic was having fun at my expense. Of all the places I ended up, I was not only in the same town as you and the same block as you, but two doors away. From you."

"What I don't get is why you didn't just tell me or talk to me."

"Other than the major stalker vibes that would've given off?"

"You know what I mean."

"I'm not sure I do. Gabe, we had a one-night stand. It wouldn't have been odd to you that I showed up in your hometown half a year later? Like I said, stalker vibes."

He held her gaze, not wanting her to shy away from this conversation. "I felt a real connection to you that night."

Understanding appeared to dawn on her face. "You're hurt," she stated, reaching over and taking his hand. "You think I didn't feel the same."

"All indications point to the contrary."

"I had to leave that night." She squeezed his hand hard. "I'd just broken up with my boyfriend a few days before. He wasn't nice to me. I knew—even with the short amount of time we spent together—I could sense the goodness in you. It felt too much like whiplash from what I'd come from, and I wasn't ready for those feelings so I left. When I saw you again, all those intense emotions came rushing back and I was overwhelmed. Then I felt foolish that you didn't recognize me, and it made everything easier to pretend we didn't know each other. Until Grey came home and made a mess of all of this."

Gabe wiped a solitary tear that had fallen from her eye. "Did he hurt you?"

At this question, tears started streaming down Devlin's face and a protectiveness coursed through Gabe, ready to battle anyone who had wronged her. "No, God no. At least physically he never hurt me. All his behaviors were emotional abuse, classic narcissism, and I stayed with him for far too long. My parents were very much the same, and I jumped from one toxic relationship to another, never thinking or knowing that I deserved more. Then I met you and I got a glimpse of what a real man should be like, and it scared me. You're so different from what I was used to my whole life, and I got spooked and ran." She grabbed a napkin from a holder at the center of the table and dried her face.

"Here I am, pouring my pathetic life story out over a game of Monopoly."

"Your life experience isn't pathetic, Devlin. It's yours and we're all shaped by ours, good or bad."

"Is it wrong to wish that mine was shaped by a trust fund, or winning the lottery?"

"No, that just makes you human." *And I love you all the more for showing me your human side.* That popped in and out of Gabe's head before he could grab a hold of it and analyze what it meant.

They played in silence for a few more rounds, exchanging rents and jabs until Gabe's pile of cash dwindled to a few dollars.

"I still don't know why Annabelle traded me Boardwalk for St. James Place," Devlin wondered as Gabe rolled an unlucky number and landed on the said property. "That property has knocked out everyone."

Gabe turned up his palms in defeat, handing over the last of his few dollars and mortgaged properties. "Let's make it official. You have won what I'm dubbing The Great Blizzard Snowed In at the Cabin Monopoly Game."

"That's catchy. You think it'll look good on a resume?"

"Monopoly master is the only thing you should need on a resume, in my opinion. It says everything one needs to know. You can manage money, you make wise real estate decisions, you're cutthroat in business and you're lucky at rolling dice."

"Lucky dice rolling is now a sought-after skill in the workplace?"

"I'm surprised more employers don't ask about it."

Devlin laughed and handed him the board. "Loser has to pack it all up." A yawn split her face and her jaw made a popping sound. "Oh, man, I'm beat. I don't think we've gotten a lot of sleep these last few days. I think Annabelle and Sebastian have it right — how does a nap sound? I think I could sleep until the morning."

Gabe was surprised to find that he was tired as well. The physicality of their lovemaking combined with the emotional conversation had worn him out.

"Then nap we shall." He stood and held out his hand, ignoring the mess of the game, a shiver of happiness rolling through him when she took it.

He was pleased to discover that he would be content to just hold her while she slept. If he couldn't slay her demons for her, he would settle for holding them at bay.

Chapter Sixteen

Almost a week had passed since they'd been able to leave the cabin and they were both busy. The college students had come back in full force after the winter break, and it hadn't slowed yet. Between coffee in the morning and booze at night, business was booming.

Devlin stood behind the counter of Books and Beans and felt a thrill pass through her when she saw one particular man in the middle of the long line of customers. They'd spent what time they could together, but their opposite hours made it difficult, so they visited each other at their respective establishments when the opportunity arose. Breakfast at Devlin's shop and lunch or dinner at Gabe's bar. Having Devlin's loft right there had been helpful for them to get some much needed alone time.

Devlin counted the days until they could be together with no other commitments, but with the Winter Wonderland activities starting today, she knew they'd have to get creative in order to spend time together. She couldn't forget the proposal deadline looming like a bucket of water held over their heads. They hadn't discussed it since the cabin by silent mutual agreement, but it was there, and she was more than aware of it.

The proposal she'd come up with at the cabin with Annabelle and Prudence was a solid one. They'd poured over her finances, forecasted profits and drawn up plans that included other options to increase her profits, including expanding her customer base and the products she offered. Between the three of them, they'd exhausted all avenues of growth and she felt better than ever with what she had to present to the town council.

Looking at Gabe now, and seeing the smile on his face, she felt a small tingle in the back of her brain. The tiniest hint of unease about her plan appeared and she faltered for a moment, burning her thumb on a coffee warmer just as Gabe reached the front of the line. She hissed in pain, blowing on the offending digit.

"You're lucky today is the ice sculpture competition." Gabe reached over the counter to take a look at her finger. "There'll be plenty around to cool off that burn."

"How can I forget? Annabelle hired someone for the newspaper to sculpt a bee and she won't stop talking about it. I don't see what's so exciting about sculpting freezing ice in freezing temperatures."

Gabe shrugged. "I wish I had a fun story to tell, like the town elders held yearly competitions to see who could come up with the best way to preserve ice year round until refrigeration was invented, but there's no story to go with this one."

"Well, I'm going to be freezing my butt off later at the hot cocoa stand. It got cold out."

Gabe tilted his gaze toward Devlin's loft. "You have time for me to warm you up?"

She glanced behind him at the line of customers still waiting. "As wonderful as that sounds, between the customers and prepping for the cocoa stand, I'm going to be busy for the rest of the afternoon. At least the contest won't go past dinnertime."

"Hey, I have the night off, why don't you come over after? I still haven't painted the basement so that was my only plan for the evening."

Devlin had only been to Gabe's house once, and that was for a quick visit. She wouldn't mind spending more time over there and getting to see the whole place.

"Now that's a plan. Should I bring painting clothes over?"

"Sure, why not? I don't know how much we'll get done, but it'll get started. I'll stop at the hot cocoa stand on my way home."

He leaned in for a quick peck then turned to leave and she watched him on the way to the door until the next customer in line cleared her throat to get her attention.

"I'm so sorry, what can I get started for you?"

* * * *

Devlin stomped her booted feet on the ground later that afternoon for the umpteenth time, trying to thaw her frozen toes. Her breath came out in white bursts and the hot cocoa cooled almost as soon as she poured it. She enjoyed the cold, but this was miserable.

The ice sculpture competition was in full swing, and the frigid temperatures sent people over in droves to get a hot beverage to warm up. She'd had to call Emma more than once to prepare extra supplies and Prudence had been kind enough to deliver them to her when she needed them. She decided that this was her last round, and she was going to pack it all in when she ran out this time.

Holding a cup of spiced cider in her frozen hands, she watched the sculptors put the final touches on their art. The loudest part had been at the beginning — most of them had used chainsaws to start — but now the gentle tink-tink of hammers on chisels was a soothing background noise.

A frisson of warmth ran through her when she spied Gabe walking toward her from across the town square. He was the most handsome man she'd seen, although that description seemed lacking. Handsome didn't convey his fit physique with long, well-muscled limbs. She recalled New Year's Eve, when she thought he had the effortless look of someone who did manual labor for a living, and she now knew she wasn't too far off with his constant movement at the bar and the strength one needed to make furniture like he did.

His smile, though — that smile was the most attractive thing about him. His lips tilted up at one corner almost all the time, like he was one moment away from breaking out into a grin, or had a good natured quip at the ready. That was something you didn't learn, and she bet that he was easy as a baby. Whenever he spoke he had a twinkle in his eye, and he listened with such compassion that she was surprised she hadn't told him her whole life story yet.

"Are you frozen?" he asked, walking behind the table and giving her a quick kiss.

"I'm so cold." She shivered, and he wrapped her in a side hug. "But you're helping a lot."

"How much time do you think you have left?"

Devlin looked around at the dwindling crowd and lifted one of her now empty carafes. "Looks like I'm done. The table is the city's, so I just have to put the supplies away."

Gabe helped her pack the few belongings before motioning toward the street. "I've got the truck since it's too cold out to walk and the heat is blasting in it already. I've got the basement prepped and ready for painting if you want to come to my place?"

"You had me at heat blasting. Lead the way."

* * * *

"My arms are burning," Devlin complained a few hours later. They'd eaten a quick dinner of leftovers and had gotten started painting the basement, speeding through the first coat and starting on the second.

"Here, you switch to the roller, I'll take over the trim."

They swapped tools and continued painting, soft music playing in the background.

They lapsed into silence again, as they had a few times over the last hour, and Devlin was grateful that neither felt like they had to fill the air with noise.

She peeked at him over her shoulder and caught him grinning, like he was in the middle of telling the most hilarious joke.

"You *were* an easy baby, weren't you?" she demanded, as if they'd been having a conversation about his childhood disposition this whole time.

"Of course I was," he answered without missing a beat. "With a kid that had the flair for the dramatic like Greyson, I must've known my parents needed a break."

"I knew it. You don't just turn into a charming man like yourself, you're born like it."

"You think I'm charming?"

"Digging for compliments, Atwood?"

"I've never had to dig for them before," Gabe admitted.

"And humble too, ladies and gentlemen," Devlin drawled.

"I just prefer to see the upside of things."

"This world has a lot of downsides."

"I know that. Of course I know that. I can only go by my experiences and upbringing, though, I have no reason to have a negative reaction if I can be positive. I see no point in that."

Well, damn. "I don't think I've met anyone else with such a positive outlook on life. You're a lucky guy, Gabe."

"I suppose that's luck. What about you? What kind of baby were you?"

"My parents never talked about me as a baby. I seem to have come out fully formed as a difficult teenager."

"Difficult? You?"

"Not everyone has a middle class suburban upbringing with the doting parents and close siblings." She ran the roller along the wall with some force, causing the paint to spatter back onto her. "Dad was there when he decided it was convenient to be there and Mom would've been happier or better off somewhere else. Anywhere else. She reminded me of that almost daily."

"I'm sorry to hear that. Do you keep in touch with them?"

"I haven't spoken to my dad in years and my mom only reaches out to me when she needs something. I didn't send her my forwarding address, so I haven't heard from her since I moved." There must have been a hint of bitterness in her voice as Gabe started to move toward her.

"Hey, Dev, my life wasn't perfect."

Devlin gestured around the room. "You're living in your childhood home. A beautiful home, one that you have fond memories of being raised in, and I've never heard you say a cross word about your parents. That alone is close to perfection to me."

"I'll grant you that. I have nothing to complain about. I'm sorry I brought this up. You don't have to tell me anything you don't want to."

Devlin waved his concern away. She was being pitiful, bringing the mood down over a past she could never change. Yes, this was her truth, her life experience, but she could recognize in herself that in the short time she'd known Gabe she'd been happier than she could remember. After her miserable upbringing and dating a series of men just as terrible as her parents, she realized she was happy. Gabe made her happy. No, she'd been happy before she met Gabe. She'd made herself happy by leaving Boston and moving to Amber Falls, but she understood that he was helping her find her inner happiness, the part of her that was begging to come out and play. The part of her that wanted to see the good in everyone, or the humor in situations that should be humorless. The eternal nature versus nurture debate, and although her nature had been stormy, she just needed someone like Gabe to nurture her.

"Enough about the past." Devlin needed to change the subject. "Have you decided what kind of games you're going to put down here?"

Gabe surveyed the large room then walked over to a corner with an egress window. "I'm going to put some walls over here and make this a guest room."

"Really?" Considering their past talk about this being a bachelor pad, Devlin was surprised at this revelation.

"Yeah. I've been thinking a lot about our conversation from the store, about leaving the upstairs rooms as family rooms and making this a guest space." She saw him visibly swallow, as if nervous about what he was going to say next. "I did remodel this house — this home — for more reasons than it needed updating, but I never let myself think about why. Until now."

"What changed?" she prodded.

Gabe was quiet for a moment. He started to speak then stopped.

Devlin realized she wasn't ready for his answer. Too much was at stake for the implied *you* to be spoken aloud. Nonetheless, he held her gaze, not letting her shy away from the emotions in his eyes despite not being able to say the word.

She coughed and cleared her throat, starting to paint again with her roller, letting the moment pass. "So, no pool table, huh?"

"No pool table." Gabe picked up his brush and kept working.

"Now that a game room is out, what else do you want to do?"

"Other than the bedroom, I'm going to get a huge fluffy sectional, and a big-screen TV would be perfect against this wall. Some recessed lighting to brighten it up, maybe."

"You still have room for some games. I've always been a fan of ping pong."

"Maybe air hockey or foosball."

She finished the last wall with a flourish, setting down the roller and stretching out her shoulders, wincing at the pain that shot through her back. "That does it, two coats on every wall."

Gabe walked over to her and took her hand, massaging it. "I think a wet bar would be nice over here."

"A wet bar, you say?"

He nodded. "Things could get very wet in this corner of the room."

Devlin put her arms around Gabe's neck and pulled him close. "What if I told you things were already wet?"

Gabe smiled. "I'd have no choice but to believe you."

She reached down and toyed with his zipper, stroking his erection once she freed it from his jeans. "Do you have a condom? My purse is upstairs."

He produced one from his wallet and after sliding it on, Gabe reached down and lifted both her skirt and her at the same time, bracing her back against the wall. She felt the tip of his cock teasing her entrance and, as she had promised, was already very wet and he slid easily into her.

She was half aware that her back was against a wall that had yet to dry. The smell of wet paint mingled with the pungent musk of sex creating yet another tantalizing scent that had no business being so carnal and she knew that wet paint would forever be an aphrodisiac.

She tangled her tongue with Gabe's and focused on the place they were joined, tightening her legs around his hips, holding on and letting him set the pace.

He snaked his hand between them, circling her clit and whispered in her ear, "I need you to come for me. Now."

She convulsed at his command, almost losing her hold on him as her body strained against him. He removed his hands and put them on the wall on either side of her head, using the new balance to pump into her. She caught his mouth again as he came, helping to calm him as he slowed his movements.

She loosened her legs from around him and lowered herself to the ground. Gabe looked at his hands that had been braced on either side of Devlin as he held her against the wall, then at his handprints on the wall and the spilled paint can on the floor.

"At least the carpet isn't down yet," he remarked, wiping his hands on his pants as he pulled them up.

"I'm scared to look at my hair." Devlin nonetheless reached up to touch her hair, her hand coming away with paint on it.

"That's the messiest thing I've done." Gabe stood back and surveyed the wall, analyzing the abstract pattern their lovemaking had made. "Call me crazy, but I'd love to frame this spot and let people wonder what the hell happened here for the rest of eternity."

Devlin turned to look. "You're not kidding, we make some good art."

"It's abstract. I'll call it *Uncontrolled Attraction*."

"Ooh, that's a good name for how we created it."

Devlin stood there, motionless, not sure what to do with the mess she'd become or the pool of paint on the concrete floor.

"I'm sorry about your clothes. I thought we were against a dry wall but once I realized we weren't, I couldn't stop."

"Then *Uncontrolled Attraction* is the correct title for what we left on that wall. I'm gonna just..." Her arms flailed. "I think these clothes are done for."

"If they're done for, I'll help you get them off."

Chapter Seventeen

Gabe didn't want Devlin to leave, but she had to open the coffee shop for her early customers by six. He had the day shift at the bar and today was chili cook-off Tuesday. Leo made chili that was nothing short of perfection and they submitted it under the Finnegan's bar name, so he had a lot at stake in the competition. Leo was an authentic chef, culinary school included, and Gabe was lucky that he'd chosen to work with him. His cooking was one of the reasons Gabe had decided on expanding the bar to include an all ages eatery — he wanted a place to feature Leo's foodie masterpieces.

He was sampling a second bowl of chili as Leo walked into the kitchen.

"Hey, leave some for the judges." Leo put the cover back on the pot after giving it a stir.

"I can't help it, if I could inject this into my veins I would."

"I hope the judges agree. I've come in second place the last two years, and I can't figure out why."

"Mrs. Crenshaw must've made a deal with the devil, that's the only way to explain how she wins every town cook-off."

"I picture her using one of those 1950's cookbooks that has ham filled Jell-O or raw beef as the featured recipes."

"I like a good steak tartare."

"That isn't tartare," Leo explained. "My grandma made a dish with seasoned raw ground beef held together with eggs. I'm not kidding when I say she served it at barbecues, just left out in the heat."

"Raw ground beef?" Gabe questioned.

"Oh yeah, we loved it as kids, but I couldn't imagine eating it now."

"I'm thankful you don't have those recipes."

"You didn't stop in here last night," Leo ventured after a moment.

"I was...busy."

"I've noticed you haven't stopped in on your days off like you usually do. Does it have anything to do with a certain barista?"

Gabe glanced toward Devlin's shop, wondering what she was doing right now.

"Ah, so it does."

"It does," Gabe admitted. "We got close at the cabin when we were snowed in and we've, uh, kept it going since we've been home."

"I'm glad to hear it. Anyone that stops you from working sixty hour weeks is worth it."

The sound of the doorbell jangled in the bar, and they heard Devlin's voice come from the main room.

"Gabe? Is anyone here?"

"Speaking of your distraction, I think you've got a visitor," Leo called as Gabe sprinted out of the kitchen.

"I'll stay back here and watch the chili. It needs to simmer for a few more hours before the cook-off tonight."

"Hey! I didn't think I'd see you until later," Gabe said, walking around the bar to give her a quick kiss before leading her to a bar stool.

"Emma came in and I had to come over and find out what this divine smell is." She closed her eyes in pleasure and took a deep breath. "I'd say it's chili, considering the contest tonight, but I've never smelled chili this good."

"I don't know how he does it, but Leo is able to take the most mundane food and elevate it to levels that I've never tasted. I still don't know how I got him to stay here."

He wanted to tell her about his plans to open an eatery to highlight Leo's talents, but they weren't at the point where they could each talk about their respective plans. He wasn't sure that, despite everything they'd done in the last few weeks, they were ready to go there.

"Just lucky, I guess," he offered.

"That's the reason I came over."

"You mean you didn't come over just to see my handsome face?"

She reached up and stroked his cheek, scratching over his day-old stubble. "That's obvious, but no, chili isn't the real reason for this visit. Annabelle called me this morning and asked if I could be a judge at the chili cook-off tonight. I wanted to let you know that Finnegan's would now have a ringer in the judging department."

"I don't know," Gabe joked, "Mrs. Crenshaw is on a roll after winning the tater tot hotdish contest in

October. I'm not sure you have the time to sway the other judges."

"You have so little faith in me." She leaned in and brushed her lips against his. "I have abundant powers of persuasion."

"You can persuade me to do just about anything, but unless you're going to seduce a bunch of octogenarians, we're just going to have to win the old fashioned way."

"Oh fine," Devlin sighed. "I was already letting the power go to my head, it's best that I don't realize my full potential." She looked at her watch before standing. "I've gotta go, I want to shower before tonight and maybe get a nap in."

"My afternoon is free," Gabe insinuated. "I can come over there later?"

"No, I really do need to nap. If you don't remember, we didn't get a lot of sleep after cleaning the paint last night, and five a.m. comes at you real fast. If I'm going to stay up to do this judging, I need to get some rest. How about I stop over when I get up, we should have time for dinner before the contest?"

"I don't know how I'm going to fill my free time, Dev."

Devlin kissed his cheek and called over her shoulder as she opened the door, "I'm sure you'll find something productive to do."

* * * *

Gabe did find something to do, and the afternoon flew by. He'd started a woodworking project in the fall—a long table to set up in the hopeful new eatery. One of the first things he'd done when renovating his parents' house was build an addition to the garage—a heated workroom where he could craft his projects year-round. He'd been sanding the large tabletop all afternoon and was sweaty enough that he'd pulled off his shirt. He'd just finished off the last section when he heard a low whistle behind him. He turned to see Devlin leaning in the doorway.

"No, please don't stop. The way your muscles move makes me think indecent thoughts."

His whole body went on high alert at her words, and he set the sandpaper down, but not before striking a pose with his muscles flexed.

"You like what you see, huh?" he joked.

"More than like," she answered as she sauntered over to him. "I rang the front doorbell but didn't get an answer, then I saw the light on back here."

All reasoning fled his brain as she ran her hands up his chest and pulled him in for a kiss.

"You have me at a disadvantage," he managed, breaking the kiss as he leaned back on the newly sanded table. "You're all fresh and showered and I've been working in here all afternoon."

She gave him a small shove and he fell back with no resistance.

"If you haven't figured out by now that I find you alluring all hot and sweaty, I'll just have to show you."

He lay back hard on the table as she undid his pants and took his cock into her mouth, sliding it into the root. The tip nudged the back of her throat before she slid up, letting it out with an audible pop before repeating the process. The swirl of her tongue over the tip every time she raised her head made him see stars. He moved his hands to her hair, running his fingers through it before holding her steady and pumping into her mouth. She brought him to the brink of release, and he let go, trying to pull her up by the shoulders.

She replaced her mouth with her hand, stroking as she leaned up to kiss him. He struggled to tame her long skirt, but she slapped away his hand after grabbing a condom out of her purse. His breath hitched in his throat as she climbed on the table and straddled him, skirt and all.

"Just lay back. You must be so tired after working all afternoon."

"I know you're teasing, but the image of you straddling me is the only thing I want to remember when I'm old and gray and I don't know my name." He hissed through his teeth as she rolled the condom over his cock.

She raised herself to her knees and positioned her skirt around them, sliding his cock into her tight pussy. He reached under her skirt and grabbed and handful of her ass, urging her into motion. Her hot breath puffed over his face as she leaned over him, her hands braced on either side of his face, raising up and slamming down, rubbing her clit against him on every downward motion.

He looked at her face, her eyes closed in concentration, and silently took back his earlier words. It didn't matter what image of her was ingrained in his psyche in old age, if the image was of her he'd die a happy man.

He held his breath when she stopped, grinding down on him as her orgasm overtook her, a loud keen coming out of her mouth and his mind snapped a mental picture of her bliss.

Gabe let her rock over him as she came down from her high until he couldn't stay still any longer, pumping into her one, two, three times until he released with a shout, and he felt his soul leave his body, the ecstasy too much to bear.

Rolling on to his side, he hugged her. He felt her run her hands, exploring over his back and butt.

"No splinters?" she asked.

"I don't think so, I wouldn't notice them even if I was a pincushion for them."

They lay side by side, legs dangling over the edge of the table, and he reached over and took her hand as she scooted closer to lie on his chest.

"You do build sturdy tables," she offered. "When did you start?"

He paused for a moment, thinking about how he'd started woodworking.

"I did some stuff with my dad, projects here and there around the house, but high school was where I found out how much I loved building things. I had the choice to take woodworking or mechanics and I chose woodworking."

"I don't know why, but I pictured you as starting later in life."

"You're sort of right. I learned the skills in school but was too young and inexperienced to do much with it until after college."

"What was your first big piece?"

"Pru requested a table from me. She needed something for her dining room and couldn't find anything she liked, so she begged me to build her one."

"She has great taste, this just proves that more."

"Her pushing is what got me back into doing it on a regular basis."

"What do you like so much about it?" She toyed with a lock of his hair as he spoke.

"Creating art from nothing is such a rush. When I'm working on a project, I feel like I'm meant to be there, in that exact moment, creating that exact thing."

"That's deep."

"I can't explain it." He shrugged. "I get a vision when I look at an unfinished piece of wood. It could be a stump, a pile of boards or a huge slab of an old torn-down barn. I just look at it and I know what the final resting shape in its life will be."

Devlin didn't speak, then blew out a breath. "I take it back — that's positively existential."

"I don't mean it to be, it's just my experience. After Pru's table, I've commissioned a few pieces for her clients that wanted something similar and made extra for the local furniture store that have sold well — side tables, coffee tables and chairs, too."

"A successful businessman twice over." A smile played on her lips. "You should have a guarantee when you sell your furniture that you tested it out and it won't collapse, even with vigorous lovemaking."

A laugh rumbled up and he shook with it at the thought of handing out 'safe for sex' certificates with each of his items.

"We'd have to test everything then." His tone turned pragmatic. "Each chair, table and bed frame."

"I'd love to be part of your quality control department."

"Tell you what, I'll make you the supervisor, as long as you're willing to take on the important responsibility of being my number one tester."

"Well hold on now, before I accept, I need to know more about the benefit package you're willing to offer me. Will I have sick time or vacation time? I think insurance will be important, because even though I trust your work, I can't guarantee that we won't get crazy and go above and beyond the line of duty."

"It'll be a full time job, so I'll offer insurance and we'll roll sick and vacation into a very competitive personal time off bundle."

"That's an offer I can't refuse." As she spoke, an alarm went off on her. "Shoot, I need to be at judging in thirty minutes." She turned off the alarm, hopped off the table and smoothed her skirt then her hair.

Gabe followed suit, setting himself to rights. "I can whip up something quick. We have time."

"No, that's okay. We're going to be eating boatloads of chili and if we're still hungry, we can eat something after."

"I'm glad they decided to have this at the library instead of the community center. They can take donations and might increase the number of people with library cards at the same time."

"Changing locations was Annabelle's suggestion, I'm glad the council went for it."

As they walked the few blocks to the library, hands clasped in solidarity with each other against the cold, Devlin spoke.

"We've talked a lot about the coffee shop, but not a lot about your bar. Why did you choose that business to open when you could've had a shop where you sold your furniture?"

He shivered against a strong gust of wind. "I worked in that bar every summer in college that I could and for a while after before I got an office job."

"I can't picture you wearing a suit every day, let alone cooped up in an office."

"I stuck it out for a long time thinking that was what I was supposed to do after getting my degree. Then one day after work I was at the bar with some co-workers and the guy who owned it was talking about selling. I saw it as my opportunity to get off the corporate merry-go-round and do something else with my life."

"What was your degree in?"

"Finance."

"That must be serving you well still."

"It is." He didn't say that his degree was helping him to secure the new space for his eatery as he opened the door, thankful they'd just gotten to the library and he didn't have to continue with the natural flow of her question.

The small one-room building was jam packed. The promise of free food never failed to get people in the door.

"Oh, this is divine," Devlin said. "Between the warmth and the delicious smell, I could hibernate in here for the rest of winter."

"Don't turn into a bear on me yet. You've got a job to do, and I want to beat Mrs. Crenshaw." He gave her butt a small pat. "Now get on over there and do whatever you need to make Finnegan's chili number one."

"What happened to winning fair and square?"

"That was before I saw this." He pointed to Mrs. Crenshaw holding court by her crockpot, wearing all her previous first place ribbons. "Now I've got something to prove."

Annabelle joined them as Gabe finished this statement.

"The only thing you have to prove is that second place is just as good as first place. She's not going to lose," Annabelle stated.

"Hey, you know I have my ringer right here. I've got this thing in the bag," Gabe declared.

An hour later, Gabe was holding his second place ribbon, perplexed.

"I tried them all. I tried them all more than once and Leo's chili was clearly the winner."

"I'm sorry." Devlin put an arm around his shoulder. "Leo's chili was better, but all the other judges liked Mrs. Crenshaw's. You were a unanimous second place, if that makes you feel better."

"Somehow I don't think that will look as good hung up in Finnegan's. 'It was unanimously decided that our chili wasn't the best.'"

"Chin up, Gabe." Annabelle threw on her coat and walked out of the door with them before veering off in the direction of her condo. "I promise that I'll give her a run for her money at the peach pie bake-off this summer."

"I'll see you tomorrow, AB," Devlin called and got a wave in response.

"What's tomorrow?" Gabe asked.

"I'm having a late lunch with AB and Pru. Lots of wine and even better company."

"I work a double tomorrow. Did you want to keep me company tonight?"

"Emma is opening in the morning, so I'd love to stay over. You've got to warm me up after this walk. It's gotten a lot colder out."

Gabe gathered her close to him as they walked the rest of the way to his house but couldn't stop thinking about what conversations Devlin would have with the other ladies tomorrow. He wasn't sure he'd come up at all and felt a pang of sadness that he might, and was sure it wouldn't be in the happiest of contexts. They were inching closer to the proposal deadline, and he'd been able to compartmentalize their situation until now, but separating themselves from the proposal was getting harder with each passing day. They'd had conversations where they'd delved into each other's histories and hopes and dreams. He was having a difficult time separating what they were doing now with what was to come. He didn't want to think about it, though, so he did what he did best when it came to Devlin and shoved the interfering thoughts into the recesses of his brain.

Chapter Eighteen

"I'll get details from you, and I'll get them today," Annabelle pressured Devlin as they sat at a table in their favorite lunch spot, The Olde Town Eatery, waiting for Prudence.

"I promise you there aren't any details."

"I don't believe you for one second. Neither Pru nor I have heard from you since we've been back in town and there must be a reason for that."

Devlin evaded Annabelle's accusing stare, toying with the menu in front of her. She did want to share what was happening with Gabe to Annabelle and Prudence, but intuition told her that if she tried to explain the connection between her and Gabe the magic would be gone, and she'd never be able to get it back.

"Ladies, ladies, I'm sorry, I'm here," breezed Prudence, swooping into a seat and exhaling hard enough to flutter the petals on the flower in the middle of the table. "Greyson—"

"Needs to get a life," Annabelle interrupted.

"Not fair, AB," Prudence shot back.

"Oh, I know," Annabelle soothed. "I was just kidding. For as long as it took for you two to get together, you deserve to be as saccharine as you want to be."

"Yes, let's talk about you and Grey," Devlin insisted, ignoring Annabelle's accusatory glance as Prudence continued.

"We've been going through the guest list for the wedding and we're at an impasse at one person." Prudence paused, letting the suspense build. "Wyatt Reed."

"The golden boy himself," Annabelle stated.

"Why would you not invite Wyatt Reed?" Devlin asked. "He does seem like a great guy."

Prudence took a sip of her wine before explaining. "You know that before Grey and I got together, he had quite the reputation as a loose cannon."

"We know now that wasn't true, though," Devlin clarified.

"Yes, for the most part, but Wyatt and Grey ran in the same circles until one day Wyatt stopped being a hellion and overnight turned himself into this...paragon of society. He started acting like a monk, serene and unflappable, and the press couldn't understand what was happening, so they took it out on Grey, making everything he did seem one thousand times worse than it was all while letting Wyatt wear a saintly halo."

"You are still sound miffed about this," Annabelle pointed out.

"A little," Prudence shrugged. "On Grey's behalf, since once Wyatt did his one-eighty Grey's life got a lot more complicated."

"It doesn't seem fair to blame Wyatt for how the press treated Grey. He, after all, was not a saint." Devlin took a sip of her wine, savoring the break in Annabelle's scrutiny.

"I know all this," Prudence affirmed. "I tried to explain it to Grey but he still doesn't want to invite him."

"Is there a reason he has to?" Annabelle asked.

"Not one in particular. I do want him to move past all that and bury the hatchet before he gets too far removed from Hollywood and spends the rest of his life nursing this one beef." Prudence waited a beat before continuing. "Plus, I'd like to be able to watch a Wyatt Reed movie without the guilt or getting a lecture on how everything he does is just for show."

"Yeah, but it can't be just for show," Devlin stated. "The tabloids would've found something on him if there was something to find."

"I think that's what kills Grey the most. That he did change." Prudence picked up her menu and flipped it open. "I'll talk to him again tonight, since we need to get the invitations sent ASAP. Now, I'm starving, are their new lunch specials out?"

Devlin's mouth started to water as she looked over her menu. "Yes they are, and I've been waiting for them to put the rib-eye on the menu."

"You haven't been eating enough meat this last week, Dev?" Annabelle questioned just as their usual waiter, an old man named Jason, sidled up to the table. Jason had started around the time Prudence and Greyson had gotten together and he was more than used to walking up to the table just as one of them dropped a ribald comment. The only thing that gave away that he'd heard anything was the slight uptick to his mouth, just as it was doing now. They turned into polite misses as they ordered, mimicking Jason's overly formal way of speaking.

"Ladies, what a pleasure to have you back. Have you had a chance to peruse our new lunch menu?"

"Jason," Prudence started, "as sad as I am to see my usual walleye sandwich go, this crispy salmon salad is intriguing me."

"A wise choice indeed." He turned to Annabelle. "And you, madam?"

"Jason, dear, I don't have a big appetite today, so I'll just go with the seared scallops and a scotch on the rocks."

"Of course. It wouldn't be lunch without some scotch." He wrote down the order and looked expectantly to Devlin. "Is there anything that caught your eye?"

"I've been dreaming about the rib-eye since I heard rumors it would be on the lunch menu, and I'd be daft if I didn't order it."

"The cut of meat is rather large, ma'am," Jason remarked, winking at Annabelle, who snorted with laughter.

"Jason, I'm going to have my steak and eat it too," Devlin stated.

"Well done, well done. I'll be back with your food." He gave a short bow before retreating to the kitchen.

Annabelle turned to Devlin and said without preamble, "Time to dish, Dev. I said I was going to get the info out of you, so let's have it."

"Can you please tell AB to stop threatening me?" Devlin implored Prudence.

"Are you threatening her, AB?"

Annabelle shot Devlin a look. "I wouldn't say threatening, just pressuring her to explain herself."

"I don't have anything to explain," Devlin insisted.

"That's bullshit and you know it. After what happened at the cabin, you can't expect me to not want to know more."

"How on earth did you know at the cabin, anyways, at least before we told everyone?" Devlin asked. "We were hiding it pretty well."

"Ha!" Annabelle exclaimed, "I knew it! And you weren't hiding it well at all."

"It's true, she has a gift," Prudence confirmed. "She knew when Grey and I first kissed. And that was just a kiss."

"A kiss is more intimate than full on sex," Annabelle explained. "A subtle shift happens with a kiss, a release of pheromones or something."

"Ok, well Gabe and I have been releasing pheromones all over the place since we got back from the cabin," Devlin admitted.

"All over the place?" Prudence asked.

Devlin buried her head in her hand and her words came out muffled. "We've had sex in every place with a flat surface. Or a horizontal surface — or any surface, really."

Jason showed up just then with their drinks and plates of food and deposited them without a word before giving a slight cough and leaving.

Annabelle looked to Prudence after taking a sip of her scotch. "I don't want to say I told you so but I sure as hell told you so."

"I figured that whatever happened at the cabin would be the end of it," Prudence said.

"That was the plan, but we decided that neither of us wanted to let go of whatever was happening between us quite yet, so we've continued seeing each other."

"Sorry for pouncing on you earlier, Dev," Annabelle offered, "but why didn't you tell us? We could've helped you navigate whatever is going on."

"I know I messed up before, but I was hoping that you trusted us now," Prudence added.

"No, you guys, that's not it. I know I've kept things from you in the past, but I think that what it comes down to is that I've never had anyone that cared enough to want to know what I was going through, or how I was handling things."

"You didn't have friends in Boston?" Prudence questioned.

"Not like you two," Devlin admitted. "Co-workers or acquaintances. Friends of boyfriends."

"That sounds like a lonely existence." Prudence speared a fork into her salad.

"I held everything in for so long that I'm still having a hard time thinking that people here care about me and want me to succeed both personally and professionally. I seem to duck back into my shell whenever I feel a hint of happiness, sure that someone is going to sabotage it."

"All we can do is to keep being here for you, Dev," Prudence told her. "If that means annoying you until you open up and let us in, so be it."

"So…" Annabelle prompted. "How is it going?"

Devlin busied herself with cutting her steak while figuring out how to answer. She did want to let them in, but she was still having a hard time with it.

"Everything is going great. He's kind and generous and—" She stopped, not sure how to continue to open up to her friends. "I don't know why this is so hard. I've already admitted my shortcomings when it comes to friends, why can't I just say it?"

"Let's start small," Annabelle compromised. "Do you like him?"

Devlin smiled—she couldn't help herself. "Of course I like him."

"Okay, that's a good start." Annabelle resumed her line of questioning. "Do you like him for more than just his body?"

Devlin pretended to think this question over. "Maybe? I mean, he is spectacular."

"Oh jeez," Prudence muttered. "I've known this kid since he was in diapers."

"Get over it," Annabelle sighed. "We have our friend to help."

"Yeah, yeah." Prudence waved her hand for Annabelle to continue.

"Okay, time for rapid-fire questions," Annabelle insisted. "Does he make you orgasm?"

"Yes."

"Multiple times?"

Devlin felt herself getting warm. "Yes."

"Do you mind his odd hours?"

"No."

"Does he mind your odd hours?"

"No."

"Do you like all the shiplap he's used in the renovations?"

"Well—"

"Don't think," Annabelle barked, "just answer!"

"Yes!"

"Do you love him?"

"Yes." Devlin gasped as she clapped her hand over her mouth. "Wait, what?"

"Rapid fire never lies," Prudence remarked.

"The truth always comes out during rapid fire," Annabelle confirmed.

"Hold on," Devlin exclaimed. "Don't use that witchcraft on me! Nobody said anything about love."

"Sorry, honey, but you just did," explained Annabelle.

Devlin's heart slammed in her chest. No, this wasn't love. A heavy dose of lust, sure, but love?

"No, it's not possible," she sputtered.

"Ok, let's try this," Prudence started. "What was the last real conversation you two had?"

Devlin tried to remember. "Before the chili cook-off. We talked about his woodworking."

"Interesting," Annabelle murmured. "He doesn't talk about that with most people and when he does, he explains woodworking like a hobby, but it's much more personal than a hobby."

"I gathered that," Devlin said. "He was so passionate about it. I got chills listening to him explain his process for creating a piece."

Prudence and Annabelle exchanged a glance. "I almost hate to tell you this based on how you responded a moment ago, but I think his feelings for you are mutual," Annabelle pointed out.

Devlin pushed the remainder of her meal away, her appetite vanishing. *If Gabe has ruined rib-eyes for me I'll never forgive him.* A laugh formed out of nowhere at this ridiculous thought.

"Are we missing something funny?" Prudence accused.

"No. No, nothing funny." She glanced around the restaurant then back at her friends. "Except that everything about all of this is funny. The universe is playing a joke on me, that's the only explanation for any of this. I leave Boston to get away from everything just to land smack dab back in Gabe's lap. The whole thing is comical."

"Maybe the universe is trying to tell you something and you're not listening to it, Dev," Annabelle said.

"You always need to listen to the universe," Prudence philosophized. "I believe divine intervention was the reason that Grey came home just as a job opened up at the college. You ended up in Amber Falls for the same reason, and I don't think you need to figure out why anymore, but how to make it work."

"It might be time to talk with Gabe about the whole proposal thing," Devlin admitted.

"Wait." Annabelle held up her hand. "You're telling me that you haven't discussed the one thing that adds the drama to this whole situation? You're banging each other's brains out, but not using those brains to figure out what the hell you're going to do?"

The sound of a throat clearing broke Devlin from her despair.

"Of course, Jason, you're back. I'd expect nothing less," Annabelle deadpanned.

"Just the checks, ladies." He deposited them on the table and did an about face with military precision before gliding off.

"Devlin, please tell me that you and Gabe have discussed your proposals or the art gallery?" Prudence echoed Annabelle's earlier words.

"Umm." Devlin tried not to give the outward appearance that she wanted to avoid the question.

"What are you going to do when one of you gets the property and the other one has to give up on their dreams?" Annabelle asked.

"I'm trying not to see it that way," Devlin explained. "We have time before anything needs to be decided."

"One day is not time. You do know the proposals are due Friday, right?" Annabelle pointed out.

"Of course I do." Devlin grew frustrated. "You don't think I know all of this?"

Seeming to sense Devlin's unease, Prudence tried another tactic. "I don't want this to come between you, but I can't think of an outcome where one of you doesn't get hurt."

A silence settled over the table, which was rare with this group. Devlin felt a stab of guilt at her irritation with her friends and tried to summon anything that would ease them back into being their easygoing selves, but was cut short when Prudence downed the last of her wine and looked at her watch.

"I've got a meeting in ten minutes, otherwise we'd continue this conversation." She sighed as she grabbed some cash from her wallet and deposited it on the table. "We're not trying to be hard on you, Dev, we're trying to help you."

Annabelle nodded, agreeing with Prudence. "Do you remember when Prudence completely overreacted at the Fall Festival street dance?"

"Hey!" Prudence exclaimed. "I had my reasons."

"They ended up being terrible reasons, but my point is that Devlin and I helped you talk it out." Annabelle laid her hand over Devlin's. "We weren't trying to prove anything or to be right about it, we just want to help, and the best way to do that is to talk it out and see the situation from all angles. A ladies lunch doesn't give us enough time to get into it, since I've gotta go, too."

Prudence and Annabelle stood and said their goodbyes, waving to Jason on their way out. This left Devlin alone in their corner booth, ruminating on the situation she'd gotten into but not yet sure how to extract herself from it.

Devlin remembered Prudence's misery from a few months ago and tried to convince herself that her situation wasn't the same. She and Gabe were adults who'd made the joint decision to pursue a relationship despite knowing the outcome. They were so wrapped up with each other that she was sure neither of them was letting reality sink in and they weren't thinking about what would happen when one got the shop and not the other.

Oh yes, it *had* crossed her mind more than once, but she'd gotten good at shoving it back to a place where it didn't need immediate attention. That place no longer existed. That place was now a cavernous hole where thoughts pinged around with a speed and clarity that made her lightheaded.

She hadn't let herself dwell on the fact that Gabe had been able to break down her walls in a matter of weeks, or what that meant. She recalled his poetic talk about his craft and wondered if that also applied to her. Maybe he saw her unfinished self and just knew what she should be, what her final shape would end up as.

The bastard from Boston dared to sneak back into her thoughts at this exact moment of clarity. He'd done a number on her, she knew that, and the fact that she was still letting him anywhere near her mental state was concerning to her. She'd been practicing mindful meditation since she moved to Amber Falls, and was starting to think she needed to kick it up a notch.

After Annabelle and Prudence had broken down her defenses, they'd made her realize that Gabe was the most exceptional person she'd met. Everything she'd told them was true. He was kind and generous and giving. She could go and make her business a success anywhere, she knew that, but she could go through the rest of her life and never find another *Gabe*. What they felt for each other might not go any further than where it already was — hell, it might not last until next week — but she was determined now to try.

Devlin sat there with the sounds of the restaurant creating a background symphony. The clink of silverware on plates, a bang from the kitchen and the murmur of voices all somehow quieted her mind.

She knew what she had to do. Gabe worked late tonight so she wouldn't see him until the next evening. She'd talk to him tomorrow and tell him that she'd decided not to submit her proposal. The time they'd spent together had given her a new outlook on her time in Amber Falls. Expansion could happen at any time but she felt like she needed to tend to her budding relationship with Gabe now, like a seed that needed water and sunlight. Devlin hoped that Gabe understood and felt the same, and that he'd let the building in between go to let their relationship grow without their businesses being involved.

Chapter Nineteen

The ladies decided to join in on tonight's dart night at Finnegan's, a rare occurrence. The Nor'easter that had passed through a few weeks ago had proven to be the exception to this year's winter rule, and the snow had all but melted, leaving clear streets and sidewalks and a town population that was excited to not be stuck in their houses. That meant good business for Gabe, as they had only so much to do in a small town after dark, even in a college town, and meeting at a bar was one of them.

"Bullseye!" Greyson crowed, hitting the center.

"Good job, honey," Prudence called from her stool at the bar.

"Way to go, Grey," Annabelle added as Devlin clapped.

Sebastian was next to go. He toed up to the line and let his dart fly, missing like he always did.

"Next time, Seb," Devlin reassured.

"Fat chance," Annabelle clipped.

"At least I'm trying to get better," Sebastian shot back.

Gabe watched Devlin swat Annabelle on the shoulder and a now familiar warmth spread throughout his chest. All night he hadn't been able to stop watching her. From the way she laughed to the way she sipped her drink to the stifling of her yawn when she thought no one was looking, he was enthralled by her every movement.

There was a lot going on with the whole group together, and Gabe got the feeling that Devlin wanted to tell him something, but every time they had a moment alone it was interrupted. They'd have plenty of one-on-one time later, and he was hungry with anticipation.

"I get why Pru and Devlin are here, but who invited the shrew?" Sebastian asked.

Grey walked off to see Prudence as he had after every turn, and as Gabe was watching Devlin, he heard Sebastian speaking but wasn't listening.

"Sure," Gabe muttered to Sebastian's question.

"The moon is full tonight. *EyeWitness* news is reporting werewolves will be overtaking Amber Falls at midnight," Sebastian stated in a matter-of-fact tone.

"That's too bad." Gabe watched Devlin as she threw her head back in laughter, her long neck begging for his attention.

"Hey, what about cults? I think I'm going to join one."

"Have fun." Gabe's mouth went dry as Devlin tucked a strand of hair behind her ear then ran the same hand to her legs to smooth out her skirt.

"I think the time has come to burn down The Bee for the insurance money."

"That's a good idea." Gabe's eyes came back into focus and his head snapped toward Sebastian. "You're not going to burn down The Bee," he insisted.

"I'm not going to join a cult or get turned into a werewolf, either. You were in lala land."

"I've been distracted."

"It looks like your distraction is just as distracted as you are." Sebastian nodded over to Devlin at the bar. "Let's call the game good and go over there. Between my inability to hit the board and your inability to pay attention, I'm sure that Grey has won. I could use a refill anyway."

Gabe was relieved now that he was on his way over to Devlin. He'd found it hard to be in the same place with her but not *with* her. He realized now what Greyson had been going through the last few months and how he felt when he and Prudence had first gotten together. He almost felt bad for the crap he'd given him. *Almost.*

Gabe had tried to pinpoint what his feelings were last night while he's been working, missing Devlin during his long shift, and decided that it wasn't the blush of first love, rather a lava flow of emotions. Gabe had been in love before—or what he believed was love—but it hadn't felt like this. His every waking thought was consumed by Devlin. If they were apart, he found himself wondering what she was doing or if her day was going well.

What caught him off guard was his need, his want, to oblige her every desire. When they were together, he was focused on making her happy, whether it was what they were eating, watching or doing in the bedroom. Any other relationship he'd had, he'd been the dutiful boyfriend, doing what he thought they wanted, or what he imagined a partner should be, going through halfhearted motions. Only after he'd met Devlin did he realize all this, and felt a small pang of guilt for girlfriends of his past.

"Hey." He rested one of his hands on her thigh when he reached her.

"Hey back."

"How long do you want to stay?" he asked, rubbing his thumb in a slow circle on her leg. "I have the day off tomorrow, if you don't mind me staying at your place."

"I'll be ready as soon as you are," she confirmed. "I wanted to talk, but we haven't had any time alone."

"I saw you yawning. A lot."

"I haven't been getting enough sleep," a gentle accusation laced her voice.

"It'll be an early night," he promised, becoming aware of the raised voices next to them and noticing a confused Sebastian.

"I only wanted to know if Devlin had submitted her proposal yet. I know Gabe did as soon as we got home from the cabin."

He saw Devlin blink rapidly, the only giveaway that she was clearly flustered by Sebastian's words, and his heart plunged into his stomach. *Critical error* sounded through his head like a warning bell.

"It's okay, Sebastian," Devlin soothed, "that's good to know. But no, I haven't submitted mine yet."

"The deadline is tomorrow, though. Will you get it there in time?" Sebastian asked.

"Are you serious, Sebastian?" Annabelle snapped. "Read the room for, fuck's sake." She lowered her face into her hands and a muffled, "I just can't with this guy," escaped.

Prudence, who had been whispering into Greyson's ear until this point, sprang to attention at the shift in conversational tone. "What's the matter?" she asked.

Gabe saw Annabelle shoot Prudence a look with a slight shake of her head. Unsure what the look was supposed to mean, he told the truth.

"I submitted my proposal to the town council the day after we got back from the cabin. It was done and as good as I could get it and I didn't see the point in waiting."

Devlin turned her back to the group and spoke to Gabe in a hushed voice. "The point might have been that we continued sleeping together when we got back."

"Yes, and we agreed to keep seeing each other, nothing else."

"I believed we had become more than that."

"Devlin." He reached out to take her hand, surprised when she pulled away. He glanced over her shoulder, very aware now that the rest of the group was silent and listening. "We didn't agree to anything else. We knew what would happen."

Her eyes widened and he heard a sharp intake of breath from someone behind her. *Fuck.* He had surpassed critical error territory—this was bordering on a full and total meltdown—but he'd already stepped in the quicksand and was getting pulled deeper and deeper.

"C'mon, Dev. Whatever happened to girl power and every man for himself?" he tried to joke.

Devlin got quieter if that was possible, and the air seemed to be sucked out of the room. "I decided not to submit my proposal. I tried to tell you tonight but we kept getting interrupted."

Gabe's head flew back as if he'd been struck. "I don't understand. We've both been planning this for a long time, long before we got together. Our plan was to take what happened after the proposals and figure it out then. We made no promises." Gabe knew he was digging a hole he might never get out of, but the words flowed out of him against his control. "Our businesses are everything." Gabe knew he was digging a hole he might never get out of, but the words flowed out of him against his control. "Our businesses are everything."

"Oh, Gabe," Prudence moaned at the same time Greyson said, "Oh no."

Devlin looked around at these exclamations, seemingly surprised that the four friends had witnessed their conversation.

"I've gotta go. Don't come over tonight." She gathered her purse and fled the bar.

Gabe stood in a stupor, staring after her. He tried to move, just like he had the first day he'd seen her in Amber Falls, but he was rooted to the spot once again.

"Gabe, what the fuck?" Annabelle's words broke him from his reverie.

"What just happened?" he asked.

"Bro, you know what happened. You told Devlin that your business came before her after she admitted she didn't submit her proposal because of you." Greyson looked perplexed. "Did you not just have that conversation with her?"

"I don't—" He was cut off by Prudence.

"How could you do that to her, Gabe?"

"I didn't do anything other than follow the plan that we came up with at the cabin."

"Those were some harsh words, though," Sebastian pointed out. "Whatever you agreed upon doesn't mean you should treat her like that."

Gabe's brain started to hurt as he had flashbacks to New Year's Eve and being yelled at in the same place by the same people about the same person. He fought the urge to relent. He should've used nicer words with Devlin, she did deserve that, but he'd only stuck with the plan they agreed upon by submitting his proposal.

"I submitted the proposal the day we got back to town. Everything that's happened since then wasn't expected."

"So what?" Greyson countered. "That was cold, and not like the Gabe Atwood I know."

"She's a human being, Gabe," Annabelle added. "Your business is just a business. She had such a hard time after she moved here making friends and opening up to people."

"I know, we've talked about it."

"Then you should know that what you just did to her was shitty," Prudence all but shouted, both her and Annabelle pulling out their phones at simultaneous pings and they compared texts, whispering to each other.

"What did she say?" Gabe asked.

Annabelle shot him a dirty look before whispering more with Prudence.

"C'mon, guys," Gabe implored. "What did she say?"

Prudence nodded and Annabelle spoke. "She's going to bed." Short and sweet. That was it.

"You guys aren't going over there?"

"Not tonight, I think she needs to be alone." Annabelle punched Gabe's arm. "What are you going to do to make this right?"

Gabe saw the look of expectation on his friends' faces, even Sebastian, who had only moved to town three months ago. His shoulders felt heavy with the burden of making five people happy. Devlin wasn't the only person that his decision would affect, but her friendship with the rest of the group lay in the balance. He knew enough of Devlin that she would back away if things went sour between them. She'd done it when she moved to Amber Falls and he believed she'd do it again.

"I'll make this right," he promised. He wasn't sure yet how to make it right without giving up on his own dreams, but he was damned sure he was going to try.

* * * *

Devlin walked the few feet to her coffee shop, her ears tuned to hear Finnegan's door opening, both hoping it would and praying it wouldn't.

You're not good enough.

The taunting voice followed her.

Everything you do is worthless.

"No!" she shouted, trying to get him out of her head. She'd left her ex in Boston yet here he was, loud and clear in her mind.

She stopped at Books and Beans and looked over one more time before unlocking the front door. The shop had just closed for the evening and Emma was behind the counter wiping it off. She smiled wide when she saw Devlin.

"I didn't expect to see you tonight, I'm just finishing up prep for the morning."

Devlin flipped the door locked again and leaned her forehead against the cool glass.

"Is everything okay?"

She exhaled a breath and watched the fog spread over the glass then disappear. She turned and walked around the counter, pulling out her phone and typing out a quick message to Annabelle and Prudence.

I'm fine. Everything is fine. I'm going to bed, we can talk tomorrow?

"Men suck."

"No, don't say that! What happened?"

"I don't know why he'd be any different, but he's just like every other man I've been with. He got what he wanted and that's it."

"Gabe isn't like that. He's one of the good guys."

"Is he? He just told me he submitted his proposal to the town council already. Like the last two weeks didn't happen."

"Oh, Dev, he didn't?"

"He did. And on top of it, he just called me out in front of everybody for not submitting mine, that it wasn't our plan."

"What was your plan?"

Devlin tried to remember their conversation, but a haze of sex and sleep deprivation tinted it.

"I don't remember exactly what was said, but I *am* sure we didn't agree to go ahead with the plan as if nothing happened between us."

Emma appeared thoughtful as she finished with the last of her prep, taking her apron off and hanging it on a hook behind the counter.

"I've been in the background for a lot that's happened the last few months, in the unique position to observe what's been going on without anyone paying attention to me. When Greyson Atwood came in to get coffee, he wasn't here to talk to the lowly barista Emma, he wanted to talk to his girlfriend's friend. He wanted to get to know you because you were important to Prudence, and the look in his eyes when he talked about her was unmistakable. He was so clearly in love that it hurt my own heart. That same look is in Gabe's eyes when he's around you. If he can look at you like that, then nothing will stand in your way, especially all this." She waved her hands around the space indicating the expansion. "I'm sorry, Devlin, it's not my place, but I wanted you to see it how I did. I'm going to put the till away then I'll go home."

She wasn't willing to hear it. Emma's youthful take on love seemed like a foreign movie with subtitles she couldn't understand. She knew what was happening but couldn't put the plot together, the nuance of it lost on her.

Devlin saw Gabe walk by her door and stop. He looked in, his face inscrutable, and she wasn't sure if he saw her, then turned and walked away. *It's not worth it*, her mind chanted while her heart broke. She'd picked up her life and moved on once before and she could do it again.

Chapter Twenty

Devlin had promised Annabelle that she'd be at the snowman building contest to help decorate for The Bee, but she just wanted to curl into the fetal position and sleep for a week. She was sure that Annabelle would let her off the hook for the day, especially after what had happened last night at Finnegan's, however she'd spent so long hiding from Gabe that she wouldn't do it anymore, so she bundled up and went to the town square.

She'd run from her problems all her life, hell, she'd moved cities when the last one was too much to bear, and she was tired. Bone tired of running and fighting. Or, rather, fighting then running. Even if she didn't end up with Gabe, that cycle needed to break.

Amber Falls was home — more of a home to her than Boston had ever been, and the friends she'd made here were closer to her than family. That was one of the reasons she left her loft when she would've been happy working or deep cleaning or doing any other menial task. Annabelle was family, and she wouldn't let her down.

The contest was in full swing as Devlin made her way across the open space. So many different kinds of snowmen were being built—some she would call snow sculptures, since they were more intricate than three large balls of snow and decorations with variations that included a sasquatch, a dragon and a bear. Annabelle was still rolling out her second ball, the middle section, when Devlin walked up.

"Finally, Dev! Where have you been?" She accepted a cup of coffee from Devlin's outstretched hand.

"I'm just a few minutes late, you started early."

"I suppose I did. I either had to start moving or freeze my butt off."

"Where is everyone else? Sebastian isn't here?"

"The Duke called me just as I got here to tell me he'd forgotten he had a spa weekend booked that was a gift from a sponsor and it would be bad etiquette to not go. He was just about to get a hot stone massage, that bastard."

"That's low, knowing you'd be out here freezing."

"I told him that and he just laughed and hung up, but I'm determined that I'm going to win this thing without him."

"Mrs. Crenshaw isn't participating, is she?"

"She would somehow figure out a way to outshine us all, if she was, like building a kitchen with a wood stove and whipping up a prize-winning dish."

Devlin bent over and helped Annabelle heave the middle ball into place, packing additional snow around to stabilize it.

"I like a lot of the snowmen, but I'm surprised that so many people are making sculptures instead."

"They won't win, the rules are clear that it has to be a snowman, but they still do it to show off."

"Did you know there's a World Snow Sculpting Championship?" Devlin asked.

"No shit. Now that must be some miserable people. What Scandinavian nation came up with that?"

"It's held in Minnesota, believe it or not."

"I believe it. Those people are about as Scandinavian as they come."

"You ever been there?"

"No, but I've watched *Fargo* and I'm sure that's an accurate portrayal."

"You betcha," Devlin joked. "Where are the accessories, or should we have brought our own?"

Annabelle pointed to some large boxes in the gazebo. "We can take whatever we need out of there."

"I'll go get some stuff while you finish rolling that."

Devlin wandered through the maze of snowmen until she reached the accessories. She was bent over one box sorting through the items when she heard a shuffle on the step.

"It'll just be a sec, there's plenty of other boxes for you to look at until I'm done."

"I'm not here to decorate," Gabe's voice came from behind her.

She shot up. "What are you doing here?"

"I came to see if Annabelle needed any help. Sebastian decided he was being clever to use the spa weekend to get out of having to build a snowman outside, so I thought I'd stop over."

Devlin crouched again and started sifting through a box marked 'gloves'. "We've got it, thanks for the offer."

She thought he'd walked away and was grateful for it until he spoke again.

"I don't want you to be mad at me."

Anger surged through Devlin at these words, words that erased his involvement in the issue and placed the blame only on her. She stood and whirled around, her face heated, and she was sure her cheeks were mottled red. The words poured out of her.

"How could you do this? Submit your proposal when I was ready to give everything up for just the possibility that you and I could be more than fuck buddies," she sputtered.

"We're more than that, Devlin, and you know it. This isn't a passing fling for me. It hasn't been a passing thing since Boston, but you were the one that hid yourself from me. I've just been playing catch-up with you from day one."

Devlin didn't know what to say to this. She did know that she had to admit some culpability for this situation. *All of it* a voice whispered, since she was the one at the cabin who'd said they had to be honest about what would happen, but she didn't want to listen to this voice. This voice had gotten her into trouble one too many times to decide now was a good time to heed its advice — case in point, not submitting her proposal.

"Why are we doing this, Gabe? Why didn't we stick to the plan at the cabin that it would be for one night. It would've been so easy to end it then."

"Easy? Ending this was impossible, that's why we didn't. Whether you like it or not, one of us is going to win and one of us is going to lose. Life works like that."

"No, it doesn't. Life isn't that cut and dried, Gabe."

"How is it not? I see no nuance in this, nothing that tells me we can figure it out as we go, even though that's what we said at the cabin. There will be resentment on one or possibly both of our ends. You for blaming me for not submitting your proposal, and me for submitting before we could start to figure things out."

"So, you admit you submitting the proposal was premature."

Gabe threw his hands into the air. "I don't want to keep going over this, Dev."

"I'll make it easy for you. I'm going to submit my proposal before this afternoon's deadline. If you insist there must be a winner and a loser, let's make it a real battle."

"I don't want to battle you."

"You already started it when we got back. You've made my choice very easy. I'm not going to lose."

She picked up her snowman accessories and stormed past him, bumping his shoulder on her way out of the gazebo.

Gabe followed her back to where Annabelle was standing, and her smile fell off her face when it became apparent that the two of them hadn't had a harmonious reunion.

"Hey," she ventured. "How's it going?"

"Devlin decided to submit her proposal," Gabe shot out. "I'm glad she's doing it, but the rest of this? She's clearly angry about something and taking it out on me."

"That's it!" Devlin yelled, dropping her belongings and scooping up some snow. She made quick work of the icy substance, forming it into a little, neat snowball. "No man is going to tell me what to do!"

And with those words, she hurled the snowball at Gabe, hitting him square in the chest. Her eyes widened and Gabe's narrowed. She backed up, almost bumping the snowman behind her over.

"Guys," Annabelle started, as Gabe made his own snowball. "Let's not get crazy here."

"Crazy?" Gabe asked. "She hits me with a snowball, and you want to caution us both to not be crazy?" He lobbed a soft throw and it appeared to go in slow motion, all three of them watching until it landed right on Devlin's head.

"When in Rome." Annabelle resigned herself to the battle and started to make a pile of snowballs as Devlin sputtered and tore her hat off, knocking the snow back onto the ground.

The rest happened so quick. Devlin was sure it would go down in town lore that no one quite knew who started the great snowball fight, but that everyone had a blast. Everyone, that is, but she and Gabe.

They both had a singular focus, throwing snowballs as fast as they could make them. Gabe had just fumbled on his latest one, he wasn't wearing gloves, and Devlin could tell his hands were red with cold.

"Always bring gloves to a snowball fight," she yelled as he charged her. She ducked behind a Bigfoot sculpture, thankful for its increased girth, but didn't notice that Gabe had come around the other side until he tackled her, both tumbling to the ground, Gabe on top of Devlin.

Their breaths came out fast, the condensation of the air mingling, their lips millimeters away from each other.

"Get off me," Devlin whispered.

"It wasn't anything personal, Devlin," Gabe whispered back.

"You can't tell me what's personal and what's not."

"That's not how any of this was supposed to happen."

Devlin lay motionless until a shout from the distance brought her back to reality. She shoved as hard as she could and pushed Gabe off her. Her life up until this point had been about restraint. Appeasing others — parents, boyfriends, teachers — anyone that she felt she needed to please.

She'd broken herself out of that cycle the night she'd met Gabe. That night had been just for her. Look where that had led her? Here, to this moment, where she was going to take what she wanted and to not be ashamed of it.

Standing up, she was tempted to reach out, an olive branch of sorts, to help Gabe up, but she couldn't bring herself to.

"I'll see you Monday," was all she said before she walked away.

Chapter Twenty-One

The next three days were the longest days of Gabe's life. Everywhere he turned, a memory of Devlin played through his head. He couldn't sleep in his bedroom, but his couch was ruined as well. The kitchen and bathroom would need complete remodels. He couldn't even escape to his shop, the unfinished table laughed at him every time he entered there.

His whole house smelled of her, sweet and intoxicating vanilla wafted at him wherever he went. He had to get out of the house, so he ended up at Finnegan's.

He'd given Devlin the space she wanted, and he'd hated every second of it. The weekend had been filled with loneliness and longing, his thoughts going from one perfect memory to another then back again, in an endless loop. The only other thing breaking into his tedium was the self-flagellation that took place when he remembered what he'd said during dart night.

He slammed his hand on the bar top, startling the customer closest to him. He was sitting at the far end by the door, a beer in his hand, but Gabe didn't remember him coming in or pouring his beer.

"Whatever is bothering you, son, dealing with it in anger is never the solution," the patron offered his sage advice.

"The only person I'm angry at is myself. I'm sorry, that's not my usual way of dealing with frustration."

The old man picked up his beer and moved down the crowded bar, finding a seat in front of Gabe.

"I've got some time. Why don't you tell me what's bothering you?"

"Isn't that backwards? You should be telling me your problems."

"I'm okay to let precedence slide if you are." He reached out his hand at Gabe's nod, shaking it as he introduced himself. "I'm Joe. So, what's the issue?"

"I met this girl," Gabe started.

"The stories are always about a girl."

"We…" Gabe wasn't sure he wanted to tell this man—who could easily be his grandfather—that he'd had a one-night stand, but he could tell his mental load was already lightening just by thinking about spilling his story to someone that didn't know either him or Devlin.

"It's okay, son. I've heard it all," Joe insisted.

"We had a one-night stand about a year and a half ago in Boston, then she moved here not knowing I was from Amber Falls. She figured out I lived here a few months after, but kept it a secret from her new friends and me. Then my brother started dating one of her friends and we got thrown together."

Joe whistled. "Now that's a doozy if I've ever heard one."

"It gets better. She avoided me for a few more months, only admitting she knew I was here when she was caught."

"Caught, now that's an interesting word. Is she a criminal?"

Gabe paused and thought about how he was portraying Devlin to a stranger. To demean her character after telling her more than once that he understood where she was coming from, that he understood why she'd hidden from him and why she had a hard time opening up to people. *Maybe because assholes like me do crap like this.*

"No, she's not a criminal. I'm sorry, that's not how she is, I don't know why I explained it like that."

"You've apologized twice to me now. I feel like you're not quite yourself."

"No, I'm not. I haven't been myself for weeks."

"Women have a strange way of doing that to you, especially when love is involved."

Gabe shouldn't have been surprised when he heard that word come out of Joe's mouth. He'd known he was in love with Devlin from the first time they met, and it had only deepened once they reconnected in Amber Falls. Everything he'd shown her about himself and everything he'd said to her after she'd explained her past had been chucked away when he submitted that proposal. He told her she could trust him, that she could let her defenses down when he was around. He'd gone so far as to wish he could slay her demons for her. Then what had he done? He turned into every bad seed she'd known and proved, in her mind, that all men were alike and not one was worth the hassle. Devlin was clearly still fighting her demons and he had to figure out how to get past her defenses.

God he *was* an asshole for doing that to her. He broke out into a cold sweat thinking of the way he spoke to her Thursday night.

"I can see the wheels turning in your head, son," Joe ventured.

"I'm replaying everything back. You can't imagine how bad I feel after talking to her like that. I'm not like that. I don't know what happened."

Joe nodded along, quieting for a moment before speaking. "I do know a little of what you're going through."

Gabe was surprised. "How so?"

"Oh, I recall many years ago, right after the Vietnam war, if you must know the timeline."

Gabe did a double take at Joe's appearance.

"There was a girl."

"Fitting," Gabe murmured.

"She was the most beautiful person I'd laid my eyes on. We'd been going steady on and off in high school, but when I went to college, I decided to sow my wild oats as it were, and having a girlfriend still in high school would cramp my style."

Gabe tried to picture a young Joe, hair long in the hippy style, wearing bell bottoms and a fringe vest, or with close-cropped hair, a skinny tie and big, black-rimmed glasses.

"Did you get as crazy as you wanted to?"

"It wasn't for a lack of trying," Joe admitted, "but my heart still belonged to Agatha, and the other ladies could see that plain as day. It took me a few miserable years before I realized what a mistake I made, but by then Agatha Sanderson had married Arthur Crenshaw and I'd lost out on the love of my life."

"*The* Mrs. Crenshaw? The one that wins all the cook-offs?"

"The one and only."

"I can't picture her as the love of anyone's life," Gabe admitted.

"She was a spitfire back in our day. Word has it that not much has changed."

"I live next door to her and she still is."

"You don't say?" Joe grew pensive and downed the last of his beer. "And how is Agatha doing?"

"Good, from what I can tell. Arthur died about five years ago and they never had any kids that I could gather," Gabe offered.

"No, no kids for them," Joe confirmed then smiled. "I know a few things, but lost track of her years ago."

"I think she's lonely. She likes to stick her nose in everybody's business. It wouldn't hurt to stop over there to say hi, would it?"

"So much time has passed, I don't know if she'd remember me."

"She'll remember you," Gabe promised.

"Yes, but how? As the man who broke her heart? She was inconsolable when I ended things, I said words that I couldn't believe were coming out of my mouth and she said she never wanted to see me again."

"Same here, Joe, same here, but she hasn't gotten to the point of telling me to get lost." Gabe picked up Joe's mug and tilted it toward him in an offer to refill it.

"That's all for me." Joe waved his hand and stood, placing some bills on the counter. "Son, don't make the mistake I did. If you know you love her, don't let her go. Hold on to her with everything you have, otherwise you'll be an old fuddy duddy like me, by myself, drinking a beer at eleven a.m. Go to your girl and make everything right, and if she doesn't want to hear it, keep reminding her that you're just human and you made a mistake. That kind of love comes around once, and she'd be crazy to let you go over your foolishness, and to not let pride or stubbornness get in the way."

Gabe turned around to deposit the mug into a sink of water and when he turned back, Joe was gone.

Taking a step back from the odd realization that Mrs. Crenshaw was the recipient of a lifetime of unrequited love, Gabe thought about the words Joe had spoken to him about pride and stubbornness. A dash of arrogance and a pinch of conceit had created the perfect recipe for his attitude on Friday.

Gabe was kicking himself for everything that had happened over the last few days—all he wanted to do was run to Devlin and beg her forgiveness. He felt like it would take more than words to forgive her, and he had the perfect plan. He just needed to be able to make it to the town council meeting tonight.

The afternoon crawled along at a snail's pace and if he didn't know the basic concepts of time, he would've sworn that the clock was ticking backward. Every person that passed by the front window caught his attention but none of them were Devlin. He was hoping to catch a glimpse of her, or that she'd come over, but neither happened and that ended up being okay. He'd planned tonight out, and he wasn't quite sure words this afternoon would hold the same influence as his gesture tonight.

Tonight, he was going to withdraw his proposal at the town meeting. By withdrawing, neither of them would know who the town council chose, but Devlin would get the building. He was sure he was making the right decision. Finnegan's was fine for now, just as it was. He wanted to focus more on his woodworking, and he had space to do that in his garage. It was smaller than he wanted, and he didn't have any place to store his creations, but he would figure that out.

He'd gotten to the town hall early so he could watch everyone come in. The meeting now was supposed to start in five minutes and Devlin still hadn't shown up. He tapped his finger on his leg, wondering why she wasn't there, frustrated from not seeing her for four days.

The door whipped open, and Annabelle whirled in, a notepad in her hand. She noticed him sitting at the front and made her way to him.

"Hi, Gabe. The meeting is almost ready to start."

"I've been very aware of time today," he admitted. "Have you seen Devlin?"

Annabelle avoided his eyes, turning around to take note of the other townspeople in the room.

"AB, have you talked to her?" he begged. "I need to know."

She sighed. "I haven't talked to her. She's kept a low profile all weekend since she got sick."

"Sick? Is she okay?"

"From what she says, yes. It seems like a normal cold, but she sounded miserable. She didn't want us over so she couldn't spread it."

"I wonder if that's why she isn't here yet. Do you know anything else?"

"I don't, we know as much as you."

"You're telling me you don't know if she ended up submitting her proposal?"

"Fine, I know everything, but she made me promise not to tell."

"Did you pinkie swear?"

"What?" Annabelle looked taken aback by the question.

"If you didn't, that promise isn't binding."

Annabelle chewed on her pen cap for a few moments before she started talking again. "She didn't submit."

"I don't understand. She was very clear that she was going to and nothing was going to stop her."

Annabelle shrugged. "We talked after and once her anger went away, she decided she just wanted to be done with it all. It wasn't worth any more mental anguish to continue to fight with you."

"She has to have submitted—my plan will only work if she does."

"She's moved on, Gabe. I hate to entertain this thought, but I think she could leave Amber Falls after this." She cocked her head. "Wait, what plan?"

"I decided that before the council make their decision, I'm going to withdraw my plan, so Devlin gets the building no matter what."

"Dang, Gabe. That's good. I'll admit, I'm impressed."

"Thank you, but I'm not doing it to impress anyone. I'm doing it because it's the right thing to do. I had no business submitting it when we got into town, especially since we hadn't talked about anything long term. I should've waited and figured it all out together with her."

"What are you going to do, then?" Annabelle asked, but his answer was cut off by the sound of the meeting starting.

Council President Reardon called the meeting to order and passed the first order of business to councilperson Campbell. "Mr. Campbell, will you please proceed with the issue of the property on Main Street and the two parties who want to buy it?"

"Yes, thank you President Reardon." He looked around the room. "Is Ms. Watkins present?" he asked.

"No, sir, just me," Gabe answered.

"That's just as well. I'll note that she didn't submit a proposal like we asked her to at the last meeting. Since Ms. Watkins did not submit a proposal, we will grant you the permit, Mr. Atwood."

Gabe took a deep breath before speaking. "I don't want the permit."

"Only one proposal is on the table—yours—and if you reject the permit we're granting, the building will go back on the market."

Gabe stood, perplexed at what was happening and not knowing what to do. His grand gesture to give the building to Devlin was backfiring.

"Mr. Atwood, can you please let us know your decision?"

"I have a question." He waited until Mr. Campbell nodded then continued. "If I'm granted the permit, can I transfer it to someone else without going through this whole process again? I promise you that Devlin will be the owner of that building." He crossed his fingers behind his back, hoping that she'd stay in Amber Falls and do just what he was promising.

Councilperson Campbell put his hand over his microphone and consulted the rest of the council before addressing Gabe again.

"Sir, only two people showed interest in the property. You and Ms. Watkins. As I stated before, since she didn't submit they will go to you, and if you refuse we start all over."

Rustling sounded from the back of the room and Mrs. Crenshaw stood. "Oh, let him do what he wants, Bob. He loves the girl and wants her to have the property. Don't be an ass, just tell him that he can pass the permit on to Ms. Watkins so she can buy the place." She turned to the people around her, explaining, "It only makes sense. What a ridiculous premise, this whole granting permits thing." She spoke to the front of the room again. "Let the boy do it, Bob."

The crowd broke into a cacophony of sound as the council yet again discussed the matter between them until they quieted when the President held up her hand, addressing him informally.

"Gabe, the whole proposal part of the building sale was made up by us at the last meeting because we'd never had two people want the same property. In the light of the fact that we made it up—" She shooed Bob away from his microphone when he tried to interrupt. "No, Bob, we did make it up and we can make up how to get this finalized. Here's what I'm going to do. Based on your words and your assurance that Ms. Watkins will still buy the property, I'm going to put the permit in her name. If you decide later that neither of you want the building, we'll just start over from scratch, but for now, we're allowing the sale to go through to Devlin Watkins."

Her last few words were drowned out by cheering in the hall. He gathered the permit, now made in Devlin's name, and walked over to Annabelle, who was writing at a furious pace.

She held up a finger to stop him from talking and finished jotting down her words.

"This is going to make a great story in the paper, I can't believe I was here for it. This stuff never happens at these meetings!" She spoke the words aloud as she wrote them. "Grand gesture made at town council meeting. Town cheers."

"You can't make a grand gesture if the other person doesn't show up."

"You sure can. And I can write about it. Now leave me alone so I can get this written while the meeting is still fresh in my mind, and go get our girl."

Chapter Twenty-Two

Gabe called Leo at the bar before he started out from the town hall asking him to pack up some soup. He figured that if he had a reason to go to Devlin's loft, she would be less likely to boot his ass out when she saw him at the door. His steps slowed as he walked from Finnegan's to Devlin's. He'd flown from town hall, his feet barely touching the ground, but his excitement waned now, not sure what he'd do if she didn't hear him out.

He hesitated a moment before opening the door of the street to her loft. He walked up the stairs, preparing himself for the real possibility that she would kick him out, not listen to his apology or both. The TV could be heard from inside, the unmistakable sounds of a game show floating through the door. He decided that he'd taken enough liberties by letting himself in downstairs and knocked. The TV went silent, and he heard footsteps approach the door. Another eternity passed until the lock clicked and the door swung open, Devlin appearing, her hair tousled and nose red.

"What do you want, Gabe?" Devlin asked, her voice nasal and hoarse.

He held up the bag from Finnegan's. "I brought soup and crackers. Annabelle told me you were sick, and I wanted to make sure you were okay."

She took the bag from his outstretched hand and started to close the door.

"Wait, Devlin, please," Gabe begged, knowing that once the door closed it would be an end to their relationship. He wasn't going to stop her, but he hoped that the tone of his voice would give her enough pause for him to plead his case before banishing him from her life forever.

"I love you," were the only words he could think of saying. He'd come up with a whole impassioned speech, all the right words to make her reconsider, but these three words—short and sweet—were the only ones that mattered now. The trajectory of the door slowed, and he saw his opening to continue, grateful he didn't have to rush when the door opened back up and she let him in. She sat on the couch and looked at him expectantly, then motioned for him to sit in a chair.

"I fell in love with you in Boston and this last month I've only fallen deeper in love with you. You said once that you didn't know what it was to be in love like nothing else in the world exists, but I do. I love you, Devlin, and nothing else matters, not the shop or my expansion. Only you. I want to see you succeed and your vision to be a reality." He shot her a rueful smile. "I had this whole thing planned out. At the meeting tonight I was going to withdraw my bid for the property. I don't need to expand now. I don't want anything to come between us." She started to speak but he had one more thing he wanted to say. "Don't give up your dreams for me. I want to be here, with you, cheering you on every step of the way."

Her eyebrows shot up at these words and he waited in misery for her to speak.

"Why did you do it?"

Gabe psychoanalyzed his whole life up until now in a split second. "I don't clue people into my plans until they're in motion or already done, and what happened here was no different. I'm not trying to deflect from my behavior, but once Grey got famous no one paid attention to me — which I didn't mind — but that meant I could do what I wanted when I wanted and no one…cared isn't the right word. People cared, but what I was doing was never as important, so I just went ahead and did stuff without telling anyone. I ended up being cautious about who comes into my life because of Grey's fame. I was always like this, but I hadn't realized how bad it had gotten until now."

Devlin closed her eyes and spoke, so softly that he moved closer to hear her.

"He weaponized intimacy."

Gabe felt his stomach turn at these words but didn't speak. He knew she needed to let this all out, but when she opened her eyes the sadness he saw there was almost unbearable.

"With him it was his way or the highway. Nothing I did was good enough and anything I wanted took a back seat to his needs. I didn't realize how much he was still affecting me and my decisions — I thought that when I left him I left him, but that's not how it works. He's this voice in my head whenever anything gets too good, or I was getting too happy that would tell me I was worthless. I should've known that you were different, that you weren't him, but I couldn't separate the two and I started making irrational decisions like pulling my proposal and expecting you to do the same and if you didn't you would be just like him. I was sabotaging us from the start and I'm sorry."

Gabe moved from the chair to the couch, taking Devlin's hands in his as he sat next to her. "I'm not him and I will do everything in my power to help you believe that."

"I can't promise that I can change overnight, but I think that together we can make this happen."

Relief washed over Gabe and his skin tingled from the emotion. He gripped Devlin's hand, hoping to never let it go. "You should've seen the face on the clerk when I went to town hall to submit. She asked me if I was sure, like she could read the hesitation on my face and wanted to stop me from making a big mistake. But why didn't you submit yours? You made it clear after you'd pelted me with at least hundreds of snowballs that you'd changed your mind."

"It wasn't hundreds," Devlin exclaimed. "I'm sorry I started that. I didn't expect the whole town to join in, either. The truth is that I was miserable after it happened. I had my proposal all printed out and ready to go when I started feeling sick. I had a fever that spiked, nausea and body aches. I felt like my bones were glass and if I moved too much I'd just break."

Gabe reached his hand and touched her forehead. "You don't feel hot now."

"My fever broke overnight." Devlin ran her thumb over his hand before continuing. "Annabelle has told me that I need to listen to the signs the universe is sending me, and I figured this was yet another sign and this time I was going to listen. So, I let myself be miserable and wallow all weekend. I watched bad movies and slept a lot. The universe was telling me that I needed to stop and think this whole thing out, to stop acting irrationally and to think something through, but I couldn't stop thinking I messed everything up. I let what happened in my past dictate how I'm acting now. You're right when you said you've just been chasing me since we met. I've led you on from day one and that's been unfair. I should've known—I do know—that you're so different from anyone else I've met, and I didn't give you enough credit that we could do this without bad feelings getting in the way. I should've recognized that, and instead of running away from it, I should've embraced it. I realize now that giving up on my dream wasn't the way to go about this. I've always tried to please other people and I was still doing that when I decided not to submit my proposal. I should've known that we'd get through whatever happened, good and bad, and to trust my feelings for you."

Gabe listened to Devlin. He knew she needed to talk through her feelings, and he was overjoyed that he was the person she decided to open herself up to. Right now he wanted to do nothing more than sit on Devlin's couch and listen to her pour her soul out to him. When she stopped speaking, he leaned over and kissed her on the mouth.

"No, don't! I'm sick and I don't want you to get anything."

"Right now, I'll take anything just to hear you say that you're mine."

"I'm yours," Devlin promised.

"Forever?" Gabe asked.

"Yes, forever yours."

Epilogue

Winter melted away and the sweet smell of spring was in the air. Trees and flowers were blooming, and Gabe couldn't stop smiling. He hadn't for months.

The Spring Fling was in full swing in Amber Falls as Memorial Day was fast approaching. They were at the Spring Fling dance, the kickoff to the annual celebration.

Gabe and Devlin were dancing, their arms around each other and everyone else tuned out. Gabe could hear the music, just enough to sway to the beat, but everything else around him was muted, quiet, so he could focus on Devlin. The music stopped and he leaned his forehead against hers, not wanting to let her go.

Her winter wear of jeans and thick sweaters had changed over to a spring wardrobe of flowy dresses, and he relished in the shape of her body under the thinner fabric. She'd pulled on a cardigan as the night took on a seasonable chill and gave a little shiver now.

"You ready to go home?" he whispered, and felt her shiver again as his warm breath hit her ear.

"I'm ready," she agreed. "Let's go."

As they were walking over to say goodbye to the rest of the group, they were stopped by a familiar face. Joe, the man that had given Gabe life changing advice, waved them down.

"You must be the girl," he stated after saying hi to Gabe.

Devlin gave Gabe a quizzical look and he just grinned back at Joe. "She's the girl."

"I'm very happy to hear it." He put his arm around Mrs. Crenshaw. "And here's mine. Agatha, these are the two I was telling you about."

"Hi, Agatha. How are you doing?" Gabe asked.

"That's Mrs. Crenshaw to you, young man."

Gabe was secretly happy at this set down, it felt strange to call her by her first name.

"I'm glad I ran into you, Gabe," Joe said. "I'm not sure if you know it, but I own the building on the other side of Finnegan's."

Gabe's eyes widened. The building had always been closed, but never run-down, taken care of enough that Gabe never gave it a second thought.

"I'm ready to sell it," Joe continued. "The old family property hasn't gotten any use in the last twenty or so years. I'm hoping to move somewhere warm soon, if I can convince Agatha that sunshine is the real fountain of youth."

"I'm far too wise now to want my youth back," Mrs. Crenshaw admitted. "I'll take you just as you are."

"I'm glad to hear that, dear. I was hoping that there would be someone who wanted to buy it and I wouldn't have to go through the hassle of listing it. If I make the deal with you, the town council will approve, I've already talked to them."

Devlin squealed with excitement. "Gabe, that's perfect!"

He agreed. Perfect was exactly how he'd describe it.

"Joe, I don't know what to say."

"You don't have to say anything yet. We can look at the building next week, and if it suits your needs, and your price point, it's yours. Now you two go and have a good rest of your night." He shook Gabe's hand and Mrs. Crenshaw led him over to the display of prize-winning jams, for which she'd won the grand prize.

Everything was falling into place, and he was going to ask Devlin to move in with him tonight. They'd been fixing up his house in their spare time and he felt now that the house was just as much hers as it was his. She'd taken over the design job, a job Prudence had given up gladly so she could spend more time with Greyson. Gabe trusted Devlin's aesthetic and it felt wrong now when he went home and she wasn't there. He was nervous and didn't want to wait until later, so he just spit it out.

"Will you move in with me, Devlin?"

"Yes!" came her immediate reply.

"The house has turned—wait, yes?" It took him off guard, though he wasn't sure why he thought he'd have to convince her to give up her loft.

"I'd love to move in with you, Gabe! I've come to love that house so much. I'm glad you feel the same way I do. In fact, I've been hinting to Emma that if she needs a new place, I might have the loft available for rent this summer."

Gabe's heart soared. He was truly the happiest he'd been, and he couldn't wait to start this next chapter of his and Devlin's lives together and maybe he'd get to use his grandma's ring after all.

He shared the good news as soon as they reached the group.

"Devlin's going to move in with me," Gabe announced.

"That's great. I've got my truck if you need help moving," Sebastian offered.

"Thanks, Seb," Devlin said. "It won't be much, I'm going to leave a lot there and rent it out, maybe to Emma."

"That makes sense, business-wise," Sebastian agreed.

"With the renovations and expansion, you're going to want to get away from that place at some point," Greyson added. "Otherwise it'll take over everything."

Gabe started to lead Devlin away when Prudence stopped them.

"Wait, before you go, I can't forget to tell you. Grey and I are going to fly out to L.A. in a few weeks for the Passel awards. The writer's strike has moved the show back so many times, but they finally picked June. Grey is begging me to come with him. He said that if I'm there, the paparazzi will be nicer to him and that I can crack the whip on anyone who tries to take advantage of him, Nadia included."

"They all think she's some sort of dominatrix that holds all the cards and they'd have to go through her to get to me," Greyson confirmed. "Plus, Nadia is scared of Pru, so hopefully she'll leave me alone."

"It'll all go smoother if I just go with."

"What about Summer Stock? Isn't that right when it's starting?" Devlin asked.

Prudence grinned. "That's the best part. Grey and Wyatt finally made peace with each other and Wyatt agreed to come and teach the first few weeks of it."

"Now we can have that Wyatt Reed movie marathon." Annabelle high-fived Prudence and Devlin. "Ladies' night!"

"A marathon of third-rate romantic comedies?" Sebastian groused. "No thanks."

"You weren't invited," Annabelle pointed out.

"Hey, he's got a lot of good action movies, too," Greyson defended Wyatt.

"I'm going to have too much to do, anyway," Sebastian explained. "My sister, Sofia, is going to be visiting for a month this summer. I'll have to make sure she's got enough to do while I'm working."

"You mentioned she might be coming here, I'm glad she can make it." Gabe noticed Devlin yawn and they said their final goodbyes.

He took Devlin's hand and they walked out into the spring night, the voices behind them fading away.

"Hey, Gabe." Devlin snuggled close to his side on their walk home. "I'm so grateful for your support with my expansion that I want to return the favor somehow."

"Believe me, you've returned the favor more than you know."

She gave him a nudge. "You know what I mean. Joe's offer got me thinking about your woodworking. You love it so much, and I think you could make a serious business out of it."

"You're a mind reader, Dev. I have so many thoughts swirling around about that, but I don't know yet how I'd do it."

"You already have your shop to build your pieces in, now you can have a place to showcase them all."

"That's a genius idea. It might be small, but that'll only highlight the pieces I put in there."

"There's a lot of planning to do, but I'm here with you for it all. I know you love Finnegan's, but this is your passion."

"You're my passion, Devlin. Nothing else matters as long as we're together."

Gabe wrapped his arm around Devlin's shoulder and a sense of peace surrounded him. He felt like he had a true partner, that they supported each other, and there was no better feeling than that. Well, maybe that they were going home — to their home — together.

Sign up for our newsletter and find out about all our romance book releases, eBook sales and promotions, sneak peeks and FREE romance books!

Want to see more from these authors? Here's a taster for you to enjoy!

Amber Falls: Inevitably Yours
Rachael Heinan and Kimberly Metcalf

Excerpt

In business one of two things happen — you win, or you lose and Sebastian Locke did not lose. Everything he touched turned to gold, his intuition was impeccable, and it had served him well. That intuition was how he found himself in Amber Falls, Massachusetts. As he sat behind his desk at the Amber Falls Bee listening to this vexing woman rail on against him for yet another decision she didn't agree with, he thought *just once*, maybe his intuition had been wrong.

"Sir, are you even listening to me?" Annabelle Winters, star reporter at the Bee, made an exasperated noise.

He closed his eyes, allowing himself a brief respite.

"Sir, I have a million other things to do to get ready for the Summer Solstice. I don't have time to watch you take a cat nap."

"Winters." Sebastian opened his eyes. "Name one thing that's important enough to warrant my attention."

"Peach pie."

Sebastian's mouth went dry. Together, the words described a delightful dessert. Separately, each word formed carnal images in his head and once he saw that picture floating around, peach pie would never be the same to him again. He'd known this was coming for months, that the town would have a peach pie bake-off, and he, in a small corner of the soul he'd never admit he had, was looking forward to this one seasonal celebration. He was from Georgia, and any good Georgian knew peach pie, dammit.

Annabelle slammed a paper on his desk, breaking him from his thoughts. "The blurb on the peach pie bake-off is just one of the items you need to approve for the layout. I have the Summer Solstice activity schedule that needs to get printed, and I need your signature to approve the outline."

Sebastian leaned back in his chair and stretched his legs out to rest on the top of his desk, crossing his ankles. He picked up the folder and flipped through it as if he had all the time in the world. Which he did — one of the perks of being the boss. But they had this conversation every three months, going over in minute detail each of the seasonal festivals Amber Falls held. Not wanting to have the same talk today, he picked up the pen and signed his name on the dotted line.

"Have a good night, Winters." He flipped the folder onto the desk and closed his eyes once again.

"What?"

Sebastian counted to five before he forced his eyes back open. "You wanted the approval, and now you have it."

Annabelle was visibly stunned at his change in attitude. In months past, they'd had vehement arguments about the tiniest details of the previous festivals. It appeared that he didn't wear acquiescence well.

"You always have something you make fun of. Just like you did for the Fall Festival and Winter Wonderland." It seemed like Spring Fling had just finished, and Sebastian was already sick of the excited anticipation the whole town had over the Summer Solstice Celebration.

"Winters, are you going to argue with me now about my not arguing?"

He lifted the folder and offered the approved layout to her again.

Annabelle narrowed her eyes at him, distrust clear on her face. "Don't you want to know who plays in the softball game? Or what happens if no one shows up?"

He set the folder down and decided to see where this went. "Go on."

"Whoever wants to. We meet on the field the morning of the game and choose teams. Before you ask, if there aren't enough people, the adults grill and the kids play in the park."

He sat in silence, willing his cheek not to twitch with amusement.

"You don't want to know who chooses the movie for the outdoor movie night?"

Gesturing with his hand, he indicated she should proceed.

"City council does. Next will come a lewd, adolescent joke about how the peach pie is delivered for judging. After which I roll my eyes and you tell me how ludicrous the whole process is, that this town is wasting time and assets that could be better spent elsewhere."

Annabelle stopped and held his gaze. He took this opportunity to look at her, to check her out. Not a leer, he was better than that, but an intense once over — the kind he *shouldn't* give his subordinate.

To call Annabelle pretty would be a gross understatement. She was gorgeous. The kind of gorgeous that should be reserved for classical paintings, but the Birth of Venus had nothing on the

Pique of Annabelle. She was a short spitfire and Sebastian was a tall man who topped her by a foot—less when she decided to wear skyscraper heels, which she often did. Her hair was an iridescent auburn that glinted a deep blue in the right light, but it was always up, never unbound so he didn't know its length. Her features were small and fit her face.

"Winters, you've just made my point for me." He slid the folder over to her.

"I know you don't get why these festivals are important to Amber Falls, but why do you have to give me a hard time every time I need the approval for one of the layouts?"

"I'd like to point out, I did sign the layout upon your first request. And I'm not giving you a hard time, I'm giving you shit. There's a difference."

"I fail to see what that difference is."

"If I were to give you a hard time, I'd have you explain in detail why each of these activities is necessary to mark the summer solstice, because I can guarantee you that the season will turn to summer even if no"—he opened the folder back up—"flea market marks the occasion. Fall came, winter came, and spring has sprung, and you celebrated it with a damn May Day Festival. It all happened and will continue to happen for the rest of time."

"Then why does it make a difference how we celebrate it?" Annabelle sat in the chair across from Sebastian and propped her legs up on the desk in the same way his were. He raised his eyebrows at her with her movement, but she didn't remove them. "We all know the seasons continue to change and time marches on, but what's so wrong with wanting to embrace those changes and be present in those moments? These are the things I remember from my childhood, the moments I remember with family and friends — the lazy days of summer vacation when there wasn't a care in the world other than staying up late to watch the baseball game or my dad counting the time between lightning and thunder during storms with me."

"I've never said I don't understand why it happens and what the town is trying to accomplish, I've just stated that there are better things to spend time and money on."

"That's not how you've portrayed it," Annabelle responded.

"Yes, well, there it is. And that's why I'll be running for mayor."

They looked at each other for another beat then Annabelle stood so fast she almost knocked her chair over and pointed toward the door.

"Get out. Go home, pack your bags and leave town."

Sebastian laughed. "Calm down, Winters, I'm joking." He could see the pink blush starting to creep along her neckline. He did enjoy getting a rise out of her. "I don't need anything else tying me to this town."

"I don't have time for your bad jokes, sir." Annabelle gathered her notebook and folders from his desk. "Don't you own your house? Isn't that the definition of putting down roots?"

Smirking, he replied, "No, that's just a good investment."

"If you don't need anything else, I'm going to leave for the night." She stood waiting, the tip of one stiletto tapping on the floor.

"I needed to ask you about one more thing." He gestured to the chair and Annabelle sat once more. He could see her fidgeting with the edge of the folder, now on her lap. "What's your rush this evening, Winters? Hot date?"

Her half grin was that of a sly fox. "If you must pry into my personal life, yes, I do have a date, and I'm already running behind. What can I help you with?"

His stomach flopped at her admission, and he stopped himself from asking any more questions. "My sister, Sofia, is coming to stay with me for a while this summer. I want to make sure she's comfortable and has what she needs to, how did you put it, be in the moment."

"Careful, sir, I might start to think you have a heart. Besides, don't you just go home on the weekends and plug into the wall like a Roomba? What could I possibly help you with."

"Winters, please." This was as close as he'd get to begging. "Prudence is busy and I could use some help making sure I have whatever she might need during her stay."

Several moments passed before she answered. "Are you saying I was your last choice?"

Undeterred, he responded, "Of course you were."

Annabelle got up and walked to the door. She'd laid one hand on the doorknob when she paused, turning back to face him. "As it should be. I want it noted that I'm only agreeing to this because I wouldn't mind a favor from Sebastion Locke in my back pocket. When does she get in?"

"On Sunday."

"Fine, I'll be at your house Saturday morning." She turned on her heel and left his office, shutting the door gently, compared to her usual slam.

Sebastian shuffled paperwork on his almost empty desk until he heard the front door to The Bee close. Slumping back in his chair, he took a fortifying breath. He wasn't sure how to best describe his relationship with Annabelle. Their relationship, or lack thereof, wasn't love/hate, more like hate/hate, or love to hate.

His mind wandered back to a few years ago in Atlanta and the reason he'd passed on a novel submitted to him by one Annabelle Winters, before she'd been an intern at his family's company, Locke Communications. He hadn't felt it. Nothing about it had been fresh or new. On top of that, she'd submitted a romance novel and romance wasn't his…thing.

The decision to reject her novel had plagued him since he'd landed in Amber Falls. As he sat behind his desk, he thought maybe he'd been wrong just once in his life. He let his mind continue to wander around the memories from years ago. He might have used the words trite and mediocre. The words derivative and execrable might have slipped out before he'd given her a harsh rejection.

Would it have been worth it? To not listen to his gut for one time in his life to have peace now?

Yes. In the deep recesses of his black heart, doubt crept in. Just once he should've taken the hit, reputation be damned.

A loud knock sounded at his office door, and he jumped in surprise. "Come in."

"Hey, boss." One of the newspaper's columnists walked into his office. "I'm about done for the night. Is there anything else you need?"

"Peter, you went on a date with Winters, right?"

Peter shrugged. "I wouldn't call it a date. She ended up being more preoccupied by someone else on New Year's Eve, if I recall."

Oh, Sebastian recalled. He recalled her dress cut so low he swore when she moved a certain way her areolas showed, and he recalled her biting words, digging into him every time he spoke that night. Devlin

Watkins and Gabe Atwood, two of their mutual friends, had reunited that evening and the drama that follow was worthy of a front page spread in *Person* magazine. What he remembered most, though, was walking Annabelle to Devlin's after Devlin had run off in a panic when she'd seen Gabe. Devlin lived above her coffee shop, Books and Beans, two doors down from Gabe's bar, Finnegan's. Midnight had passed and Annabelle had been preparing to leave to see if Devlin was okay. Leaving Sofia at the bar, he'd informed Annabelle he was walking her over despite her protestations.

Annabelle had had plenty to drink that night, and had rocked a bit on her heels as he'd held the door open for them to exit, catching the tip of her shoe on the landing. She'd reached out, in what he could only assume was knee-jerk reaction, and grabbed his hand to steady herself. What surprised him most was that she hadn't let go for the twenty or so feet it took to get to Devlin's door. They'd stood at the entrance to Devlin's loft, Annabelle swaying and Sebastian standing motionless, afraid that if he moved she'd break her intense gaze. He'd lowered his head, eyes now transfixed on her plump lips, and he was a hairsbreadth away, the warm puff of her breath warming his cold lips when a raucous group of drinkers from Finnegan's burst out of the bar and the moment was broken. Annabelle had turned and unlocked Devlin's door, retreating inside and it closed with a resounding thud.

Devlin and Gabe were now exclusive, and Sebastian and Annabelle hadn't spoken of that night since.

"Boss?" Peter interrupted his thoughts. "You still with me?"

"Sorry, Peter." Sebastian shook his head to clear his thoughts.

"That was the one and only time we went out and I think we were in each other's company for maybe ten minutes total. That's okay, though, makes things less awkward around here."

"You had your eyes set on my sister, didn't you?"

"Um, so anyway, you need me for anything else?"

Sebastian wasn't about to let him off easy. He liked watching people squirm. "What piece are you working on?"

"Annabelle has—has me—" He stuttered at Sebastian's raised eyebrows and corrected himself. "*I'm* working on this month's birth's layout."

"How many storks flew into Amber Falls this last month?"

"Twenty-one babies were born this month."

Sebastian whistled. "That's more than usual. The town has been busy."

"We had an unseasonable cold snap in August, right before you got here. We always have extra births nine months after those."

A cold front had moved through that foretold Sebastian's arrival. He liked that imagery.

He waved his hand toward the door. "You can go. I'm about done here myself."

"All right, boss, I'll see you tomorrow."

Sebastian was once again alone in his office and a now familiar feeling crept over him. It had come out of nowhere a few weeks ago. He'd never been restless before. Since he was a child, he'd known what he was supposed to do. He had an innate sense of internal direction, one that pointed him to his true north at every turn and was propelled forward by this.

He reached up and loosened his tie, a tightness there that wouldn't go away even with the release of his shirt's top button. He wasn't restless to *leave* Amber Falls, and that was the part that was confusing him. The obvious assumption would be that this small town had gotten under his skin to the point where he needed to get out. To go far away from the festivals and the baby announcements and the peach pies. But he'd made friends here, friends he had more of a bond with than the trust fund cohorts he grew up with.

And the newspaper. Locke Communications was in the business of publishing and they had never owned a paper before The Amber Falls Bee, and Sebastian found that he was enjoying running it. Branching out into a world that was considered a dying business wasn't easy, but these small newspapers were holding on. They were holding on despite all odds and that had a lot to do with the locals.

The *locals*. That was a loaded term. Sebastian had become friends with a handful of people born and raised in Amber Falls. Other than Gabe and Devlin, he'd met Prudence Hardwick, an interior designer and her fiancé, Greyson Atwood, the retired movie star. Devlin was a recent transplant to Amber Falls, much like himself, but the others had known each other since they were kids. The link that connected them all was Annabelle.

He straightened out his desk while he contemplated where life had taken him. Atlanta was where he grew up and was also the headquarters of Locke Communications. Before that he'd gone where he was told—New York, Boston, Paris, London—anywhere the company was acquiring something or trying to build into emerging markets. His youth had been shaped by boarding schools and his adulthood by his job. He didn't want to paint a bad picture, though. He was closer to his family than most people with his same upbringing and for that he was grateful.

Where did Amber Falls fit into all of this? A small town with a thriving college scene didn't seem like any place that an up-and-coming thirty-something would find themselves, but here he was, approving birth announcements and thinking ahead to when the next dart night would be.

His eyebrows crinkled in confusion. Was Sebastian becoming a…local? Was he on the same level as Mrs. Crenshaw, everyone's favorite nosy neighbor? He shuddered at the thought while the simultaneous thought popped into his head that becoming an Amber Falls local wouldn't be the worst thing that ever happened to him.

About the Authors

Rachael Heinan

Rachael's love of books started at a young age. Her love of romance novels started in university when she couldn't stand to read another textbook and picked up her first pure romance.

Rachael co-authors with Kimberly Metcalf. They met in the corporate world and their friendship flowed seamlessly into the real world.

Rachael lives in Minnesota, USA with her husband, daughter and four cats.

Kimberly Metcalf

Kimberly is an avid reader who managed to convince her best friend they could put their stories on paper. She is so excited to share them with you.

Based in North Dakota, USA, when not writing she can be found spending time with her family, cooking, or curled up in her favorite armchair with a book.

Rachael and Kimberly love to hear from readers. You can find their contact information, website details and author profile page at https://www.firstforromance.com

ENTWINED PUBLISHING